JONATHAN FIERO

BE PREPARED TO DIE

There are tears of sadness and tears of joy.
Then there are those tears that fall in between.
I at first called them tears of love.
But tears of love are tears of joy.
Those in-between tears, they are tears of misery.
Despair passes, and joy has fleeting wings.
But misery grips us tightly with uncertainty.

~

For my little rebel.

CONTENTS

BE PREPARED TO DIE

PROLOGUE
EscapeMentality

Escapement: the mechanism in a timepiece that controls the
transfer of energy

Act I: Year Two

Scene One: The Last Day of Summer

Hindsight. It's Twenty-Twenty. I am haunted by the ghost of a spirit that still lives. A loss, though old and healed, that seems anew with every break of day. The spirit still calls out to me, asking me to wait, ensuring me its temporal vessel will return. But I can't allow myself this belief any longer. It'll have to be in another lifetime. Hopefully then, whatever conscious mind I might inhabit will understand the difference between honesty and truth. Truth, it is relative to time; but honesty, it is eternal.

I've taken refuge in passion, though once released, I find my mind scanning the ethereal radio waves pulsating from my heart. Even naked, in the closeness of companionship and lust, I feel distant and lost; fully clothed, yet freezing in a vast wilderness. I have no map or compass, and the clouded mind blocks both Sun and stars; stealing from me, any ability to sense in what direction I should walk.

Ah, but truth is also relative to knowledge. The question is, is knowledge only attainable through our five temporal senses? Can the heart learn? Can the soul? Is there really a soul within each of us? Are souls contained within all living things? All matter? Or must there be a brain, or a heart; or both? Does the idea that only humans have souls necessitate that there must be a higher power? Or are souls born from the unique cognitive consciousness of humans? In other words, is it possible that our ability to create eternity goes beyond such earthly collectivism as literature and music? Perhaps the radio waves of the minds and hearts carry on long after we are gone. Or, is it simpler than that? Is this phantom sense something that merely needs to be taught and learned?

I rarely see hearts anymore. Maybe I just stopped looking, they're as meaningless to me as the Voice in my head. The relativity of truth to time and knowledge shows the reality of honesty, the reality of this material world can never be fully known. Everything is always changing. The truth is, at one point, I came into existence as a conscious being; and at another point, the conscious being I am will cease to exist. After and before my existence, it would be a lie to say I exist; but in this current moment, my existence is a truth. The truth must be continuously altered in order for honesty to remain a constant.

I still see everything else though. Maybe not so much the colors. Blue and yellow no longer inflame my heart as they used to. But the omens, they're still there; wrapped up in the books I read, the music I hear, the numerology, the acronyms... Maybe they'll all fade away like the colors and the hearts. Regardless, this love that still permeates my existence, I know it is not merely true love; it is an honest love, flowing on the vibrating planes of existence.

That is why I know the Voice in my head is real. It's only meaningless because nothing ever seems to come from listening to it. There have been more instances than I can remember where the Voice in my head proved its existence. The omens, they're a subconscious map of coincidences that are fueled by my desires. But the Voice, it is a reality, one that does not seem likely to ever abate. I suppose this means I must keep listening.

What is the reality of the Voice though? Has the truth of the Voice's reality changed? Or is it an honest voice, always there regardless of momentary truths? Perhaps this is why my own emotions and those of the Voice are so often in conflict.

The omens, though coincidences, create a reality within my mind, a path for me to follow. So they are real, just as the Voice is; but they are momentary truths, created by the meaning I give to them, much in the way a cross is seen as a religious symbol. But objects like a cross are part of the collective knowledge; individual omens are not, they cease existing with the individual who brought meaning to them. In this way, curiously, the temporal world seems to have gained eternity through collectivism. But a discussion for later, right now I must discover the truth of the Voice.

Sitting at the park, there's a persistent breeze, my Oak Tree leaves mute most nearby conversation. The gusts are heavy, and persistent as well, sweeping into this river valley city with the Summer ocean's warmth. No clouds. The blue sky is paling with the setting Sun; it hardly even looks blue to me.

Scene Two: Don't Call it Fall

Sometimes the earth seems to move. Vibrations of a sort. Not tremors, not a quaking earth. Surface vibrations. Sometimes they flow softly, like the ocean's pulse on a calm day. Other times it's rapid, and harder to explain. What does this have to do with the Voice? What does truth and honesty? Nothing... Everything.

I spoke to the Voice today. Not that I don't every day. Today was just different, like it used to be. I learn lessons that seem as if they should be unbeknownst to me. Conclusions are reached using knowledge I never gained. This is why the Voice is real, it seemingly informs and instructs from a source outside of myself.

It seems like, well, feels like, hell, it even looks like Judgment Day. The wind picked up, breezes turned to gusts, gusts have become howls. The Voice has quieted, yet I still feel its presence in my heart. A sort of spiritual renewal of two souls that refuse to release from one another. I know I need to stop looking backward, but the past can't die until a new future is born. And I'm exhausted with living in the moment.

These moments keep stringing together, though it does seem the cord has wound around me. It isn't tightly wrapped, not yet at least; I can still free myself. But escape must take place again. It was easier in my younger years, even if I still live with the same, or probably even more, detachment from people and possessions alike. Granted, the cord wrapped around me is far tighter than it has ever been.

What a fool I am, trying to live an *honest* life in this world of greed and dishonesty. The trouble is, I rely on employers... I rely on regulations, and economic fairness. All this reliance gets me nowhere. It's a depraved dependency, expecting those with wealth and power to actually create a society in which people can succeed through a fair and just system. Such a thing does not exist in America. You're either born with wealth and/or power (though power seldom exists without wealth), or you step on others to gain them.

So much of nature is viewed with destruction in mind. Yet environmental damage caused by humans is too often celebrated as progress. The majority of us demand change! We are told truths rather than being given honesty. From the ruling class viewpoint, this seems logical. Uninformed people are too ignorant to handle honesty. In a sense, certain people will always ignore a truth that questions their personal beliefs. And people will use that belief against them to gain advantage through guile and grifting.

Before information, and misinformation, could be spread across the world in a matter of seconds, the ignorant had little power. Until the existence of the internet, and even more so, social media, *the truth*, even in this supposed 'land of the free', came from two sources, bureaucratic performers and pawns, or the journalistic media. Any other information source was largely viewed as tabloid trash, and anyone who derived opinions from them was not to be trusted or listened to. Then the media became an arm of the government, both sides, the liberals and the conservatives.

Such things no longer break my heart though. Not to say I lack empathy, it's just that their willful ignorance has become a badge of honor, rather than the black-eye it used to be. Conspiracies have taken a dive down the rabbit hole, becoming more like tabloid magazines with their stories of lizard people and alien invasions. These sordid conspiracies also help to discredit actual ones, such as the thought that JFK and MLK Jr. were both assassinated in effort to derail their messages, that social welfare must take priority over economic excess. I don't contend these conspiracies any more than known evidence can allow, but the Romans killed Jesus for similar reasons, he was a political threat to the status quo.

Of course, in response to his crucifixion, the followers of Christianity have gone on to purport one of the most enduring conspiracies humanity has ever known. Sadly, his political message of equality has been overshadowed by two millennia of promises, granting those who worship him eternal life in Paradise. This plays harshly on the ignorant of America. They've come to believe that the lives of the meek don't truly matter; that as long as they accept Jesus, and worship the cross, Eternal Paradise awaits them. As they see it, inequality doesn't matter on Earth because it is a temporary state.

This is how the beggar, the mother whose child was stolen by an early death, the politician selling out constituents to corporate profits, they are all able to claim their lives are part of some divine plan. Such conspiracies as we are seeing today play off the same human weakness; that of the ego. 'I exist, therefore I *must* matter.' The truth is, we are only as free as our most oppressed.

Scene Three: When does Autumn Start?

"To rule is not a right of the elite; it is a primary duty of the elite." This quote from Jean-Paul Sartre's novel *Nausea*, at first seemed to ignite the anarchist within me. Why should the elite be the only ones to rule?! But while I still don't altogether agree, I can see the wisdom in such a claim. Socrates felt no different. Yes, surely the most educated and informed among us should see to societal oversight.

What is it to be elite though? One must have access to a better education, which costs money; one would need to have the free time to keep informed of societal matters, from the local level to the global. Wealth has become the judge of a person's elite status. Academic and societal knowledge are automatically assumed of the wealthy. This is why we live in a world where celebrities and CEOs garner more attention and fame, to the point of worship, than do scientists and authors. It wasn't long ago that fame followed people like Einstein and Hemingway, as it now looks to the most well-known actors and athletes, and the wealthy owners of corporations and sports teams.

We all have voices in our heads, internal dialogue between the conscious and subconscious. Such conscious voices tell us things like, "I deserve that promotion," "It's wrong of my part-ner to treat me that way," "This food was served to me cold," etc. But these are socially acceptable thoughts, and so we feel comfortable acting on what the subconscious voice tells us to do. We ask for the promotion, end a relationship, request our food be warmed... Since these are normal actions by the col-lective standard, and more importantly, since no one is being physically harmed, we view these voices as intuition. In a way, we congratulate ourselves, the ego, for being strong or direct. The commonplace of voices like these also helps the individual to see the voice as their own.

I'm stuck though, (or trapped, not sure which), in two reali-ties, (or between the two). This question of the voice(s) within us must first be answered before any philosophical debate on honesty (and this includes the honesty of the ruling class) can be had. For if we don't know or understand the truth of our existence, how can we honestly assess the best way to construct a society, or even more so, how we decide to define morality?

Fantasy poisons the mind with unrealistic possibilities if not contemplated on with regard to known reality. The trouble, as I believe it to be, is that most have not been properly instructed on the human spirit. How can we be certain of an unseeable and unverifiable reality if we never learned anything of that reality? This is why we see so many turning away from modern science.

To the uneducated, anything deemed unexplainable is sub-ject to be seen as impossible, something that cannot exist with-in their known reality. But education broadens both individ-ual perspective and possibility exponentially. Without knowing that the Sun is the center of our solar system, and without the knowledge of the periodic elements, or that there are spectrums of light invisible to the human eye, it would be nothing more than a guess to say that both our Sun and every other star were formed from the same creation process. The same could be said of something as simple as teaching a person the names we've given to colors. If they are only told the names, it would only be by chance that they properly attribute each word to its corresponding color. One can be taught that blue is called yellow, just the same as one might incorrectly learn that our Sun is not a star.

Much like the science fiction writer that knows little of scientific truths, I theorize on omens and unseeable forces with no true understanding of, what most would call, the mystical world. I have no knowledge of what is possible and what isn't. To me, this possibility of the outside voice exists because of biological evidence. We are a product of evolution, and somewhere within us is a latent ability.

My issue here again is the lack of prior education on these matters. Under normal circumstances, I would further educate myself, but the subject of mysticism is fraught with rabbit holes for a beginner, especially one learning only through text. Books can be troublesome for unverifiable topics; they are ripe for subjectivity from the reader, and, in that the main purpose for many authors in writing and publishing a book is sales. I can trust the novelist to write an honest story, the historian and scientist to provide verifiable honest accounts, the philosopher to put forth honest thought. But can I trust the author of a guide to the occult? Without honesty being apparent, I risk, not simply falling down the rabbit holes, but being trapped within them. In this way, it becomes no different than the conspiratorial world. As I see it, it's just better to instruct oneself when the information being consumed is a known honest source.

The Sun has been out far more often than the weather report predicted. A light breeze, clouds streaking at atmospheric heights; one of those so-called *Second Summer* days. I'm abandoning this project, with good reason. It's irrelevant, the words of a boy who is lost...

PART ONE
BaseMentality

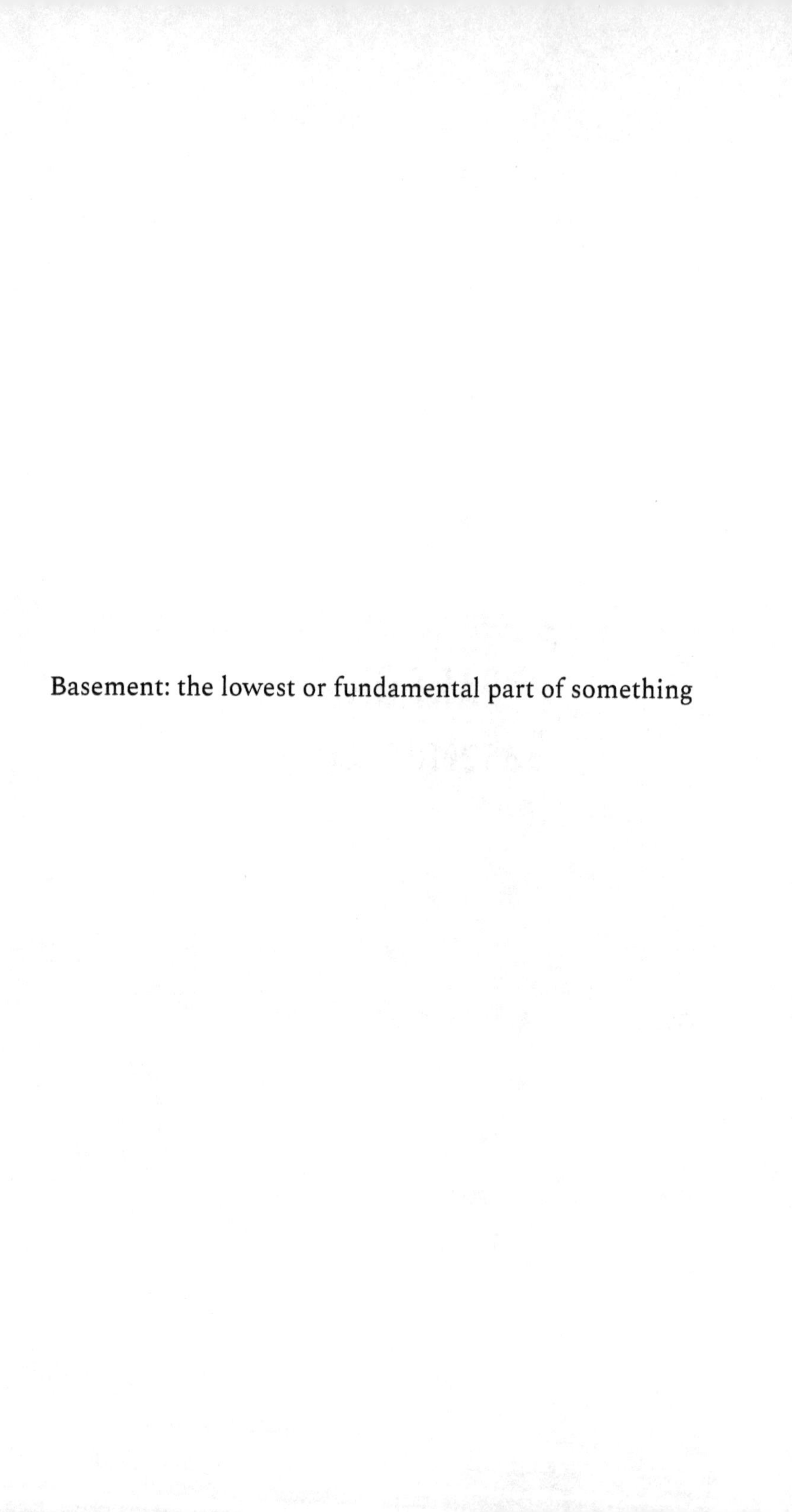

Basement: the lowest or fundamental part of something

Act II: Year Three

Scene One: June the Fifteenth
TO STAY OR <u>LEAVE</u>

The Old Crow, she basically loaded the bullet into the chamber that would be the first shot to fire when the trigger was pulled. There was no spinning of the cylinder, no blind chance. It was murder through and through. Sure, I knew the odds of death were one in six. But no one ever talks of those five chances at life! In this case though, my chances for survival were more like one in a hundred. They say to not waste good liquor on mixers. Sure, I agree. But I'd add, don't waste a good cocktail on cheap liquor. This hangover tomorrow will be the death of me...

That was earlier. A quarter of a day ago. All these constructs of time, just ways to add up insignificance. It's the existentialist in me. He emerged too young to understand the words that then directed his life with blind luck. Maybe it wasn't blind, I just wasn't really searching *for* anything. I only sought to escape from the things I found I didn't want. And so existentialism was my unknowing guide, pressed somewhere in my subconscious, leading me to drift aimlessly for that first decade of adulthood. Eyes always for the horizon, even if they, often too frequently, drifted into the mundane trap of the consumerist life. A white picket fence. Could a more oppressive symbol exist? Indeed it does, the fence is easily seen, easily avoided, easily climbed over or broken through. It is the White Curtain that immures so many.

No one really dies in this story. Then again, no one really dies in any story. It's just the constant cycle of death and rebirth every time a story is began anew. Maybe that's what our agrarian tribal ancestors meant with their various concepts of reincarnation. The trouble is we never know of the knowledge we need until it is needed. How else would you describe blind luck? C'est la vie.

The hangover already came and passed. The Sun, both culprit and remedy. I thought maybe it was depression, then perhaps the melancholia of Sartre's *Nausea*. (I don't get seasick, but there is certainly humor in the relationship there.) But it wasn't any of that. I'm happy at times. My existentialism though, it isn't the humanist of Sartre and his bourgeois upbringing (and for similar reasons I rebuke Marx). As much as I respect the man's work and mind, his status in society (as it was with Marx) both afforded him opportunities not available to those born on the lower rungs, and saved him from knowing the true struggle, the suffering, of the proletariat.

Ah, but I'm preaching politics. That is not this story... My existentialist soul, it is that of Camus's absurdist rebel. At least it was. It's absurd to be a rebel. More so though, in this world, it's rebellious to be absurd. That consumerist life I mentioned, that is not absurdity, it's commodified conformity. Still, no, it's not an existentialist absurdity anymore that guides me. I've gone backward in time. I'm now the Nietzschean nihilist, Dostoevsky's man from the Underground. Maybe I'll be a Christian when I die after all.

Unlikely. It's my own Underground that's brought me to nihilism, both physically and emotionally. My mental state is fine, mostly. The Sun helps. The warm weather more so... He's banging on the floor again. The Man Above from my place in the Underground. Banging the floor and making his noises, a mixture of agony and pleasure. I've no interest in knowing the truth of what happens above me. My ears have already translated enough information I wish to not have. I suppose that's why I'm writing this, well, about that specific thing. To make you suffer just a fraction of what I have endured.

No, no! It's not out of spite! I couldn't just simply tell you that a wine tastes *good*, could I? Well, my friend, it's the same for the bad. You must at least taste some form of my suffering to come to an understanding with my world. There are many other things I'd prefer to taste than suffering though. The peaches around here are quite delicious. It's almost Summer. I'm not certain how to feel about that.

It's become almost pleasant when the noises are mostly just muffled voices from the television and the sound system's bass sub-woofer shocks. It wouldn't bother me so much if it weren't for the vacant third story he never utilizes. It wouldn't bother me so much if I didn't live here either. But then again, it doesn't bother me so much really. It's more that I don't even want to be here, in this city. But hope for a future not living paycheck to paycheck is a powerful drug. More powerful than the drugs that the Man Above feeds on to fuel his marathon bouts of self-flagellation. The trouble is the rent. Wall Street is pricing people out from being able to live on their own.

There I go with the politics again. Do you think the queen of an ant colony or bee hive knows when a drone dies? Do they care? Is there any recognition amongst any of them when one from the tribe dies? I know mammals mourn, as do the birds. I saw them, the birds. The murder of crows circling their departed, crying out in chaotic unison; that came first, but that didn't mean anything. The ones I saw, I didn't see them really. I don't know if they were sparrows or swallows (or some other small bird), but they were huddled around one of their own deceased, like motionless humans, heads somberly bent over a freshly dug grave. I thought they were just debris in the snow-covered road… Mourning makes life so vulnerable. Their cries of terror still haunt me.

They were chirping outside my window this morning, some small birds. Another night of partial insomnia, waking at two, only falling back to sleep once the Sun quelled the darkness. I heard their calls before any crow. Maybe it's the heat, and the cloudless sky. There's also the wind. It's funny, that same wind that can make a mild sunny Winter day so intolerable, it can turn the sweltering late Spring Sun into a pleasant incubator to thaw a frozen heart. It's a beacon of some sort, my heart. I haven't quite figured that out yet.

Do I want another drink? Certainly! Will I get another? Probably not. I'm no good at figuring out much of anything these days. I've lost the shade that allied the wind. The Sun is becoming oppressive. (How are they so bad at parking? It's really no matter.) That poor man though. I think he just wanted to feel like he was among people. No one seemed particularly bothered by him initially. I never thought I'd see the day when cigarette smoke bothered hipsters. I figured it out though. They're something new. Yuppie hipsters. All the terrible style with a bourgeois elitist attitude.

They really have been quiet today. The crows. It's as if they mimic my silence. But it's not my own silence. It's the Silence I met three years ago. I wonder if the Man Upstairs hears my classical and jazz, or my reading to the Silence aloud. Or does he only hear the breakdowns, as infrequent as they now are? But breakdowns *ain't* fractures. And that will always keep me going, to sustain my hope and belief.

I was often admonished for saying ain't when I was of school age, that it wasn't a word. But the dictionary disagrees. It's a conservative ideology, deciding what's 'proper' English. But it's not even their own past conservatives hold onto. It's a collective past of humanity's failures, or antiquated successes that have since evolved, for better or worse. Liberals, in a way, seem to be developing their own form of conservatism.

There I go. The politics again. I'm going to escape this White Curtain that has draped over me, but this may be the last real chance I have. I have always supposed a life of *contentment* could suffice.

Scene Two: June the Seventeenth
FROM BELOW TO <u>ABOVE</u>

I came out through a tunnel of clouds, the light first splintering out of the forest canopy, then expanding into that blue dome of nothingness. Nothingness. I finally grasp what Sartre meant. Nothingness is nihilism... Someone should put him out of his misery. The Man Above me.

He told me he was suicidal, of his addiction. I gave the best advice I could think of. Fuck. It was all money related. He paid off his debt to the man who supplies his pills. And it's back to the normal routine. I feel somewhat responsible. I know the cash I give him for rent just goes toward his injurious habit. There was a lull when he was supposedly suicidal. No doubt his supplier cut him off when the tab came due. The suicidal thoughts, a product of withdrawal. He's miserable. Even worse, he has no courage. No confidence. A gripping fear of change.

Am I any different though? I fear the mundane. A life of routine is a life spent digging a grave. I am different, certainly. I'd be on a Mediterranean beach if I had his current situation. Hell, I'd have a sailboat docked in Monaco, rolling dice, driving Ferraris. Sell the house and take that pension. He's talked about it. But that's all he does. No, instead this fucker snorts fentanyl and Greco-Roman wrestles with ghosts for six hours a night, give or take a few hours. My solace is found in the hope that one day someone else might keep me up at night.

Currently, I favor misery over contentment. At least I feel like I'm working toward something. I always thought of nothingness as the antithesis of being, but I see now they are of the same substance, opposites residing at the ends of the scale of existence. I interpreted that nothingness as it sounds, the absence of reality. But reality isn't the same as actuality. What's real to me might not seem real to you. This is the 'being' of Sartre's philosophy, the existentialist's ability to find meaning in life. Nothingness, it is the nihilist's apathy toward finding meaning. What is 'actual', that's just the whole of existence. And existence is lived through being and nothingness.

To me, at this moment, being is like when you think there are clear skies coming, but it's just a clouded horizon of bluish-gray. It's that same bluish-gray that appears on the asphalt once a cooling Summer storm has passed, in those moments of rising steam, before the Sun evaporates the reflective sheen; and the oppressive heat returns. I prefer the nothingness of the rain or cloudless sky, they offer no hope of what's to come.

I'm sure I'll be charged with cynicism or pessimism, or both. It's no matter to me though. I've embraced being for over a decade, and it's only kept me trapped by the commodified life. I suppose it was a mistake to think I could use the system as a means to escape from it.

I know of what can change me, but it's no longer in my control. Eventually though, the ebb of misery will flow back toward contentment... It's like a drummer with no rhythm, love with no soul. The Man Above. Imagine a stampeding bull elephant having a seizure, while being 'milked'. The drummer analogy is probably better. Either way, it's fucking maddening. There's so much more to this story, but madness consumes me. I suppose that's why I've turned towards nihilism. I don't care if I go mad. At least I won't have to care anymore.

Perhaps he is suicidal. That's why I've reduced my criticisms of him to a character in this story. Rather than tell him what a pathetic lost soul I think he is. Could you imagine having the means and health to travel the world, maybe not always in luxury, but certainly in style; yet choosing to work 10-12 hours, six days a week? All to come home to an empty house, without even so much as a fish tank (let alone the cat he always mentions wanting), just to get high and physically abuse yourself?

If this were merely a matter of personal enjoyment, it would be no matter to me, (other than the noises). But he's made it my matter. So long as I'm here, his potential dead body will be my responsibility. Suicide is a selfish act, in most cases at least. I won't blame the young or the elderly. Both subjectively mind you. I did talk him out of it. I'm glad I did as well. That's never the correct answer (save perhaps to alleviate terminal suffering). It just aggravates me that it was clearly never about the addiction or depression as was claimed. It was about money. And that's why his story is relevant to this one.

These hours of darkness are the most peaceful, when Saturday turns to Sunday. Sunday being the Man Above's day of rest. He creates nothing though. Only misery within himself, and pity and scorn from those who've known him. And if the few stories I've heard are any indication, the scorn seems to be most prevalent among those he was closest to.

Day has broken once again. A certainty if there ever was one, based on our collective knowledge of the past. A bright morning. But the sky is pure white. Not a shadow of gray nor sliver of blue is visible. How can a day appear both cloudless and sunless at once? Then again, are there not times when there is both sunshine and rain?

Maybe I sympathize with him because of the stories he's told me. The cheating wife (and subsequent girlfriend), the son who doesn't speak with him, the physical ailments, the friends who used him, the coworkers who killed themselves. But I don't know any story but his, and in his versions, he's always the victim. Such a thing must be considered, that it's likely his behavior that creates these reactions. That, or he's far too trusting and a terrible judge of character. I suppose it could be a combination. Either way, he gave me an affordable place to live when the Bungalow Room I was renting across the street from his house was sold out from under me.

Still, I must contest the former is far more likely. I've been here for a year, but have no intent in forming a relationship beyond living below him in the Underground. It's not just that he's a bore, a self-proclaimed intellectual, and a misogynistic creep; though those are all enough to keep me at distance. No, my charge against him is that I've heard the same four or so stories over and over. And they're always just as long and drawn out as the first time I heard them. It's like he can't break free of his past.

Above all though, as grateful as I am to have a place to lay my head at night, I often get a sense of purposeful inconsideration. I know that might sound crazy, and it's likely a matter of obliviousness coupled with his drug addiction. But that really only explains his insomniac actions. I stopped cooking in the kitchen within the first month, save for frying some eggs in the morning once he's gone for work. He was adamantly obsessed with my cleanliness, while always leaving the sink full of dishes. So what could I do? It was a catch-22. There's also the various yard work that he's always mentioning needs doing, and then, seemingly with an air of passive aggressiveness, his mentioning of when the yard work has been completed. Yet there's often still a mess around my entrance to the Underground. But I'm not a roommate or housemate, I'm his tenant.

And then there's the peculiarity of the creaking floorboards that sing for minutes at a time, and the Godzilla stomping back and forth to the kitchen for his frozen pizza and fifteen diet colas. Aware or not, such inconsiderate behavior is clearly a pattern, and almost certainly the cause of his unwanted solitude. Pair that with his fear of change, and the man, any man becomes insufferable. Still, the empath in me endures him, not for any benefit to myself, but because I believe he can change, that he can find his happiness, and hopefully stop treating people in a manner that clearly pushes them away. But such is the case with far too many in this country, chasing and holding onto things we don't actually want, just because we were programmed to want them.

I say programmed rather than raised because that's just what a consumerist society with an instilled nationalistic pride is. *Programmed.* I don't claim that I never was, nor that I'm completely free of it. Only that I'm aware of it, and I desire to escape it. That was my suggestion to the Man Above. To break free of his self-made prison.

It's no concern of mine really. I just believe the world would be better if people sought out the things that bring them joy, rather than hoping for happiness to find them, or to hope to find happiness in the very things that are the cause of their misery.

I see it on the streets everywhere, even more so now, after the past year of accelerated social decline. People on the streets, still hoarding their possessions. I don't mean to make light of their struggles; I just can't image looking to commodities for comfort if my life were in such disarray. It just seems like they've given up on bettering their situation in an attempt to hold onto the things that used to bring them comfort.

It's no different with the Man Above. He's lived in the same city his entire life, worked the same job for thirty-five years, been in the same house for nearly thirty. People can change. It's just rare that people like him do. I didn't mean what I wrote, that someone should put him out of his misery. Only he should have a say in that. Just as only I do in taking myself out of mine.

I like to think of misery, not as an endpoint, but rather the middle point between joy and despair... Sometimes it sounds like a space shuttle launch. The banging from the Man Above. As I wrote, maddening. Maddening enough to jar me from my thoughts. My point. It is much easier to release from misery than it is to let go of joy or escape from despair.

I'm glad I wore my fingerless gloves, but fuck, why do I still need gloves? It's nearly Summer. He was always outside on his porch when I met him the beginning of last Summer. And through the Summer. But that was when he was almost recovered from one of his ailments, before he went, well, had to go back to work. Clearly his work, though it's all he knows or has, is the cause of his misery. And with every decision he makes based on staying at his job, he falls further into despair.

And here, at this tipping point from misery to despair, is where so many Americans, so many consumerists around the world find themselves. The culprit? It isn't the corporations and their advertisements, nor the state-structured education with its cog and drone manufacturing curriculum. It's this idea that has been warped under a guise of virtuosity; it's a facade of free expression that hides an ideology of selfishness. Understand this first, all 'isms' lead to absolutism. Maybe not for you personally, but any single ideology will have followers and detractors, and inevitably, defenders and revolters.

Individualism. Please take notice of the suffix. Individualism is *not* individuality. Individualism is an ideology, it is a way to structure a society, or rather, those living in it. However, in my view, individualism is far more dangerous to the well-being of a society than any other 'ism', simply because all other 'isms' at least hold some belief in a collective of individuals. This is why the collective individualism of a society that embraces authoritarianism is so dangerous.

The Man Above me, he's been programmed by the cult of individualism; hilarious for someone who delivers packages while wearing a mandated uniform for a living. Uniform. The antithesis of individuality. How do I know of his support for individualism? I'm sure there are many examples I could dig through my memory for, but the most recent occurrence is probably the most relevant anyway. As I wrote, the man is a misogynist. An 'ist' falls not far from an 'ism'.

I bought us dinner recently, suggested we eat on the porch. Spring was singing, our neighborhood, anxious to return to the outside world they once knew. A woman and her husband and two children passed by, the husband lagging just behind with the slightly older, more inquisitive child. "You know what he's thinking about?" Knowing him nearly a year, I tried to diffuse the conversation by placating him. My response was simply what I thought any husband would think walking behind the woman he loves. "I can't wait to get home and put the kids to sleep..."

But no. His response wasn't the benign "ya bro!" and locker room high-five I expected. No. He pushed on. His claim then became that the husband was thinking about getting 'something better'. I was almost speechless, especially with that woman being at least as physically fit as any other woman I've heard him objectify over the past year.

Before I said anything though, he continued, how it was biological. That all men thought that way. That all men are always looking for something physically better. It was such an easy riposte. "I didn't think that husband was looking for anything better." And that, for the first time, silenced him. So what does this have to do with individualism? Nothing, if you want to be blind. Everything, if you see the assumption he made. "Everyone is just as selfish as I am." And that is the thought that pervades the collective minds of those trapped behind the White Curtain.

Scene Three: June the Nineteenth
TO CONFORM OR <u>RESIST</u>

The crows are vocal again. And even more so with the brooding. Farther above, the clouds seem locked in battle with the Sun. Their gray underbellies curving around that solar disk like giant hands grasping at a gold coin. The Sun, pushing back with its fiery light, dissipating those that seek to consume it. But the clouds are many to the power of one star. These aren't philosophical thoughts, they're observations of nature turned into philosophical allegory. Such are days of harmony, when even the tree tops and their crow nests receive shade.

The clouds seem to be growing heavier. Though, I had not heard that they plan to fall from the sky today. But how often do they not make their descent when I am told they will? I can't control the weather. I can only prepare for it. These days, I find I must simultaneously expect both the best and the worst. Considering how quickly the best conditions can deteriorate, one wonders why the worst can't be more like the passing rain? This is where humanity splits with nature. Nature never mistakes a short Spring storm for a hurricane. Nature never feels the cold sting of Winter in these lengthened days.

Isn't it all allegory though? The Sun doesn't actually rise or set, or move across the sky. Nor is the Sun even stationary. Nothing is. Everything is in constant motion. We humans are just the only entity we know of who can understand that. It's impossible to not be in constant motion. So I strive to avoid motion in excess. That sounds lazy. I just mean I try to not waste energy. And in order to not waste energy, one must recognize how and when (and *why*) it is used. Such an endeavor is found if we follow the path of least resistance.

Surely another thought lethargic in appearance, but I assure you, in my world, it is not. The day is not so harmonious to me. A chill when the clouds maintain their cover, a sultry luminosity when they are dispersed. I could just move into the shade of a tree when the heat becomes too much, or remove my outer layer.

But then, when the largest of the clouds pass under the Sun, or coalesce, the chill would have my actions reverse. Such would be wasted energy for only a slight variance in comfort. *This* is my path of least resistance.

If you were to discern the psychological definition of the path of least resistance, you would see that it's extremely biased with its attachment to nature. It is, "to choose the easiest way to do something instead of trying to choose the best way." Gravity is the universal path of least resistance. If we were to view this logically, as contemplating beings, we can observe that, for one, the 'easiest way' is a subjective concept; and secondly, that the easiest way, in fact, often incurs the most resistance. This is why humans have come to build bridges and tunnels.

Let me return to nature. Even here, with their definition based on the Natural World, humanity fails to properly interpret its own observations. The flow of a river (often a metaphor for this topic) is seen as a single force, finding the easiest route to reach the ocean. But I don't see it that way. To me, the river is avoiding anything and everything that stands in its way, in order to reach its goal. Oh, I've piqued your curiosity have I? But I can push further. That river, if we are to use it as an accurate comparison to humanity, that river is all of us combined.

It all starts with singular raindrops falling into an alpine lake. This is each individual being born into a collective world. Some raindrops might stay their entire existence in that lake, some might sink into the shoreline. But there are those adventurous raindrops, the ones that avoided the thirsty deer, the ones that managed to not simply splatter and evaporate on a rock; the ones that escaped from all that tried to prevent them from plunging into the sea.

You're likely not convinced. Aren't I using my own biased attachment to nature? Perhaps. So let us explore this path, not with regards to Human Nature or the Natural World, but with our thoughts directed toward human action. After all, isn't selecting a path for our individual lives a matter of contemplation, rather than instinct?

Human Nature is no different than nature. As it is with all of nature's evolutionary successes, Human Nature is programmed for adaptation. This is why people so easily fall in line with government mandates. In a sense, conformity enables evolution. Evolution itself is a sort of programming. It's just left to instinct and chance, rather than contemplation and knowledge.

...I feel as if I'm stepping up to the guillotine again, or walking the plank. Not sure how many times this makes. The silence of my Underground devours me. Not with despair, or frankly even misery, at least not anymore. No, it's the contemplation of the Silence that's driving me mad. It's so loud in my mind, I feel it in my heart, I see it in my soul, yet the Silence remains, enveloping my temporal world. If only the Man Above were silent instead. Or at least as well.

So what path to take now? I suppose there is one more sunrise before that question becomes actuality. Such contemplation, an analysis of the clouds' direction, of the strength of the wind, it's all too varying. It's good advice to stay ahead of the storm, but such actions will eventually fade one's endurance. To constantly be striving toward a goal is often seen as virtuous; the epitome of taking the hard route to success, whatever success may mean to you.

I wouldn't say such actions are not virtuous, but eventually it does seem foolish. I say just head another direction, away from the storm. Life is difficult enough to navigate without constantly challenging one's self, or competing with others for success. If there is no other direction, just stop, and let the storm pass over. Certainly the emerging rays of Sun will cast light on something worthy of your time where you currently stand. You're just as likely to find some profit digging down as you are venturing forward.

I've been a bit abstract with my explanation. Apologies. I've much on my mind. As I wrote, I'm once again preparing for death. No, enough with the philosophical allegory. I know you require concrete examples to be convinced that such a path is not passive or apathetic. But I assure you, there is far more pride to be found in oneself if we put our energy into our immediate surroundings, rather than what we hope lies ahead. I know, this sounds like I'm advising you to only strive for that which is instantaneously within your reach. But there is fertile earth below you, and many others will be passing through on the pathway you once walked. There's something cathartic about just calmly watching the crowds pass by.

The crowds. In America, the crowds really only seem to bother people when they're in auto traffic. Obviously, you'll always encounter impatient people in any setting with social interaction. It just seems that the ratio of patient/impatient people is reversed when they are in auto traffic, compared to most other social instances. That's not to say we're all just fine with waiting in lines, or trying to maneuver through crowded areas when on foot. But there is a cohesive unity of individual understanding that most people will adhere to. This is not conformity so much as it is respect for other individuals.

However, the impatience of American drivers is not my main concern. My only care is to avoid the rush hour and weekend crowds that so many find themselves trapped within. My patience is more than enough for the vast majority of traffic incidents I find myself in. No, my concern is for the non-auto crowds. That's not entirely true. I had meant to provide an example for you, as it relates to the path of least resistance.

For some time I lived near the corner of a busy street. To turn right was never an issue, but making a left was nearly impossible during most hours of the day. Yet a block or two down was a traffic light. So instead of fighting the constant flow of traffic and blind corners, I would travel around my block, probably even adding time to my journey. But I tired of the risk of accident. So I chose the path of least resistance. I could give you a thousand examples of similar decisions as it relates to driving; though with driving, my concern is safety, not adventure.

Another example then? Very well, I'll give you one from my travels. In a place beyond the White Curtain where cars are not allowed. The Cinque Terre of Italy. I could tell you of the trek I made from Riomaggiore to Manarola on a steep hot desolate trail, instead of taking the overly crowded train. Or of the 33 flights of stairs I climbed four times up to the village of Corniglia, over waiting for and taking a bus with tourists packed in like sardines. But those examples, they are not a path everyone can take. And so, though they were my easiest paths forward; they are certainly not *the* path of least resistance for everyone. As with most things, it's a subjective concept.

Monterosso al Mare. After funneling through the train doors onto the bright platform basking in the beach Sun, blinded travelers follow the signs, and each other, through a dark congested tunnel into the Old Town. Always wanting to take in my new surroundings before venturing forward, I found myself sufficiently behind the pack. Or flock. Flock is more accurate. I knew it wouldn't take very long to trod behind the mass of conformity in front of me, but I spotted a path just to the right that followed in the direction of the tunnel, only with a slight incline, and a spectacular view of the sea. I couldn't believe it, no one else had taken the detour.

I ended up at the church and cemetery that sit atop the hill everyone else had likely already finished tunneling through, but had I simply continued along the cliff-side path, I would have certainly entered the village before at least half of the horde that departed from the train I arrived on. Imagine, a path so easily traveled, and so full of beauty and discovery, and thinking that cramming through a poorly lit tunnel with a few hundred other people is the path of least resistance. Simply because it's a short flat path. Resistance isn't about difficulty, it's the catalyst of conformity.

That's enough philosophy. I'm sure you get the point now. How does it pertain to this story, to my place in the Underground? Well, I'm not quite sure. That's why I'm writing this story. I can tell you what I think though...

The Man Above, he always follows the least difficult path. Yet he's been nowhere beyond where he was the day he was born. He's gone abroad, been to the coast, visited towns distant and near. But he is always planning to return to where he was. For some, this life of stagnation, with occasional travel, might be exactly what they desire. Is this not how towns are formed? The

Man Above though, he's told me of his wanderlust dreams. So why does he stay?

Lack of courage, fear of change, those certainly play a role. But it's far more than that. He doesn't recognize his own programmed conformity. "Hard work is the surest way to avoid taking the path of least resistance", or so he would have been taught. He believes his labor to be of the highest calling for a human. And in his constant struggle to fight his desire for escape, instead of seeking what he wants, he drowns himself in his drug-induced loneliness. To me, the path of least resistance is the path which most resists the urge (instinct) to conform.

Scene Four: June the Twenty-First
FROM INSIDE TO <u>OUTSIDE</u>

If you couldn't tell from my nature based allegory, the observations I make of the Natural World, my place in the Underground is located near a park. It's the only solace I truly have in this city. And aside from my employer, and the Man Above me, it is often my only non-consumer engagement with other people. The past year certainly dampened social interaction, but this city does not seem to have the butterflies floating among the barflies, as my last city did.

By definition I am certainly not an introvert, I talk far too much for that. But nor am I the typical 'life of the party' extrovert. In most instances of large gatherings, while the egocentric personalities are all vying for engagement, I will likely be found in a corner. Not hiding from or avoiding social interaction, just observing, listening. And on the best occasions, it's a small selective conversation of intrigue that provides for me on the perimeter. The entire aspect of introvert/extrovert psychological framework is completely lacking a gray area. As it is with all opposing forces, the introvert and extrovert are not simply opposites, they're polar endpoints found on a scale, or in a spectrum, whichever measure you prefer.

My current city, it has introverted me. The people, the culture, they're stale. Even with the influx of domestic migrants (Americans who relocate to new cities for employment opportunities), there's a pervasive homogeneous aura that eats at my soul. My last city, even excluding socialization with others at my place of employment, I was never devoid of gainful conversation. I didn't make any friends in my wanderings, at least not in the definitive sense. I don't even recall any names really. But we all knew each other. Intangible acquaintances. I gained more knowledge and understanding of the world in that year of random conversation and exploration, than I did from any academic setting. That city, my last city. The Emerald Realm, it's alive.

Far more alive than the city that birthed me in the middle of the night. Maybe that's why I never sleep... That's not fair. I never lived there with the mind of an adult. I'm sure it's just as alive, if not more so. On second thought though, that place is why I am the way I am. I'm conflating the idea of what it means to be alive. I don't simply mean a beating heart and cognitive awareness. One can never sleep, yet still never live a day. Just ask the Man Above me.

My mind is a bit frozen from the nihilism at the moment. At least it's no longer from the weather. Still, I'm having a hard time formulating my thoughts for you. But I just heard someone in passing, commenting on this past year that forced the world to close. "I'm an extrovert yo! I need to get out after all this shit." He was young. An adult, but still young. Kid, we all need to get out after the past year. This is why this topic is important to this story. Misconception. Those with more introverted tendencies aren't necessarily shut-ins. And though a shut-in personality type is most likely a polar introvert, there is always the possibility of unknown life circumstances being the cause of the shut-in's behavior.

The Man Above, I can't say how this past year has affected him, not having known him before. He makes claims of activities he used to partake in, and that he will be resuming them in earnest, now that things are getting better. He never does though. He just continues on with his cyclical routine. He speaks of friends I never see, all while keeping himself imprisoned by his work and habit. He seems an extrovert, talkative with me, always greeting those who pass by when he's outside on the porch. But his actions, the way he lives, hiding behind closed shades, only venturing out to hide behind a uniform and the boxes he delivers, or to procurer his frozen pizzas and diet colas. Are these not the actions of an introvert?

This past year, it's hardly affected me. People in my current city seem collectively anti-social. It's different in the park outside from my room in the Underground. People have become familiar with me and my dog Azzura (Zura for short), so there's decent passing conversation. But in my last city, conversation with strangers was common. It was more common at bars of course, but any public gathering space in that city was a potential for random meaningful conversation. And it could come from anywhere, well, anyone. I've never lived anywhere with a citizen base so interested in furthering their knowledge beyond academics, and then sharing that knowledge with anyone interested in listening, generally without a hint of pretentiousness or conceit.

I suppose if I'm to stay in this city, I should find my extrovert needs out in nature. I know, I'm conflating, in direct opposition to my contrasting introverts and shut-ins. But I can speak to the trees and the river, and the individual snowflakes and raindrops that comprise the river. The birds always have something to say. And then there's always the disconnect from the civilized world, which extroverts the mind from commonality.

This modern consumerist society, especially behind this White Curtain, it makes us introverts to ourselves. We find ourselves focusing more on what others think of us, over what we think of ourselves, what we want *for* ourselves. This is why I left the city, the region, that birthed me. All that mattered there was achieving the predetermined American Dream.

Maybe that should be in quotes. 'The American Dream'. It's a scam, and a sham. Under the best circumstances, it's programmed passivity; at its very worst, it's an endeavor of complete self-absorption. Another conflation to delve into at another time, but being self-absorbed is not synonymous with being self-centered. It's polar selfishness through and through. With selflessness being the polar opposite. Self-centered, well, it's in the center of that spectrum... The 'Dream' used to be much simpler, a house, a family, and a well-paying productive job to support it all. Much has changed since my grandparents were of my age group though. Much has changed respectively, with regards to my parents' generation as well.

All the 'Dream' has become is commodified desire. It's nothing more than a throwback to the Romantic Era, excluding the *romance* itself. I don't mean romance in the common sense, the love between two enamored souls; that will always exist.

No, I mean it with the entirety of the Romantic Era, poetry, art, literature, music, and intellectuality. There is *none* of that now. At least with Old World Romanticism there was individuality within a mass cultural movement. People had paintings and interior decoration commissioned to their specified tastes. Granted such things were largely only afforded to the aristocratic class. But now, mostly everyone chooses from the same mass-produced catalogs of design. The only variation being societal status allowing access to slightly more expensive and 'rare' mass-produced goods. We live in a culture that defines itself through the commodities its people utilize as emotional representation.

But it's not just the expressive homogeneity that covers the walls of our homes, and to a lesser extent, our bodies that causes issue. As it was in the Romantics' rejection of Enlightenment philosophy and its rationalism, the modern consumerist is rejecting logic and reason for a false sense of importance and personal satisfaction. Individual belief has become more important than factual understanding. This can be seen in any consumerist society. But behind the White Curtain, with its penchant for individualism, society, across the political spectrum, is deteriorating into extreme tribalism. This of course creates a culture of introverted minds.

Culture itself always plays a large role for an individual's expression. This is where the introversion of a personality in a cognitive being who is part of a social species is created. What do I mean by this? It's simple. No one is truly an introvert. It's only displacement from and rejection of social norms that introverts an individual. One group's introvert can easily be the extrovert within a different group, or in a different setting. Or even under different circumstances. I've known the most lively of people to be near mute in my presence, and I, so quiet out among their liveliness, unable to contain my extroversion when the scene turns intimate.

But I want to talk to you a bit more about culture, and how an individual is raised within a culture, it can affect how introverted or extroverted they behave. I don't intend to alter the definition of culture here. My purpose is to point out the importance of being cultural and embracing a multicultural society. If everyone gathered in the liveliest group at a party all refused to engage with anyone else at the party, could we honestly classify them as extroverts, simply based on decibel output?

This is not to say that homogeneous culture is necessarily bad, just that it is generally tribalist in nature. On a small scale, in a rural setting, especially in less developed nations, the tribalist mentality is more a method of group customs and survival measures than about celebrating culture. And so instead of displeasure with the society one is born to being the cause of personality introversion, it's generally prowess and intellect that instead draws out extroversion in individuals.

In fact, I'd argue that culture can only exist if one society intersects with another. As much as we may be born into our culture, our knowledge of other cultures creates an a priori choice. I say it's a priori because even if an individual finds no commonality with, or place within the cultures they've been introduced to, there's still the knowledge that other cultures exist elsewhere. Tribalism asserts that a specific way of life is the only possibility for that society to function.

Culture then becomes a cult, when a specific culture within a multicultural society imposes its homogeneity on everyone, be it through direct force or legislative authority. It's a rejection of multicultural society for tribalism. And though the followers of such homogeneity may become collectively extroverted with their large gatherings and rehearsed chants, their minds all become introverted. And for this reason, the mass of introverted minds found behind the White Curtain, I find it necessary to include these ramblings in this story.

If I believed in such things, I'd say it was the greatest trick the Devil ever pulled. Really it's just modern aristocratic rule. The White Curtain is the *Tribe of Consumerism*, and it has been so artfully draped over a multicultural society. One can grow up to be anything they want to be, so long as they stay within the consumerist system. One can move from coast to coast searching for a culture that feels like home, yet it must be achieved under the consumerist guidelines. But you can't just get a job and buy a house anymore. Everything must follow the order of consumerism, if you want to live a dignified life.

Really though, what is a dignified life anymore? For most, that dignity is a number with a dollar sign in front of it; some certainly more in need of that sum than others. Still, it's servitude to culture all the same. One who thinks there could be no dignity without simply owning a house, is really no different than one who sees a collection of suits and watches, and an expensive car as a measure that their life is dignified. It's an introverted thought process through and through, where one allows cultural programming to dictate their external needs.

As I've wrote, I am not immune to this system, I am merely aware of it, and allow myself to be caught too easily in its traps. It's not that I seek the comfort of its traps, I just utilize them to pass the time. And as time passes, I amass consumerism out of sheer boredom. If I were given a proper reason and a clear path, as I have progressively done several times in my past, I could easily leave it all behind. Well, nearly all of it, there are items which hold value beyond their commodified stature or sentimentality. And of course, there's Zura, and my hope of breaking the Silence. It's this thought though, or perhaps ability, that has always cast me as an introvert to others. To be able to just move through life with fleeting attachment.

I suppose this is why I feel so introverted here in this city. I'm uncertain where to move on to. I hate going backward. But I was done with the Land of Eternal Summer. Not so much with the Emerald Realm. And anything here that I've yet to explore is well within driving distance for a short trip. Still though, my goal is not the Emerald Realm, it is escape from the White Curtain. And this is where my mind is, where my current wager is being placed. Of the paths before me, which is of the least resistance?

My concern for this introverted city is something I can endure, so long as there is light at the end of the proverbial tunnel. Yet I feel with every moment I spend here, the tunnel just lengthens. I find myself constantly needing to invest In the current moment, instead of preparing for escape. Whether that be mentally or financially, it takes much from my focus and energy. And far too often, it takes from the sum I need to properly escape.

Scene Five: July the First
TO WORK OR <u>LIVE</u>

Most people programmed by and trapped within this consumerist society exist with the thought that being happy with what they do for a living is more important than being happy with where they live. This is why so many people will move to a new city. Not for a change of culture or scenery, but to love what they do to earn an income. Now don't get me wrong, we should all enjoy, at least on some level, whatever it is we do to get paid. It's just, the phrase "do you live to work or work to live" has always seemed like it was missing from consumerist thought. And as is such, people find themselves working a job they thought they'd love, living in a city that seemed it would be of no consequential difference.

Yet the reality is, too many end up unhappy with their lives. Only being able to find a shred of happiness in the commodities they surround themselves with. To me, there is far more worth in working to live. A job will always become aggravating at some point, regardless of how enjoyable it generally may be. So we may as well love where we live and how we spend our free time.

The trouble is, I'm potentially so close to an end to my endeavor; to escape the White Curtain. And so, my idea to live, and only concern myself with work, so as to provide a sufficient income toward the life I want, is finding itself at a crossroad along the path of least resistance. If I truly work to live, should that not focus on the future, instead of being happy with my temporary immediate state of being? If the future was guaranteed, sure, maybe. But at this point, concerns for my future from anyone other than myself are nothing but mere platitudes. Recognition of my fading interest.

I don't think I'll ever truly like anything I do for a living. That sounds awful coming from an aspiring writer, I know. But as it often is with me, my thoughts are on a different level from commonality. I enjoy writing. It's no different from the happiness I find in cooking. I just can't see myself ever churning out words simply to sell them, just so I can eat and pay my bills. I've nothing against finding success in my passions, I just won't commodify them to survive, or even thrive. There's a reason I never went the culinary route as a profession, even with my passion for cooking, and all the restaurant experience I've acquired. I never met a chef who liked cooking at home. Inevitably, if you try to turn a passion into a career, at some point it becomes arduous labor.

There are two (or three) ways around this issue, in any modern, capitalist economy based state. The first is to outright own your productivity; work only for yourself, and employ no one. Obviously, this greatly limits both the options of the industry one can operate in, and the ability to grow the business. Second, and this can also mix in with the first (hence, "or three"), one can choose to simply save and find a property cheap enough, and live as archaically as they so desire.

Of course, there's the issue of needing to be a part of the capitalist world, in order to earn enough to buy your land; but frugal living is easy enough if you have a goal, and know how to avoid the consumerist pitfalls. And once land is acquired, it can then be utilized for profit, if you would prefer to remain in contact with society. In a sense, this third option is the same as the first, though you wouldn't need to lease space for a business. As the landowner, whatever your profit may be, you own the productivity. And if your operation is small enough, the idea would be to create a craft product; be it agricultural based or providing hospitality to travelers.

But I'm not there yet. At this moment, I don't have the proper resources to escape. If I leave now, I risk entering the perpetuity of laboring for another's profits. Not that I'm not doing that right now, but I have a fair amount of freedom within, and control over the environment I am employed in. And even still, in reality, I'm earning more than I ever did working in restaurants. That is if you calculate my wage hourly, and ignore the thirty percent increase in rent prices over the past five years. In actuality, I'm not earning more. At the end of the year, it's been no different than any other. The same bottom line, more or less, but with inflation on where that bottom line goes.

Perpetuity. I seek to avoid that most of all. An endless cycle of attempting success in a world that requires resources for successes to be achieved, if you don't want to completely sell decades of your life to labor for another's profits. A life where you're only finding enjoyment in commodified activities, spending your free hours trapped by the consumerist crowds you have conformed to.

But I see perpetuity in both paths laid before me. It's just that one path contains certain happiness, and possibly joy. Whereas the other path is a stale circle of contentment. Or worse.

Contentment is an interesting state of being, isn't it? I would compare it to Limbo, a state of nothingness. Nothingness in the actual sense, not nihilistic. Limbo, contentment, they're outside of existence. This is that absurdist moment Camus speaks of, where we are looking outward for opportunity. For something to give life meaning, to have a purpose for our individual existence.

Once we find that meaning, that object or experience, or person, that gives us purpose, we move out of Limbo, finding ourselves in Purgatory. And as contentment is to Limbo, we find misery being our state in Purgatory. Why misery? Because we believe we are so close to the joy of Heaven, but are all too wary of Hell's despair. And that misery is further compounded when we neither rise nor fall, when we are stranded in motion, waiting for judgment. Add to this the Siren call from Limbo, clamoring for us to return to contentment and search for a different path to Heaven.

That stale circle, it is the city I currently find myself in. An urban prison, guarded by nature. A massive river to the north, desolation south, the east and west flanked by mountains. With the ever-watchful eye of the Hooded Giant always blocking the rising Sun. That call back to Limbo. It is a call from my past as well. The Purgatory of which I was the closest to reaching Heaven. That Emerald Realm paved with its Golden Rays of Light.

I was always wary of the diversion I took, but even the Emerald Realm is cloaked by the White Curtain. In certain ways, even more so than within this open enclosure I currently reside. But it's really all the same no matter where the White Curtain drapes over you. It's just some areas have a stronger breeze that creates openings in the curtain, should one wish to escape. That's why I came here. The opening seemed larger. My path to escape shorter, easier. Why wouldn't I take that opportunity?

There's not much difference in the bars or stores, or the availability of the few commodities I still embrace. I can always find happiness, so long as I can eat and drink to my, somewhat lofty, acquired taste. Yet here, I find myself wandering, unable to get lost. Whereas under the Emerald Foliage and Golden Sky, I could so easily get lost knowing exactly where I was going.

The real issue here, this place, this city, it is inherently one dimensional. There may be several universes of existence, but they all lack layers. It's a collective of varying homogeneity. That was always my issue with living in the Land of Eternal Summer. It's hard to find people in such places who embrace all that life has to offer. Instead, as it is with most communities behind the White Curtain, most people settle into a specific niche of existence. Only ever furthering their *selective* knowledge (if furthered at all), and associating with those of like mind.

I prefer people and places that encourage cultural sharing. This city, like many other smaller cities, lacks a web of diversity, even if diversity is present in demographics. And I don't mean this just in the typical sense of ethnicity, but in societal cultures, like exercise or gaming. This isn't to say everyone in this city stays within their homogeneous interests, or that everyone in larger cities delve into a multitude of activities. It's just the ratio generally seems skewed depending on those measures.

Here, it's as if most people only have singular interests. A group I'm friendly with, they're runners, and that's about it. If they aren't at work, they're training for some organized run, or just hanging out with their runner friends. That's it. There's never any discourse of art or philosophy, science or politics. Conversations tend to be about their work lives, or stories of their athletic accomplishments, with random spatterings of dialogue pertaining to professional sports. And it's the same with any artists I've encountered, or those engaged in political action. Homogeneity of interests.

I'm rambling. The point is, I'm not happy here. But my job is rarely aggravating, and I could likely escape this country within a couple of years. Whereas if I move back to where I was, my escape becomes an indefinite Purgatory. But I'm far more in control of that Purgatory than my current one. As always, it's risk assessment, coupled with the heart's desire. Could I endure another two years displeased with where I live? Certainly. It just doesn't seem at current that two years will see me where I want to be. I know moving back to my last city won't either, but at least I'll enjoy the ride.

Watching the Sun creep across the sky, it makes me question why I even came here. Is feeling more free at work really more important than not feeling imprisoned when outside of work? It's not the job itself that I take issue with, as I wrote, there's a freedom there that I won't find with other employers. But the job requires my constant presence, keeping me from even temporary escape. I can make advanced plans for reprieve, it's just that those plans must be made for specific, preset times.

There's freedom in being a cog, so long as you're aware of your state. You may have no control over the labor that is required of you, but once you clock out, you are as free as your income and environment will allow. The same can't be said for drones though. What's the difference? Well, drones are more free to fly when they can find free time; it's just their connectivity to their place of employment infiltrates their lives outside of work. The division between the two is generally one of acquired skills and knowledge, with education being the main form of acquisition, followed by a distant second of on-the-job experience. But me, I'd rather be a cog than a drone.

Our celebration of 'Freedom' is nearing. Do you feel free? People are funny to me, they lose their minds collectively, one way or the other, over temporary mandates. Mandates that are generally, quite frankly, necessary, even if poorly executed or disastrously misinformed. Yet how many people will stand at a corner, waiting for the little white man to tell them it is safe to cross the street, when there isn't a car in sight? Most people only act like rebels when it's safe to do so.

Scene Six: July the Fourth
FROM EFFECT TO <u>CAUSE</u>

This heat is far more than oppressive, it's downright merciless. But for me, I enjoy such stillness of life. It's even more quiet than the start of last year. Even the air is still. The smoke from my cigarette is sticking to my fingers, slightly inflaming my hand before dissipating up my forearm. It really shouldn't be this hot. The alarm has been rightly sounded, but too many see the effects as causes. And a further too many see those effects as inconsequential.

They all have their heads in the sand. Those in denial of course, but also those who believe, those who see the signs for what they are, a manufactured Armageddon. Those in denial, they are held by the same conservative ideology that evolution, the progress of humanity, has always been able to overcome. But society has never faced such a large collective of liberal progression being blinded by hate for conservatism. There I go. The politics again.

I'm not wrong though. It's not the oil, or the plastic we make from it that is the *cause* of decay. They are merely the consequences of consumerism. They are the *effect* of domination through the consumer market. So many of us are trapped by our reliance on crude oil, myself included. Much of consumer product and food packaging is made from petroleum. The food packaging is what really gets me. Especially since there are plant based alternatives. They'll tell us that the consumer will bear the brunt of the cost. That altering the materials the industry uses to create plastic will result in millions of jobs lost.

Of course this isn't true though, it's capitalist, well, corporatist propaganda. Lies they tell to keep and increase their financial profits. What is the cost of ingesting petroleum byproducts though, as they leach into the prepackaged foods we consume? Companies would certainly have to increase expenditure in the short term if they were to transition from petrol based to plant based plastics. Costs mainly being equipment upgrades and labor training for new material. But no one *need* lose their job, and no one needs to see an inflation of cost for goods for this to happen. Instead, the corporatists need to properly adhere to their supposed capitalist ideology, and forego short-term financial profit in exchange for investing in a stable future.

I'm sure many will disagree, but the actual purpose of capitalism *is* to increase productivity in the commercial sector through innovation, in order to provide for everyone, the life of leisure that was previously only afforded to the aristocratic class and those above them. The trouble is, too many trapped within the consumerist mindset mistake leisure as luxury, and a further too many view leisure as a privilege to be earned through labor. I was going to explore this thought with regards to the cliché of comparing the US with European countries, in this case, specifically the paid leave governments mandate for employees (the EU itself requires a minimum of four weeks for member nations). But on that research, I came upon something far more damning to America's claim of 'Land of the Free'.

Behind this White Curtain, this consumerist trap, this country full of corporatist politicians clamoring how they represent the will of the people, there is no minimum requirement for paid time off, neither on the federal level nor by *any* state. Maybe this doesn't seem like an issue to some, after all, are we not free to choose where we work? The American capitalist will tell you to find a job that provides the benefits you desire. But even the average days of paid vacation employers offer in the US is only twenty days, and that after twenty years of service. And it must be with the same company! What then if you're laid off, or simply want to try your hand at something new?

This mockery of freedom is further compounded when you find out that Afghanistan, a country that has been portrayed as the antithesis of freedom to American citizens for the last twenty years, requires fifteen days of paid public holidays, with most workers getting twenty days of paid recreational leave as well. Russia, America's greatest adversary, and opponent to democracy; they mandate twenty-eight days of paid personal leave, on top of fourteen paid public holidays. Even the authoritarian government of China, with its autocratic dictatorship, requires paid leave for employees.

I know the rebuttal, that this is why America is so great, so exceptional. Because our government doesn't mandate requirements on how businesses choose to treat their employees. I suppose there is some freedom in the self-determination that arises out of the worker's need to be protective and act with self-interest. But as I've seen it, this creates competition in areas, or societal sectors, where there should be collaboration and cooperation. After all, aren't we a social species?

And this here is the actual *cause* of the world burning. Competition. Greed is merely a catalyst for a sociopathic society to compete with each other, rather than working together. Even in business we find tribalism. It's only acceptable to work cooperatively if working for the same company, or toward a mutual goal with other companies, once terms are agreed upon with lawyers and contracts. This goes against Human Nature, against nature itself, and the effect is the Earth reacting with volatility. For every action...

That's why it's so fucking hot. I'm not claiming the planet to be sentient, but if you start a fire, expect it to spread if there's nothing to contain it and nothing is done to put it out. The trajectory is already irreparable, all that can be hoped for at this point is that world governments will collectively act fast enough to stop already known irreversible changes from becoming inevitably catastrophic. We know there's no going back to how things were, but if changes are made to the consumerist market to restrict planetary damage for financial profit, the living beings of this planet might only need to evolve or migrate, instead of facing complete devastation and likely extinction. Consumerism has become too pervasive throughout the world, and with it, pollution of all kinds. The cause of want creates the effect of decay.

I walked for several miles, it's 112°. I suppose my time in the desert has something to do with my sense of immunity to this heat. That's what sparked these thoughts, my survival in such conditions. Obviously there is a threshold for any life form, but

I had a thought, to say people are fainting (or in the worst case, dying), because of the heat; I ask, is the heat truly the cause? I'd argue no, it's the individual's lack of conditioning, or inability to function in high temperatures (or ignorance of the body's warnings of danger) that caused their body to shut down. The heat is the catalyst.

There is never just cause and effect, or reactive energies if we want to be scientific with this discourse. No, every instance of cause and effect *needs* a catalyst. Something to set process into motion. Sure, energy can never truly be destroyed, but it can be inert, and so, requires a stimulant to force it into action. There is no fire without a spark, no inferno without the free air.

So what of escape? That's why I'm writing this story, isn't it? My goal, to escape the White Curtain, it is simply the effect of multiple causes. The catalyst is just my point of view concerning those causes. I can't say they were always causes for my escape, most aspects were a desire to strive for whatever it was society had programmed me to believe I wanted. I never desired fame or immense wealth; though I did want to be 'well-off'. I saw no need for a mansion or an overly fancy car, no thought toward owning a yacht, or any objects of pure excess. What is excess though? I did want a 'nice' house, and a car of moderate luxury, along with a decent sport boat and all the unnecessary 'necessities' we're told define our success.

However, these were not causes, they were effects, goals. The cause was the programming, as it is with most of the en-shrouded. The catalyst, indoctrination into the White Curtain, propaganda that teaches children to measure financial profit as the ultimate virtue. The programming, that was done by our teachers and family, and anyone else we were led to believe held wisdom and guidance we could trust, though they too had been programmed. Still, even at six, my first flash of a refusal to conform illuminated my young mind when I saw the maze of cubicles in my mother's office. I knew from that early age, my path would never lead to a job in an office building.

I enjoyed art and music, and hockey. I can't even say sports as a whole. Other than that, I had limited interests. Television and video games were just passive entertainment, as they held no meaning toward any thoughts I had for my future. I did plenty of other things throughout my youth, but none of them held the vision of a career path. Of course hockey was a fool's dream; did I really believe I could play hockey for a profession? With my reflexes, certainly. Maybe I'd never play in the top tier, but I was more than content with the idea of earning a modest income for some minor team. It was my congenital heart defect that ensured that dream remained unattainable. And quite frankly, I have no innate talent for music.

So some form of art seemed the best route to follow. I wanted to avoid the aesthetics for aesthetic purpose, the visual arts, painting, sculpture, photography. There was no 'career' in fine art enterprise. Hell, nearly every famous artist we learned of through grade school, they were a cautionary tale, that works of genius are rarely recognized during an artist's lifetime. So I looked toward the commercial arts. This is how our educational system functions though, it encourages young minds to contemplate the needs of the consumer over their personal passions, and I've been fighting that indoctrination for well over a decade. The ever-changing societal landscape of this country making that fight harder.

I enrolled in a program for industrial design, the consumerist path for someone with a passion for sculpture. There are a multitude of specialty fields within industrial design, but by nature, they all exhibit the same commodified intent. Sell. Sell a movie with special effects, sell a product designed for function, sell others' products through enticing displays. All that matters is that what you design can be used to sell something to consumers. I wanted out halfway through the program. Not out of morality though, as I see it now in hindsight.

As thankful as I am now, that I avoided a life both of servitude to consumerism, and being a perpetuator of the consumerist apocalypse, my reasoning to choose a different path was born of self-preservation. There was a slight influence of disdain for consumerism that grew in me as I sought to become an educator, believing that instructing our youth would at least prove to be a noble endeavor. Even here though, once the thin veneer of the White Curtain had been peered through, I saw that all I would be doing was helping to send children down the same path of the consumerist trap.

And I saw firsthand how it was getting worse. The bureaucrats will say it's for the purpose of academic success. But kindergartners learning to repeat things without yet being able to comprehend the subject matter, that isn't about education, it's to create unquestioning laborers. The focus on academics is just to ensure the most intelligent slip through the proverbial cracks of mass-produced mediocrity. This is further compounded by the diminishing time and resources allotted toward socialization and extracurriculars.

I no longer believed in a future; the only purpose in life, as I saw it anymore, was to seek adventure. Initially, I still believed this could be done during my Summers as an educator, hopefully injecting some free will into my students as they passed through my life. That quickly dissolved once I couldn't find teaching jobs in a place I'd want to live. Then I saw the splendor of the West, life on the Pacific Coast. I had no plan, no place to live.

I looked around at all my worthless accumulations. Other people's ideas of what we want. I was living in a city I never... Ah, that's a story in of itself, my journey from *there* to *here*, my first story of escape. The point is, I began to see all the effects I sought as ends, turn to a cause of solidarity within myself to escape the life I had so long been told I wanted. I left then, because I knew I didn't want the life of *success* as it had been defined to me.

And that's where I am in this current moment. I suppose you could say I grew impatient in my cause, and that's how I became trapped again. It's simplifying it, but accurate. The truth is, I've found myself in a place, or a state of mind, I thought I'd never be, accepting a life of comfort; settling for stability over adventure. My adventures have become meager vacations. That's why I'm leaving, I won't settle. And that's all there is here, settled silence.

I won't lie, I thought the Silence could be broken in this place, but as time passes, it seems that will never be so. My wager now, that this is the reason for such deafening silence, it's a constant call for me to escape. It's been two years after all. Two years lost out in the wilderness, surrounded by the March of Time, looking for smoke rising on the horizon, or a river to follow. Whatever I can find to help me escape the silence of the trees. Only the moss gives me direction. There's space for life to grow to the north.

I never felt as if I was wasting my time when I look at the past lives I've lived. I was always enjoying myself in the moment. That isn't entirely true... There have been times when I followed my mind over my heart. That's what I've done these past two years, isn't it? What have I even gained? Better question. What have I possibly lost? I wasn't even seeking fame or wealth, just basic financial stability. Behind the White Curtain, such a thing is only attainable at a loss of individual freedom. The Sun is setting on my time in this city. In my mind, in my heart, I am already gone.

PART TWO
DepartMentality

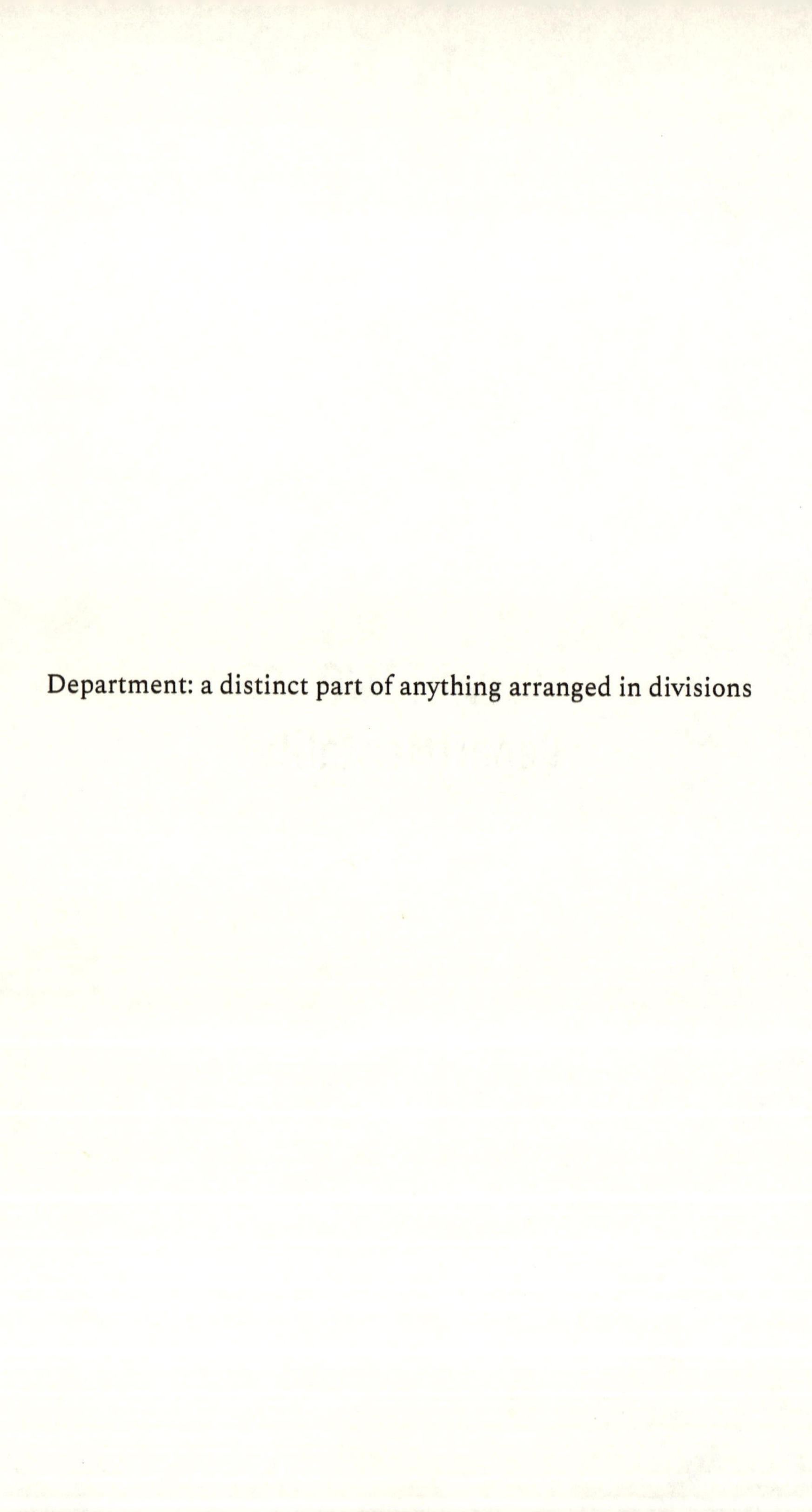

Department: a distinct part of anything arranged in divisions

Act III: Year Three

Scene One: July the Twenty-Sixth
TO CONTRAST OR <u>COMPARE</u>

We are who we are...

The thickness of the White Curtain, it both varies and is indistinguishable. My college years ended, and what we are told is life was to begin. I knew there was no place for me in the land that birthed me, the northeastern section of this country. I had spent the latter half of my childhood living in a town that fell somewhere between suburban and rural. It was too far from any city to truly be labeled as suburban. And far too commercialized to be considered rural. In reality, that didn't matter though; the homogeneity of the region touched even the smallest remote village size towns.

You could compare it to a European nation. An Italian from the Sicilian countryside has more in common with a cosmopolitan Milanese than with the most provincial Spaniard. But contrasting it to the regions spread throughout these lands, the people of the Northeast have little in common with the rest, beyond waving the same national flag. Such could be said for all of the regions here, there's just a broader spectrum of cultural diversity between their urban and rural areas.

I had intended to venture west; the southwestern beaches had always seemed the most promising to me. There was no plan of fame, just a desire to drink on the sand in the Sun year-round. At that young age though, barely out of college, the prospect of doing it alone wasn't even a thought in my mind. It was actually my friend's idea. I truly had no concept of what to do with my future. I was already back at home in that rural suburbia. But he quickly changed course, deciding on the Oaken Commonwealth over the Angelic Kingdom. Little to compare, much to contrast.

So I went south instead of west. How could I go west alone?! I knew no one, and had no real experience or skills to find a job so far from the comfort of what I knew. But for the first time in my life, I chose to dive into the unknown, to seek a future with no plan; to follow my heart, instead of my mind.

I was tired of doing what societal structures thought best for me. My parents questioned me with ferocity, what would I do there?! How could I possibly survive? I did what I knew, serving people food and drinks. I had a job within a week of my arrival. We, my friend and I, quickly fell back into form from our not-so-distant college days. Now without having to attend classes. Work and bars, and drinking too much at home. There wasn't really a difference in my lifestyle after the move, but I felt free.

Contrastingly, I was free. No longer being back at home lifted the weight of living somewhere I knew I didn't want to live. But comparatively, nothing really changed other than my location. The apartment we found to rent was right in the middle of commercialized suburbia, excluding the restaurant I worked at and the bar across the parking lot. Sure, they were standalone small businesses, but they were in a strip mall parking lot, twenty minutes outside of the downtown area. It was suburbia through and through; 'cookie cutter' housing developments, apartment complexes, strip malls, and corporate eateries. The charm of being somewhere new quickly dissipated.

We had things to do though. My friend's brother moved in with us. We rented a three bedroom apartment in anticipation of my friend's girlfriend moving in with us initially, but that person decided on a different path for her life. I felt bad for my friend, of course, but I was happy to have his brother there instead. Much better to live as *The Three Amigos* than a 'third wheel'.

The three of us, along with the cook at my restaurant, we filled our free time with anything that revolved around smoking and booze. Pool halls, bowling alleys, and public golf courses. And of course, football Sunday... All things I don't give a fuck about now. But then, that was life. That was all life *there* really seemed to offer. I even started smoking on occasion, ignoring concern for my heart. I certainly never became the textbook definition of a smoker though. Rarely would I smoke more than a pack every two weeks.

As I wrote though, the charm wore off. Especially being as far as I was from the city center, and farther from the mountains and ocean than I had ever lived before. My friend I moved down with started a long distance relationship with a girl he knew back up north, he was leaving when our lease was up.

Then there was the bartender from work, and his drunken bullshit. One night, leaving the bar, he pushed my friend against my car. I was certainly pissed at him for assaulting my friend, but I also became way too incensed about the small elbow size dent the altercation had left in my car door. That dent, along with all the other dents and scratches, and the fading paint; they became akin to the scars I have on my body. Badges of pride and honor.

But then, I was not even remotely in control of my reactionary nature. And as embarrassing as my reaction is to admit, I'm thankful for it to this day. My friend leaving, my understanding there was no way I could make that move back up the interstate, my not wanting to work with that bartender ever again; I completely lost myself. I called out of work the next day, something I had only ever done when physically unable to work. (More out of the need to survive than on some virtuous principle.)

I drove west. No, not all the way west, at least not yet. I went to the Little City in the Mountains. I'd slept in my car on several occasions before, mostly just passing out on the rear seats at some shore bar back home, knowing I was too drunk to drive. This was different though, I'd never purposefully spent the night sleeping in my car while fairly sober. I say fairly because of course I had to indulge myself at the local bars.

I spent the night in a hotel parking lot. Maybe it was a motel, though I think it was actually a Holiday Inn. I awoke in a panic a few times, the worst of them being when my fear seeped into my dream. I shot awake, confused and alarmed. It felt like my car was being towed. It wasn't. My guess, the slight tremor of a passing car in the parking lot, perhaps a truck rumbling by on the nearby road. Hell, it could've been some drunks walking by, noticing me sleeping in the back. No matter. There was no tow truck. As I wrote, I immediately realized it was the fear that penetrates dreams.

But I didn't go out there just to wander the town and sleep in my car. I went there to backpack out into the wilderness of Mount Mitchell. It's fucking hilarious to contrast that 'adventure' with what I've done since reaching the West Coast. Comparatively though, to what I had previously done, this wasn't something I was prepared for. Fear easily conquered the courage that had led me to that mountain peak.

I make myself sound heroic if you don't know Mount Mitchell. The peak is a parking lot. The previous Summer I had backpacked in the Catskills with two friends. It was arduous, and I was in far better shape then, than I had become with the substance abuse extracurriculars of my Southern Lifestyle. What I remember most from that, even to this day; the cliff where we made camp, and the stars of my childhood. The night sky before I became enamored with urban life. That was what guided me to those Mountain Ridges of the Deepest Blue, the thought of seeing all those distant spheres of fire light up the black firmament.

My bag was loaded with all the gear and provisions I would need. I knew the route from studying the trail map, and also had a GPS with me in case I became lost. The first leg of the journey was pleasant, some open meadows, some tree tunnels, fairly flat terrain that gently descended from my mountain top start. I was already beginning to regret the journey back though. All uphill. Then I hit the switchbacks on what was basically a near vertical cliff. I'm not certain how far I got, but it wasn't very far. The trail narrowed with every about-faced turn.

It wasn't so much the rest of that part of the descent that seeded my fear and doubts. I was more concerned with what lay ahead, the unknown terrain of the journey that removed me farther from civilization, and help if I needed it. My subconscious suddenly spoke as a parent. I had told no one of my plans, where I was going, how long I'd be gone for. Call it fear, call it cowardice, I won't even necessarily disagree with you in regards to that moment. But something else was born in me there, not wanting to be a statistic. Even more than that though, I became aware of something within me (though I could not say I was yet fully conscious of the thought); I don't fear death, but I will always attempt to place myself on the side of life. If I believe I'm staring death in the face, I will turn and walk away.

So I retreated back to the Oaken Commonwealth. Back to working. The bartender soon after was fired. Unrelated to me, though I was certainly happy for it. But soon after I had taken over as the bartender, I quit. It was too much standard bullshit from the typical capitalist business, with nepotistic management and absentee ownerism. In the meantime, I had also moved to an area just outside of downtown. It was close enough that you could go for a long walk and end up downtown, but far enough away that you couldn't just walk downtown at leisure.

There was a row of shops, restaurants, and bars nearby, not really a short walk, but close enough that it was easy, especially the drunken walks back home. It was more easily reached on bicycle though. Quickly as well. So I found a job along that street at some modernesque 'eclectic' restaurant that catered to the pretentious yuppie types; along with the atrocious club above it so they could all feel like they lived in a city worthy of mention. As uncouth as the patrons were though, as much as the owner was the same to the last, the chef wasn't, nor was management. Nor were most of the employees in the restaurant. One man I knew there, he owned no telephone, no computer, no television; only books. Admiration though, not emulation. I understand a necessity for survival in this world when I see one.

It was February when I took a plane to the Angelic Kingdom. An old friend lived there, having moved west just after my move south. Within less than twenty-four hours I laid out on a warm Sun drenched beach, explored the High Desert of Yuccas, and rode the slopes of a snow covered mountain. Then I took a quick trip south to my future home, to the Land of Eternal Summer. I set a goal for November. In November I would finally go west!

The debt I accumulated for that move, it will *never* be paid back. And I suppose I should thank the man who preceded America's Caesar, though the help I received was altruistic bullshit through and through. I was still working on a master in education degree, which I abandoned after completing the certification aspect of the program. I couldn't take the bureaucratic nonsense. Or the ridiculously overbearing parents.

That was it, in nine months I'd be gone. But the finances I would need weren't quite there yet. And were it not for the increased living expenditure for my degree loan, the aforementioned debt, I may have just found myself in a different Southern city. One nearer to the mountains or the coast. I was actually visiting one of those prospective cities when I received the notification of the increased funds. This was sometime in August of that year. Then November arrived. I planned it out to near perfection, even the one last drunken night I spent on a friend's couch. That hangover the next morning tried its best to delay me, but my wheels were rolling westward before eight.

Scene Two: August the Eighth
FROM THERE TO <u>HERE</u>

Four days until I leave this City that Imprisoned Me...

I left the East behind. My plan was five stops en-route to my future home. The first three were campsites I had done minimal research for, with the last two nights planning on cheap motels. I would've preferred to take longer, but my car was packed full. And I didn't think sightseeing with all of my possessions protected by easily broken glass would be wise.

I crossed into the Whiskey State, making my way down from the Great Mountains of Smoke. Camp was much farther from my place of departure than I thought. I arrived after sunset, and scrambled in the fading light to set up my tent. With the hang-over still plaguing me, I just went to sleep. Quite an uneventful day. Other than leaving everything I knew and understood on a mere whim. I can't even say I was looking for a life of adventure yet. I was still in the mindset of trying to find a place that I felt I could call home.

The next day was a blur of driving, wanting to at least enjoy some aspects of camping with the late-day Sun as company. On some lone hill in the Ozarks (they called it a mountain), I watched my companion's daily descent. I started a fire, then primed my camp stove. It had been some time since I'd used the stove. I'm lucky to have escaped injury, and thankful I was wise enough to keep the stove far from the campfire. I hadn't turned the primer off, nor, in the fading twilight, did I see the fuel trail leaving it on had made. Nearly the entire picnic table was covered in flames.

There, atop that hill, halfway across the country, completely on my own for the first time; I somehow didn't panic. It was far worse than the first time I had made that mistake, several years prior. But being that I had made that mistake before, the flames didn't have the chance to strengthen. Once that was settled, I settled in and enjoyed the night.

Early to the road the next morning, watching the prairies wake up at seventy miles an hour. Soon the rolling treeless grasslands gave way to a desert of plateaus, scattered about the landscape in every direction, as far as the horizon reached. Toppled tombstones, all pointing west. I stopped along the road at some point, an interstate rest area. The beauty of the terrain was suddenly marred. Modernity has a way of obscuring much of nature when not in motion.

On I went, the once flat straight road now gently winding, sloping up and down. The scenery became more jagged, more vibrant, more beautiful. More resembling the Rugged West I sought. I was no longer going west just to sit on a sunny beach with drink in hand, though that remained a strong feature. No, I wanted to see it all, the deserts, forests, mountains, and coast in all their various glories.

My camp for the night was my first true experience of such discovery. Getting to the park entrance took no time at all; getting to the campsite was a different story. I suppose I didn't research quite enough, as I was not expecting a slow hairpin plunge into the nation's second-largest canyon. Once parked, the evening unfolded much like the last, setting up camp, starting a fire, and watching the landscape swallow the Sun. I did manage to properly operate my stove at least.

Once the light of day had completely faded though, I learned three things that night. The first I knew of, but had yet to actually experience. The true chill of a desert night. Something I would never be ill-prepared for again. The courage of a coyote under the cover of darkness was also quite surprising, but of little consequence. Their bravery seemed to have been tempered from attempting a full approach. The third thing imparted on me from that cold deserted hole in the earth... There is no better place to view the stars than the arid inland sands.

The fourth day of travel was the shortest. I tried to fill the drive with ghost town visits, but the first one was certainly quite populated, as much as it still carried a vibe of creepy abandonment. The other was little more than a roadside stop at one point, now with a stray dog as its sole resident; perhaps there was a human inhabiting one of the few structures. As I safely sped away I was thankful for being able to avoid the chasing dog. Of course for itself, as I certainly had no desire to hurt that poor lonely creature. But even more so, agony crept into my mind at the thought of accidentally killing the possible human's only friend.

I realized that 'ghost towns' were not actual *ghost towns* along this heavily traveled route, that it would be best to avoid the rest, and to not again risk adding further despair to these wretched souls, stuck living their lives in the middle of nowhere. As uninteresting as it seems to me now, my destination for the day was a golf course. I'd always wanted to play a Southwest Desert course with mountains enveloping the backdrop. A short hike would've yielded the same results, but still, it is a fond memory.

I also wandered the nearby City of Enchantment. Thankfully I didn't make any wrong turns. I visited a few bars, ate some local food, nothing too eventful. Honestly, the best thing I found there was beef jerky. This probably doesn't sound very appetizing, but it was like beef-flavored leather chewing gum. So tasty. But it was far more useful the next day, as sustenance, and to keep myself conscious, for what became the longest stretch of my journey toward the Setting Sun.

My adventure for the day was a petrified forest, rather than ghost towns. The views became more spectacular the farther in I ventured. Hills of wind and alluvial deposits, painted by nature, eroded by time. Cones of varying sediment jutting out from the ground like a bed of dull spikes. And the mesas with their treacherous canyons. Unfortunately, I had made the most amateur of road trip mistakes, not filling up with fuel before turning off the highway. I was wise enough to be wary though, and turned back the way I came before I'd have to truly begin to worry about being stranded in the desert.

I was to spend the night in a mountain town, but the motel I found wasn't as well situated as the previous night. I was fairly sure if I had spent the night there, I'd have woken up with my possessions no longer in my car. A call to my friend in the Angelic Kingdom after consulting the remaining length of my journey, and I was flying through the Mountain Desert, with the stars guiding me toward the Pacific. The last part of my journey that would take me from there to here.

A midnight arrival in the Angelic Kingdom. A twelve-hour drive, sixteen with the exploratory detour. Eleven hours had been my previous record some years ago. I stayed for the week-end, enjoying the string of beach towns south of the airport. But I still had two more hours to complete my journey. The Land of Eternal Summer called me home. I had the brilliant idea to stay at a beach-side hostel. It was an enjoyable two weeks while I searched for a place to live. Not the wisest decision for a place to stay when it came to looking for a job though.

Still, finding a job proved far more difficult than I could have ever anticipated. It took nearly four months for me to find work in a restaurant. I was at a breaking point, if I wasn't employed soon, I'd be back in that rural suburbia of the Northeast.

It was a country club where I first found work. Notoriously known as the 'cheap club' in the area. Not just in cost to join, but a fair amount of the members clearly viewed the staff as servants, and not club employees. At least the club itself treated us fairly well. My employment there was largely uneventful, as most jobs are. But two aspects of note changed the trajectory of my life. First and foremost, working at a country club. I had worked at expensive restaurants, but membership to a club creates a level of entitlement I had not yet encountered through personal experience. This is where I truly began to see the facade of 'The American Dream'. My first visions of the White Curtain that drapes over us all.

The second aspect, though not as immediately impactful, was more of a directional determination, rather than philosophical, as the first was. A series of fortunate events, and me just being who I am. One of the employees I worked with, we became friends, and soon after, I was living with two of his friends near the Cliffs where the Sun Sets. That Little Beach Town was to be my home for longer than any community I had previously (and even to this present point) lived in as an adult. Still, in those four years, I lived in three different homes. Ever the nomad.

In that first couple months though, before the Little Beach Town, before I even found work, when I lived up on the mesa, I also began my explorations of the desert that lies beyond the beaches. A friend from back home came out to visit, and we drove east for an hour or so. The southwestern most desert, Big Horn Borregos. Our destination was a palm tree oasis. It was straight out of the storybooks of my childhood. I instantly fell in love with the desert. A barren wasteland it is not.

Scene Three: August the Thirteenth
TO SURVIVE OR <u>THRIVE</u>

Another night not stargazing...

The aforementioned directional events, they began with that friend from work inviting me to a party at his house. A Fourth of July party, ironically, considering the purpose of this story. There had been two grand setbacks to the Nation's celebratory freedom in that city that year, arising from instances of the previous year. Again, quite ironic considering... The most lively beach town had had a massive gathering on their shores. American excessiveness met American over-reactionism. Drinking on the beaches, in all of the beach towns of the Land of Eternal Summer had been completely banned. And year-round at that, not just for the Day of 'Independence'; what is it exactly that we have independence from? One would think a more sensible, tempered discretionary decision would be fair and just.

The other setback? Closer to where my friend from work lived, on the hills between the beaches and the mesas, the park there canceled the fireworks display. Well, not the park itself, the city did the canceling. The police likely didn't have enough boots to enforce the draconian prohibition-era law along the shores of the overcrowded beach towns, as well as controlling the masses gathered up on that hill. I suppose those in charge of our freedoms thought withholding the annual explosives at the park would stem the peasants from congregating up there.

I can't say it was the largest gathering for that day upon that hill, but it was probably the second largest July Fourth crowd experience I'd been a part of. (The first being when I was fifteen, somewhere in Colorado.) Needless to say, nearly everyone I encountered was sufficiently drunk. My friend's friend, my future roommate in my Little Beach Town, he was certainly among the worst off. As drunk as I was, I was my ever-steady inebriated self that I had learned to be in my latter college days.

A quick side story to back then. My roommates there, at that time, in the Citadel of Brothers, they called me Fiasco. And I wore that fucking nickname with pride and glory! I'll spare the details, but I thrashed the apartment I had previously lived in, with still another two roommates.

Some friends from work then called me off to a late-night feast in Chinatown. I rode my bike everywhere in that city. Not having a car certainly played a role. But the city hardly had any hills, and most of the streets ran one-way. I knew the city by heart at that point. My drunkenness, and thereby, bullishness was furthered even more so by the continuation of alcohol consumption, rather than stemmed by the food. After the feast, I raced off for home at my usual maximum pedal speed. I knew which streets ran which way on their singular trajectory. If a light was red, I'd simply slow my pace, and look for cars coming down the one way. If no cars were present, I would proceed through the red light. There was that parental voice, my subconscious. It screamed at me, telling me to pull on my break leavers, that the one-way sign I was trusting in was backward. And so I did, as a car flew through the intersection. My subconscious, ever my guide and protector.

Back to that hill, and our restricted celebration of 'freedom'…

I carried my future roommate, essentially a stranger to me at that point, bearing most of his weight upon my right shoulder as his feet staggered him along with me. A mile and a half walk. His friends we had come with had left us there with no ride back. (Not my friend from work, he was working.) As drunk as my dead-weight passenger was, he never forgot my assistance that night.

Soon after, two or three months, we moved to that Little Beach Town, with one of his friends who had left us upon the hill. That first year at the beach was spent much like the first year I spent in the Oaken Commonwealth. Smoking and drinking too much. Though the cigarettes were replaced largely with cannabis. And the drinking was far more excessive, with the lack of needing to get my car home from the bars. But still, my income was hardly enough to support my lifestyle, along with the debt and regular bills of a life spent living moment to moment.

I decided to go back to school, for photography. But really, photography was just what I wanted to learn about, and I could have gained the same photographic knowledge for far less a sum by other means. I actually returned to formal education for two reasons; the more immediate concern was for the living expense funds the education loans would provide. And the more distant thought was toward being able to obtain a certification to teach English abroad, preferably in Europe, France or Italy. Not yet a plan to escape the White Curtain, but a realization of the need to be prepared.

After a year of that blur of cannabis fueled drunkenness, and menial restaurant labor, the second roommate moved on, and me and my stumbling friend moved into my second dwelling of that Little Beach Town near the Cliffs where the Sun Sets. I had also switched from the country club back to serving the pretentious yuppie crowd at a restaurant my roommate worked at. But the living expense funds afforded me to finally thrive in life, rather than merely surviving, as I had been doing for several years. Had I been more capitalistic with those funds, rather than struck by a mix of consumerism and adventure, I'd be thriving now. But I certainly would not be writing this story. Nor would I be so close to breaking the Silence I endured while in the Underground.

It was actually these two homes and the Palms Hotel, as well as farther back, in that apartment I thoroughly thrashed, in which I found my ability to endure that basement room, and the Man Above me. The first, my room was in the living room, shared with the communal couch and television set. My bed, behind the couch, only separated by a thick drape. The beach town, with the three of us, my room was only accessed through the secondary roommate's room; awkward nights when he had company. And lastly, my tiny room which hardly fit a queen mattress, even without the bed frame. At least that tiny room was quiet. I'll save the story of the Palms Hotel for later.

But none of those pertain to the directional events I write of. They were just rocking waves on the current of my heart's desire, preparation for my future adventures. The friend I still lived with, he had a friend who was beginning a cannabis delivery service. He told me he would need a driver once business became more steady. And soon after, I no longer needed to serve pretentious yuppies their overpriced mediocre food and drinks.

My roommate, as they seem to do, was moving on, returning to school in the State's Northern Territory. During his lengthy seclusive preparation for this, his girlfriend and I became fairly close friends. I'm not certain how she felt about me, but while I greatly enjoyed her friendship, I can honestly say I had no interest in her in any romantic way. So she and I planned to find a place together while my friend was at school. Then they broke up, my friend was still leaving, she and I were still friends. What was I supposed to do? I didn't think I could afford a place on my own, at least not without falling back into a life of survival.

A month or two makes a hell of a difference. My friend's now ex-girlfriend, my future roommate, she started seeing some guy she had previously known. I thought it quite odd of her, the night we went out to celebrate our new apartment, she only had one drink. Usually I was trying to keep pace with her. I even asked her if she was suddenly expecting. She lied.

Perhaps I was colder than I should have been, but it was the lying that most incensed me. Not even the lying really, because I came to understand why she had lied. It was the lack of trust in my kindness and understanding nature. It wasn't necessarily a betrayal of my friendship, I just felt let down. I still do. It wasn't too awkward though, less awkward than the last few months living with my departing roommate. She and I were still friends after all. But what was once an open friendship, turned to passive cordiality. Like two people with nothing in common, assigned to share a dorm, by a computer. My best friend of the moment had become a stranger to me.

I could have backed out of living with her altogether, but knowing she would struggle with the rent, that seemed far too mean. And with my plans to thrive, and considering the apartment itself, I wanted to live there. It was nearly beachfront, less than fifty yards from my door to the sand. The living room had floor-to-ceiling windows with an ocean view; and with their size came the constant sweet smell of the salty air. Most important though, the apartment sat above the garage, where I planned to grow cannabis to sell through the delivery service. Besides, she had agreed to move out before the baby was due.

And so she did. I had only lived on my own once. My last year of college. I was quite lonely living there. Not here though. I had friends I had made around town, I had the beach, and I had the plants, now growing in the spare bedroom she had vacated. We had also begun to run the delivery service from my apartment. This all worked out quite well in my favor, as the rent I received from housing the delivery service, and the plants I was harvesting for it both helped to supplement the loss of having a person to split rent with. I was even able to reduce my work week from five days down to just two. But this was done mostly so I could focus on my photography degree, as the simple projects made way for the thesis, thus requiring much more of my energy and time.

I was in my mid-twenties, living a life of semi-retirement. A long-term goal of those behind the White Curtain, accomplished with a short-term mindset. I knew it couldn't last, but I enjoyed every moment of it. Within three years I went from wanting to be a teacher, and having no interest in ever moving away from that Little Beach Town, to living a life of little concern for my future, only in want of freedom and adventure. Where I would find adventure, how I would secure my freedom, I still wasn't certain. The very things I once wanted had become the very reason for no longer wanting them. My goals, those *effects* I sought from my labor, they became the cause for that freedom I wanted, and from that freedom would come adventure. This was my state of thriving. But what was truly the catalyst of these realizations? The opening of my mind. My internal vision of the external world.

It began in that first year, the secondary roommate's birthday, and my first experience altering my perception of reality. The scientific terminology, Psilocybe cubensis, psilocybin. Magic mushrooms. Or as we so affectionately called them, goombas. Along with the two roommates, and the friend who ran the delivery service, we set off to that place I had first discovered the wondrous desert, almost exactly two years prior, before I had even made my journey from there to here. The High Desert of Yuccas. They were all sold on such a location from some television program. And had also all previously consumed the mind-altering fungi.

For me, it was pure adventure. I couldn't wait to again set my gaze upon that high desert wonderland. I was somewhat nervous about ingesting the poison, largely because of my supposed heart condition, but I wanted, no, needed to test my mind, to see the world before me transform into something my thought process could not explain. For them, this was a tourist excursion, behavior influenced by programming. For me, it was an exploration into the unknown.

We set up camp, ate our dried psychedelics, and headed off to the nearest pile of boulders. Roughly two hundred yards from our camp. I doubt there is a safer environment for such a trial. Perched high on the massive boulder stack, a commanding panoramic view, reliable experienced friends, and the most tolerable warmth of the mid-Winter desert Sun. I was warned of a possible stomach ache, the delivery service friend succumbed to such directly in front of me, but some eight feet down on his own boulder. With us all having chosen our own monstrous rocks as a means of seclusion from each other, and anything that might alter the pureness of thought we all hoped to find, I settled myself with the breathtaking landscape.

I ignored his cries of agony, more out of self-preservation than apathy. I worried that if I engaged with him in my altered state, that I would be susceptible to his pain. And so I stared straight off into the desert, his curled up body just barely encroaching on my lower periphery. His discomfort soon passed, and I was left to myself.

A small lone mountain in the distance. My point of focus. The sky illuminated, its various blue hues all becoming ever more vibrant as I held my gaze. Then, the mountain dropped, as if softly impacted by an invisible meteorite, cratering the once lofty landscape. Then, it rose, and rose farther, to heights well beyond its temporal state of existence.

Amazement at my vision would be an understatement. Especially considering the clarity with which I still remember the vision to this day. The mountain itself appeared to be breathing. I understood almost immediately after some introspective thought. It was the psychedelic effect of my breath on the Natural World around me. Then one of my roommates pointed out the Yuccas to me, their spiny features vibrating in a harmonious visual refrain while bursting forth from the sand. The other roommate was in his own world, completely consumed by the clouds.

From here I went slightly mad I suppose. I remember exploring a small cavern under the pile of boulders. There, all alone, I had a strange conversation with my oldest friend. Of course he was not actually there, but the conversation seemed as real as everything else that occurred during the four hours we spent on that secluded mound of stones.

The Sun was suddenly disappearing with rapidity. And like the Sun, we descended from our desert perch back down onto the earthly horizon.

A poem...

Bounce

The full Moon
  was already high
  enough in the celestial night
  to provide for us
  what seemed nearly daylight.
  Our fully dilated pupils
  no doubt helped our sight.
  After hours
  climbing around on such solid mass,
  the sand below

felt as if it provided
a bounce to our flight.
And so off we went
back toward our camp, unsure,
but hoping our direction was right.
Two hundred yards
four full-grown men
bounding through the desert night
like children playing spaceman.

The exertion of our little game did quite well to sober us up, at least to a fairly normal state of mind. After a quick riposte at camp, we set off under the moonlight, this time in the opposite direction. We were searching for a place to perform the post-trip ritual. I had saved a joint from my first dispensary visit for the occasion, and we couldn't have found a better spot. Some hollowed historical ruins, from a time before the West was tamed.

Twice more I would set off on similar adventures. A few months later, without the delivery service friend. And the following year, down yet another, the secondary roommate. Both instances taking place on or near my day of birth.

The first of the two, I pushed myself farther, ingesting twice the amount than I had for the High Desert of Yuccas excursion. We also had a sober friend guiding us, though at times he only served to test my sanity more than I cared for. I could tell you of the military helicopters we pretended were chasing us all day, or the distant castle we saw at the end of the path, that though silhouetted by the setting Sun, it seemed to glow with an unnatural iridescence. Or of the galactic space cruiser that appeared above us on our frantic trek back in the dark. But those were all some variation of a trick of the mind and eyes, instigated by imagination.

What is still with me today though, more so than those imaginative visual stimulations? The contemplative thought that had been lost to my mind for several years, until my time in the Underground, and the nihilistic state of my being refreshed it. Our guide kept on about some fantastic location at the end of the trail, but everywhere along the route captivated me quite well already. I was tired of the seemingly endless march to nowhere, and wanted to simply enjoy the scenery as I had in the High Desert of Yuccas. His response inevitably became the cliché so many are told, "the journey is the destination". For years that became a thought of my own. I remembered his words as my own. Imaginary profundity of a boring cliché.

But that wasn't my thought. My thought was a rebuttal to his pedantic mind. A resounding rejection of its philosophical intent. You see, the journey is not the destination. It's the other way around. The destination is the journey, it's living *in* the moment. Otherwise you'll spend life wandering from moment to moment, always looking for what comes next, not appreciating what already surrounds you.

The next experience was fairly benign, choosing the day of a partial solar eclipse. Visually stimulating, but nothing much more. Other than the delayed understanding of the sudden temperature drop. The eclipse occurring around sunset, us being in the desert, I thought the coolness was merely the coming desert night. Perplexing as it was once we returned to the car and soon began to profusely sweat, it only took a few moments for my mind to remember basic science, and recognize that the return of the heat was caused by the termination of the Moon's transit between Earth and Sun.

No. The adventures that day happened on the drive, both there and back. We initially sought out what we thought was a remote waterfall, only to discover a stagnant shallow pool with a bare trickle descending down the rocks. We were quite excited though for the day, and I, sufficiently uncaring of legality as it pertained to driving. It was a fun dirt road, and I wanted to test my car's all-wheel capability more than I ever previously had. We were drinking beers and passing a joint back and forth as I flew by a park ranger. I suppose I didn't feel I was being that reckless. I still marvel at how he pulled me over while going in reverse on such treacherous terrain. And I still marvel at how he let us go, completely unfettered beyond a slightly stern warning. My assumption is that we weren't bothered further because we told him of our plans for watching the eclipse. I believe they likely have more issues with the locals there than with people visiting from the city.

Then, there was the drive back. But first, a preface. The prior year, once we escaped the darkness, we returned to our guide's home. There were others there; his girlfriend, some other friends. My two roommates had more or less returned to a fairly sober state. Not me though. I sat in their rattan bowl chair, fixated on the grotesque modern art painting on their wall. Still feeling the effects of my double dose, I had my headphones on, playing the *Tron Legacy* soundtrack composed by Daft Punk. The painting, it danced. I felt as if I suddenly could understand modern art.

That soundtrack, as it was with smoking a joint, became a part of my post-trip ritual. We got on the freeway heading home, and I turned the music up to eleven. Then, my roommate and I were suddenly hit with a second wave. And at the worst time as well. Rush hour, while passing through the largest of the desert cities in that region. Keep focus, especially on the car directly in front of me. It was marvelously difficult to ignore the multicolored mountains pulsing in the distance. I quickly realized the music needed to be silenced for my focus to be steady, and I made our way to an exit I was familiar with. There, we found a parking lot and sweated out the rest of the poisonous effects before safely continuing home. Such is how I learned what thriving means to me.

Scene Four: August the Twenty-Fifth
FROM RICHES TO RAGS

It's Wednesday. In the Park. I saw a silhouette, I thought
I was dreaming. I wasn't...

I left the beach town behind, quite reluctantly at that. I was in search of power. No, not the power of the wealthy elites that control everything from behind the White Curtain. Electrical power. For my plants. The delivery service came with me, as did its assistance with my rent. I lost the beach, and the breeze, and the proximity to all that I had come to enjoy, all that I had come to call home.

I moved back up to the mesas. Closer to the desert. A house with adequate power was impossible to find any farther west than I had found; if I was to remain living alone. The house came with a small detached studio in the backyard. The nearby dryer outlet providing the needed power. In hindsight, I didn't take enough of a risk. I only utilized about one-quarter of the room. Closer to one-fifth once the walls of the insulated room are accounted for. But I didn't build for the future, I built for a supplemental income.

I rarely went out to bars anymore; living too far from the beach town, and not having much around me, including friends. So I would go east instead, exploring the interior region that sits between the arid coast and inland desert. Some of the parks seemed desert enough, others were furnished with spires of pines. All mountainous though, all greatly lacking in water as well. But I wasn't alone, I found Azzura, my shepherd heeler, with her silvery white coat, warming smile, and intelligent eyes.

So how did I manage to squander such an opportunity to create a sustainable life of leisure? Simple. I chose adventure. My meager explorations into the surrounding landscape did nothing to ease my wanderlust. In fact, it was only exacerbated.

Fueled by the thesis project I decided to endeavor upon. My passion for photography had always been rooted in nature.

What a great idea I had come to! Traveling to the most famous National and State Parks in the State of Gold. Not to just capture their landscapes though. Far too many before me had already done so. No. My concept was to insert the allegory of the traveler into those landscapes. And to mimic the religiosity of cathedral frescoes from the Renaissance Age. But I wanted to replace the deities those famed artists portrayed, and in their place, display true nature. The apple is not a sin, but a miracle for all to enjoy.

My first expedition was straight east, past the Borregos and oasis I had already seen. Beyond the mountainous terrain, on the border with the Saguaro Forests. Out there lies the dunes of an ancient sea. I had seen the beach dunes of this country's eastern shores. But never had my eyes fallen upon the expansive dunes of a desert. Ever moving, yet always the same. At this point though, I was only seeking to capture the essence of the landscape. The parks I chose mattered little. This meant there was nothing to define the places I sought; and therefore, no actual reason to undertake so many journeys that would have me incur such a high financial cost.

So the project had to be reworked. The problem I needed to solve was a matter of capturing solitude in areas laden with tourists. Recognizable landmarks in these Western Parks are rarely found in desolation. But what's to differentiate the forests within the Valley Wonderland from those surrounding it?

I decided on representation over reproduction. Photographic based artwork, instead of pure photography. Symmetrical digital manipulations. I called them photographic mandalas. All the famed locations would be discernible if one peered closely enough at the imagery. But I still wanted the works to produce a sense of the traveler's allegory in the viewer. The images I had created to this point were flat and uninteresting.

The program I was enrolled in had an option to study abroad for a semester. And what luck I thought! That semester was to be in the Renaissance City itself. Firenze! Florence, Italy. But the semester length would cost me far too much without my plants being tended to, and it would have kept me abroad for far too long. Not that I didn't want to be gone for so long, I simply could not have done it. I now had my dog, Zura.

Still, the desire to cross the Atlantic was strong. I planned for two weeks. All the time I could truly spare without overly relying on others. A flight east. Then Liberty Metro to Milan. It was the cheapest flight I found to Romantic Europe. I was to only land in Milan initially, my first scheduled night was in Florence, with four more there to follow. The next three nights were to be spent among one of the five medieval villages that cling to the northern cliffs of the Azure Sea. Then four nights experiencing the leisure of the French Riviera. My journey set to conclude back in Milan for Easter Sunday and Monday. But this wasn't a vacation. I wasn't on holiday. This was a journey to find my life's direction.

The flight was a red-eye. I hardly slept. A simple lack of sleep was nothing new to me. Ever the partial insomniac. I never cared to count my sleep hours. My life thus far on the West Coast had only amplified that sentiment. Why should I not face this new adventure as I had with most others, where I overcome the exhaustion with my endurance and exploratory disposition? The train into Milan from the airport provided me with a decent hour of respite, though still no sleep. I had planned to leave my bags at the ticket counter of the city train station, and then head off for a quick meal near the Duomo.

Before this moment, I had never been surrounded by a mass of voices speaking in a language foreign to me. My weary mind simply could not take this extra task of basic translations. Instead of a few hours of exploration, I wandered around the transit corridors, looking for both food and a place of temporary rest. I didn't want to allow my eyes to close though, worried I'd miss my train to Florence. I found a small cafe, somewhat reluctantly, and marginally despondent at my first taste of Italy being from nothing more than a commuter hub. It was basic at best. Caffe'e cornetto.

By midday, I was crossing the Arno River in search of the accommodations I had set up for my stay under the Tuscan Sun.

Other than the first few days being dampened by clouds heavy with water, everything there was just as I had hoped. The cafes and restaurants, the delicatessens and wine shops, the museums and parks, the cobbled streets and sidewalks, the centuries-old architecture. I could go on endlessly about all that. But that is not this story.

My thoughts here are far more concerned with the experiences that showed me a life beyond the White Curtain. A life that isn't consumed by consumerism. A life that doesn't seek to commodify every aspect of our personal realities. Of course the tourist hordes were there, they're everywhere. Along with those looking to take advantage of their consumerist mindsets by selling them worthless commodities. I just flowed through them like I would anywhere else.

The first thing I truly took notice of? The way leisure takes precedence over labor. Of course capitalism moves our modern world, for better or worse. But even in a city such as Florence, itself a living museum, the citizens there seem to collectively work to live. The working class, behind the White Curtain, I came to the full realization at last. Most of us, myself included, we are not seen as working class. Rather, we are the servant class. To be working class in America, you must adhere to the ideology that work comes before life. That the most important thing in life is to love what you do to earn an income. And the second most important thing is to use that income to amass more expensive objects than those in your community. Programmed competition.

This is not to say that commodified culture doesn't exist in Europe, it's just not dominant among how people choose to live their lives. But there, the working class income is earned to enjoy a life of leisure, as capitalism had once promised us behind the White Curtain. To some, personal freedom is being able to exploit labor for personal profit. To others though, personal freedom is more about freedom of expression. Which in order to be fully realized, such requires freedom from worrying about if you'll be able to afford rent and bills... and especially, the cost of medical care. That's what drives most behind the White Curtain to give up their freedom for those that provide employment. Employer provided benefits; most importantly, health insurance. Healthcare cannot be a business if a country's government is to honestly provide for its citizens.

When a person is paid a living wage, and provided with basic healthcare, even the seemingly most undignified job allows the laborer, the worker, to live not just a life of dignity, but a dignified life with ample leisurely moments. There are those who try to make their own way, as there are anywhere. But the social safety net there is far wider, ensuring that those striving to survive aren't mired in complete destitution, should they happen to be unsuccessful with their endeavors. But in any nation that allows for self-determination and individual expression, you will inevitably find some form of destitution.

I only mention this so as to not paint a picture made of only roses and gold. My point is more simply that self-determination is more of a possibility for an individual, in some places located outside of the White Curtain. When everyone who provides a service, even if that's just their individual labor, is in turn provided with a social safety net, those citizens are then able to live without succumbing to a life of struggling to survive.

Individual freedom struck me next, and continued to do so for the remainder of my trip abroad. It wasn't quite late night, but it was night enough. Past the hours when the streets would still be flooded with tourists looking for a place to dine. Most restaurants were closed or closing. Corner shops and bars still open. I sat on the steps of the famed cathedral where the Medicis are entombed. Ironic, the corrupt bankers they were. A slice of street pizza and a beer. A police car... They kept driving. There's no such thing as open container laws there. And if there are, they certainly were not enforced. All I mean by mentioning this is that adults should be able to sit on a sidewalk (or at the beach) and drink a beer in a *free* society.

Lastly, the man at the American bar. And the bit of serendipity that followed once I escaped conversation with him. It wasn't that he was an American, in that American bar, that bothered me so much. After all, I was there. It was why he was there.

He wanted to find a place of comfort; he was in that city for work, and missed his home comforts. I was there, at that bar, in hopes of watching a soccer match. The Italian national team was featured, and the few bars I initially ventured into showed little promise of local fanfare. So I tried the American bar.

That American, who sat at the bar next to me, two stools over. He was from the city I was living in at that moment. That Land of Eternal Summer. Somehow, even being from the State of Gold, he was spewing the anti-cannabis government propaganda, as so many behind the White Curtain have been programmed to do. His inquiries of small talk led him to disagree with what I did to earn an income. This was when I knew it was time to take my leave. And how thankful I was for what followed my drunken wanderings.

It was my last night in Florence. Regardless of all the wine, and the cheese and cured meats I had consumed already, I had not had my fill. But I had yet to find that quintessential Florentine wine bar. Half drunk, I roamed the alleys and side streets. Searching, ever seemingly in vain, for that perfect place to lounge.

Call it luck, call it intuition, it matters not. I had nearly reached the bridge back to my accommodations across the Arno, when suddenly, I found myself peering through the windows of a dining establishment, at a wall of wine bottles. It wasn't just the randomness of having found a wine bar so near to my giving up. It was the bar itself. I had done a fair amount of research for the trip, even making a small guidebook for myself. Ranking all of the varying places I wanted to visit (parks, museums, cafes, bakeries, wine shops, etc.), based on my personal preferences. That wine bar I randomly, and quite literally stumbled upon, it was the first on my list of wine bars. As I wrote, serendipity.

It was time to move on from the capital of Tuscany. The Cinque Terre was next. I couldn't say what specifics from my days and nights there held more meaning toward the purpose of this story. As it was the same with Nice to follow. That entire six nights and their days of exploration were ethereal direction, leading me to understand that I had no honest future behind the White Curtain, that escape must be my ambition. And so, I believe, for the purpose of this story, my journal from those travels will best portray the significance of my fleeting time abroad.

A Poor Man's Guide to the Riviera

With some of the business proceeds, the father sent the son, at twenty-six, to France to be treated for what both agreed was chronic shyness, particularly of girls. Something in the Mediterranean air began the cure before Rashid set foot on European soil. Landing at Marseilles, he began building a new personality with rubber cheeks...

The Cinque Terre: Day One

I first read this prefaced quote from *The Rich Man's Guide to the Riviera* by mystery novelist David Dodge on my way from Firenze to these Five Lands, and I could not resist smiling as the northern Italian countryside flew by with its motionless blur. Though the incidents pertaining to the young Rashid are far from my experiences, the Riviera does seem to free the demons of solitude, even when traveling alone.

My journey began quite differently of course. I was not sent to a foreign country by my father, nor are my travels taking place in the 1950s. Surely this Azure coastline was much less adapted to average tourism than today, making my experience both wonderful and frustrating; the former for the ease of navigation and interaction, and the latter, because of the massive crowds all lost in their own little worlds.

Florence was an amazing experience, but there is not much to tell of my time there, other than how lovely it was to walk the streets of the city that birthed the Renaissance. It was as if I was wandering through a museum, instead of alleys and avenues. My highlights were the three hours I spent in awe of Michelangelo's David and the four hours of aimless strolling through the Boboli Gardens.

After departing Florence, I found myself on two regional trains, with the views tainted by unkempt towns, gray skies; and on the second train, a horrid waft from the toilet, as others passed through my train car to the next. Luckily, I suppose, the windows on that train did open, allowing for some fresh air to distill the acrid smell of shit.

I arrived in La Spezia around midday, the southern gateway to the Cinque Terre. It's a dirty looking harbor town, that on second thought I decided not to explore, especially on consideration of what to do with my bags. I was tired from travel and longed to find out if the room I had rented was indeed the one pictured with a spectacular balcony view. I immediately headed to the train that would transport me on this final leg of my day's journey to the tiniest of the five villages. The middle hamlet Corniglia, perched some three hundred meters above the Mediterranean, with its waves battering the base of the cliffs below.

It was at the bottom of those cliffs that the train doors opened, as I was greeted by the tourist hordes I had read about while researching for the trip. One would think that perhaps fellow travelers would clear a space for the man standing at the door with multiple bags slung over his shoulders ready to exit the train. But in typical touristic fashion, they all jammed up the door before I had a chance to move. It was as if they thought the train would somehow leave them behind, along with the hundreds of people standing behind them on the platform. Finally, there were two kind souls who understood the etiquette of letting people off the train before they board.

What followed was a grueling trek up 33 flights of stairs, composed of 382 steps that I was determined to climb, rather than taking the shuttle bus up the steep winding road. Of course I struggled with all those bags and had to take several short reprieves. I had learned long ago though, from hiking and cycling, don't look up. If you need to stop, just turn and enjoy the view of what you've conquered thus far. The view, I must say it surpassed magnificent, with the village of Manarola off in the distance, nestled in the narrow valley, the Sun's rays lighting it up like a pastel Christmas Town.

I made it to my check-in and was led up more stairs to the entrance of the building I would be staying in. Then up another two flights I climbed, the door opened for me by my gracious hostess Cristina, as realization set in that my room was indeed the one I had hoped. The French doors swung open to greet me with what I thought must be the greatest view in the Mediterranean. With my guide gone, I reopened my wine from the night before and set out the delicacies that remained from my last Florentine excursion. I swear, simple meats and cheeses, even a day old and warm from travel, have never tasted so delicious. The wine, coupled with the tiring day's journey, put me out. When I regained consciousness I was left with little options or energy to get a proper evening meal.

This first endeavor into the local eateries of the Cinque Terre was of profound disappointment. After ordering, I watched the bar attendant tear the plastic film from a prepacked dish of gnocchi with pesto; even more appalled by the fact that this region is the birthplace of the basil sauce. I put it out of my mind and heaped on the grated parmigiana; that was at least fresh. I do have to say though, the local white wine, DOC Cinque Terre was quite superb, as was the espresso; though that I had come to expect, as I had not had a bad one yet (even from the Boboli Garden's toilet vending machines). Marginally satisfied in the culinary sense, I returned to my room to regain energy for today.

I awoke to a somewhat cloudy greeting, which, along with lingering exhaustion, kept me in bed till around nine. I knew

I had few sights to see other than the streets of the two southernmost villages, and there was nothing of interest in Corniglia for this evening that would have drawn me back early. Off to Riomaggiore I headed, after my typical Italian breakfast of a cornetto, an espresso, and a glass of my seasonal favorite, freshly squeezed blood orange juice; all acquired from the cafe Cristina runs with her husband Stefano. This meager morning meal was something I had become quite accustomed to during my previous days in Florence.

The industrious first town of the Cinque Terre didn't offer much of interest to me. My first stop was the main street and a taste of a local specialty, the mixed calamari, which also includes whole fried sardines, from Mamma Mia's. From there I followed a path south of the train station to take in some coastal viewpoints, of which there were plenty available for those not so brave, when standing fifty meters above crashing waves and jagged rocks. And even better ones for those with a little courage, keen balance, and sure footing. To the north of the village lies the start of the Via Delle Amore, but it was closed for repairs. So instead I sat above it at Bar e Vini a Piè de Mà, enjoying a beer and some fresh warm focaccia, another specialty of the region, while daydreaming of the day I would return to walk the lover's footpath with the love I had not yet met.

With the short coastal path impassable, I decided on a trek over the hill that separates Riomaggiore from Manarola. Footpath 531, the Beccara trail climbs over 200 meters in roughly just half of the 1.5km hike; the other half being the delightful descent. Climbing the steep dusty Sun drenched trail, aided by a walking stick someone had left from their trek in the opposite direction, I eclipsed the peak, leaving one panoramic view for another. Invigorated from the effort, I glided down into this second medieval village bounding like a mountain lion, only stopping momentarily to remove my shirt and dry it in the pleasant breeze.

As I came through the maze of narrow alleys and salmon-colored homes, I found myself conveniently placed in front of the

Gelateria Cinque Terre. Being the local flavor, I cooled my body and soul with pistachio gelato while resting on a bench. After retiring my walking stick in a pile at the base of the trail, I strolled deeper into town and found a warm, Sun filled cement block to lie on and observe the passing clouds. I tried to read for a bit, but quickly scolded myself for burying my face in a book, instead of enjoying the scenery I had traveled so far to see.

I soon became restless and headed toward the tiny harbor. It was La Passeggiata, and the entire town, tourists and locals alike, were out for a stroll up to the garden, the church, and the adjoining graveyard that encompassed the wine bar with the best view in town. Nessun Dorma. Sipping on a glass of the local Cinque Terre blanco I had enjoyed last night, I gazed off toward the sea, watching its waves crash against the wall of rocks, intended to protect the tiny harbor below. After capturing some photos, I decided to head back and enjoy my balcony view with some antipasto and a bottle of that local white. The antipasto of course was of local flavor as well; anchovies, artichokes, and olives, all locally procured, all marinated in a local olive oil, perfect for dipping the locally baked bread in, and accompanied by stracchino, a locally produced cheese.

The Sun sank into the Mediterranean coastline as I finished my appetizers. After a short riposo, I set out for dinner. The meal is delicious, the service is excellent, and this evening absolutely made up for the microwaved gnocchi pesto from last night; as Ristorante Cecio clearly uses nothing but fresh *local* ingredients. The interior even further enhances the dining experience. Upon entering guests are immediately met by the old-world charm of the dining room, with its stone walls and wrought iron chandeliers. I feel as a king in a castle, even including the jesters to my right. Two Americans, loudly conversing about their medical procedures as I eat.

The Cinque Terre: Day Two

This morning I set off much earlier for Vernazza than I had for Riomaggiore yesterday, finding myself on a nearly empty footpath for the first half of the 4km trek. The views looking back toward Corniglia in that early light were mesmerizing, the trail adorned with wildflowers and hidden pockets born of romantic fantasy. Most of the hike was accompanied by a cool morning breeze, and by the time the Sun had broken through the marine layer of clouds, I was already on the descent toward the most picturesque view these *Five Lands* have to offer. The Tower of the Doria Castle stands prominently above the town and harbor, with the sparkling azure waters of the Mediterranean stretching off into an ocean-like horizon.

After familiarizing myself with the main street I wandered down to the harbor, finding, what seemed would be the best view, by climbing around the exposed stones of Chiesa di Santa Margherita in the sloshing low-tide. After some peaceful reflection within the church, I was greeted again by the castle tower, this time framed by a tattered blue sky and a mix of illumination and shadow on the pastel facades. Looking at the little boats rocking, I daydreamed of returning once again, for a stay long enough that would allow me to take one of those boats out and catch my own fish.

Just one euro to climb the tower; the view itself is certainly worth it, but with the use of toilet included, it's a must visit. After my spiral descent, I wandered back up through the heart of town and out through the gate that keeps the streets pedestrian friendly. I found myself in an almost deserted piazza, my only company, a friendly orange tabby. He probably thought I had fish… One of the pleasures of traveling alone is connecting with everything you encounter. When not lost in conversation, the eyes can see so much more. Vernazza was too overran with tourists for me, so I decided to delay eating, and instead find a more leisurely dining experience once in Monterosso.

A quick train ride and the doors opened to the modern pedestrian promenade that runs from the train station located on the fringe of Monterosso al Mare's New Town to the tunnel that takes the guidebook flocks into the Old Town on the other side of San Cristoforo Hill. Rather than following the herd, I veered to the right and found myself alone on a coastal path that climbed gently along the rugged cliffside. Passing some historical remnants resembling a gated prison window, I couldn't help but find irony in the 'lover's locks' that were all attached. It's freedom or *love*, at least that's what they say.

At the top of the trail stood a free man, chained by god. San Francesco d'Assisi and his tamed Lupo di Gobbio. The patron Saint of the Animals with his wolf. He died an outcast leper, abandoned by his god. Fitting I should find the church next, and the graveyard behind it. I only feel an aesthetic spirituality in these places. Beyond the graveyard was an encompassing view of the Old Town below. I followed a dirt trail, through some vineyards, and into the back alleys; as those before me had been doing for centuries. The least traveled route is often the longest, but you get to see what others don't. It's hard to get lost in a village that likely doesn't even exceed a square mile anyway.

I was quickly out on the main street with all the tourists that flooded off the train before me. It seemed to be lunchtime for most people, and the dining establishments appeared far more equipped to cater to the masses. So I went down a side street. Looking for a quieter place to dine. And to write. I'm not certain where I was, but I had the mussels. I held off on writing though. My breath taken away by beauty. She dropped her keys. Before she could even contemplate how to retrieve them, with her hands overloaded holding several bags, I was up out of my patio seat, placing the keys back in her hand. If only I spoke Italian, or her, English.

I'm back here now, in Monterosso's Old Town for dinner, hoping to see her again. Pizzeria La Smorfia. I thought I saw her when I had returned to my balcony earlier, after my daytime wanderings through this seaside village. Why she would have been two communities south, I can't say. It was obviously unlikely. But the bags I saw her carrying earlier, they were those of a housekeeper. Likely, like my hostess and her husband, this belladonna I locked eyes with is a proprietor of rental guest rooms. Why should she not also have a property in Corniglia she tends to?

I sat on the balcony, masquerading as a true Italian Romeo. Repeating the call, "belladonna" with a lyricism I had not known I was capable of. Obviously it was to no avail, as I sit here alone, writing, finishing this pizza and bottle of wine meant for two. Perhaps I'll have better luck in Nice, I'm staying in a hostel after all.

<u>Nice: Day One</u>

I wanted to wake up before the Sun today. I wasn't far behind. Yesterday was travel, from the Cinque Terre to this city of leisure. Nissa, as the Italians call it. Nice sure is nice. But yesterday, I left the Cinque Terre. The train schedule had me departing early for Genoa, and leaving there late. Luckily the train station there was far from overwhelming, and the baggage storage was easy to find. There were a few historic palaces I had planned on visiting. I only saw one. Choosing instead to explore the urban port town, from downtown to the harbor.

The palace was quite stunning, rivaling almost anything I saw in Florence, save perhaps the Uffizi. But the mix of cosmopolitan life and a gritty seaport reminded me quite fondly of Seattle, that Emerald City I visited for the first time last year. But still, this was a mere layover before reaching the French Riviera.

Darkness had already blanketed the sky by the time my train arrived, but it was still early, and the streets were filled with both people and light. After reaching the hostel, I made acquaintance with a few fellow travelers, all readying themselves for a night of drinking. I was tired, yet couldn't resist joining the fun. I didn't quite drink too much, though I certainly drank more than enough. After some bars, we stopped at a corner store for more alcohol to drink along the dark shoreline. We threw a frisbee on the pebbled beach. Impossible footing, the frisbee often hit the ground. We also marveled at two boys throwing rocks far out into the night sea. None of us could toss a stone a quarter as far as they could. I told them they could be baseball outfielders.

We returned to the hostel shortly after, but quite late. That's why I lost my race with the Sun. The morning was spent at the Colline du Château, and wandering the eastern walls of Nice's port area, following the curving shoreline around the base of the Castle Hill. I then stopped back at the hostel for a short rest and a shower. Easily the worst accommodations of my trip, but the hostel I had first stayed in when I arrived in San Diego was far far worse.

I had planned for a short bus ride to the outlying neighborhood of Cimiez. Some ancient Roman ruins, and the Matisse Museum. I even had the chance to watch some locals play a game of Pétanque in the adjacent park, Jardin des Arenes, where I found a light lunch as well. I'm under one of the garden's trees now, writing this. I'll be heading back soon, the beach calls.

<u>Nice: Day Two</u>

I had planned on much more for two nights ago, but on returning down to the shore, I felt overcome by illness. Initially, I thought it was food poisoning, but the symptoms that are generally attributed to food poisoning, thankfully never came. Still, I felt weak. Hardly able to drag my body back to the hostel from where it had essentially collapsed along the Promenade des Anglais. Some of those in the room I shared tried to rouse me for another drunken night. I could hardly move. Temporary inertia.

I awoke fairly early. Feeling like my normal self again. Still uncertain of what possessed my body, causing the depletion of all my energy. Then I realized I slept nearly fourteen hours.

I had never suffered from exhaustion before. I didn't realize exhaustion could make one feel so sick and helpless.

But had that exhaustion held off, had I gone out drinking the previous night, I surely would not have been in the hostel's kitchen to offer the girl from Vancouver some tea, as I was making mine. I had no real plans for the day, just what was in the guidebook I conscripted for this trip.

So instead of exploring on our own, we decided to wander together for a bit around the city. We then agreed to catch a bus up to the medieval village of Eze, and on the way back to the hostel to ready ourselves for dinner, we splashed around in the fountains at the Promenade du Paillon.

Our first stop was for some aperitifs and appetizers. The night was coming and the street lamps all began to illuminate. Such a lovely little sidewalk cafe we found. And then, we were unexpectedly treated to a spectacle of reverence. A candlelight procession for Good Friday. Neither of us was particularly moved by the piety of the ceremony, but it was a beautiful aesthetic display of humanity and light.

It was getting late into the dinner hours so we took our leave from the cafe and ventured out toward the city harbor. We both thought a local catch from the sea would be the perfect ending to our day together. The meal was delicious, and of course there was more wine to accompany our meal. How I was not falling over drunk, I'll never know.

We were both in excellent spirits as we walked along the promenade, cutting through the crowded streets towards Place Massena, where we sat on a bench to watch the people pass. I was terrified in the best way possible as I leaned in to kiss her, the flutters from earlier now racing at the thought of this fairy tale day, with its fairy tale ending. We went to find a corner store that was still open to acquire yet another bottle of wine.

Back down on the beach, we lay on the strangely comfortable rocks, the darkness of the Mediterranean cloaking us from the few people wandering the shore at that late hour. The violin serenaded us from my speaker. We fell into a doze, waking in the middle of the night, slightly shivering, we set off back to our separate hostel dorms.

<u>Nice: Day Three</u>

She left this morning to head back to Barcelona, where she's teaching English. She's there for another six months. Vancouver isn't so far away. But I'm alone again. Wandering alone. I hadn't had any escargot yet. So that's where I went to write my entry from yesterday. That balcony overlooking the sea would've been so much better were I not alone. But the escargot and rosé certainly helped to alleviate the loneliness.

I'm back at the hostel now. My bags are all packed for the morning. I don't want to leave this city. It's like San Diego, weather and all. But without the crass American culture, or the surfer bros. There is certainly no market in San Diego like the one I went to today. One of the guys here, he basically lives at the hostel. A Brit. But he claims Nice as home when he's not at sea. He told me he stays in the hostel just so he can meet more people.

I hadn't cooked this entire trip. The Brit fancies himself quite the chef. So we set off to the market together, we decided to prepare a feast, and invite anyone who cared to join us. Snails, clams, pasta, bread, charcuterie, wine; we supplied all of it, splitting the cost just between us two. I tried rallying him, along with some of our diners to go to watch the Nice football team. No one wanted to go, and watching a soccer match alone hardly seemed like it would be fun.

So we hit some cafes and bars instead. I hadn't smoked a cigarette in so long, but when in France… The evening was fun enough. Nothing much more to really record in these pages. I guess that's it. I'll be leaving the Riviera for Milan once the Sun again appears.

And so I was in Milan, readying for my return to be once again cloaked by the White Curtain. But my eyes had been fully opened. I was to return to the house I didn't own, and to the plants that kept me feeling more trapped, than providing me the freedom I thought they would, the freedom I wanted. Milan was more like Florence. Nearly impossible for the traveler to not be a tourist. Still, I managed as best I could to create adventure on a path so frequently traveled.

The one thing I'd say stood out as something of a memory, one that still directs my quest for escape, the thirty minutes I spent sleeping on the roof of Milan's famed cathedral. A glass of Prosecco and a bottle of red wine washed down my midday meal before I ascended the Duomo stairs. Arduous climbing with the combination of the slow moving tourists, and the alcohol settling into my veins. The Sun was quite pleasant that day. I suppose it would be more accurate to say I passed out, rather than that I was sleeping. I can't say for certain, but I doubt most famous landmarks behind the White Curtain would allow for a visitor to pass out drunk. Most of the places I've lived won't even allow you to pass out drunk on the beach.

It wasn't just direction for my life I discovered on that trip. There was also the thought I came to, the idea of not just seeking adventure, but with it, love. I also found direction for my thesis project, which in turn, kept evolving my life's direction. The evolution of my personal freedom.

I quickly became fixated on seeking a life of both adventure and love. Six months on and I still could not let go of what seemed such a perfect day in Nice. After all, the western Northland border wasn't all that far from the Land of Eternal Summer. I planned for a second trip to my current city (as of writing today's entry). The Emerald Realm. *Vancouver* had returned from Barcelona. We were to meet under the blue Summer skies. I should have seen it then for what it was. An actual lack of interest. I suppose she had initially become just as swept up in our day on the Riviera as I had. But I suppose the six months that followed likely had the opposite effect.

So I crossed the border to the Northland since she wouldn't come south. Splitting my four days between there and the Emerald Realm. My friends I visited in the latter, they brought me to a Pass of Deception. What confidence I gained that trip, both in my prowess for adventure, and my capacity for love. I came away on the train from the Northland bursting with poetry. And so knowledgeably guided my friends away from deception and encroaching darkness. The poetry, that's self-explanatory. And certainly no longer relevant with regards to *Vancouver*. The Silence now owns my poetic soul.

But the deception. And the fading light. We had wandered fairly far, to some rock outcroppings and a secret beach. The descent was treacherous, the ascent seemingly more so. For this though, we were all more than capable. It was some moments later, back on the relatively flat, well-traveled trail. We went right at a junction. The trail soon became visibly overgrown. The path we came by had obvious signs of frequent use. The trail we were on showed alarmingly little wear. A lesson. The direction you need to be heading isn't always the direction you need to go.

Life back in the Land of Eternal Summer continued to feel more and more like an endless trap. My vacations were held to days because of my plants. The system I operated was automated, but the plants still needed tending to, almost daily. I would venture off between grow cycles, but couldn't afford to delay the start of another cycle for more than a week. To add to this, my thesis project was ever in need of more attention. And I needed to leave the life of stagnation that I so suddenly realized I was living. Simply, I was living to work.

I came across some serendipity again. Random junk mail. Three pieces for that day. The first contained my friend's last name, the one who lived in the Emerald Realm. Nothing too auspicious, just the name of a town the mail was sent from. The second piece, it looked quite similar to the change of address envelopes I had become so accustomed to. The third, an Explorer magazine. But after all, I was already contemplating that move to the Northwest.

It still had to be planned of course. And I still had a couple months left on my lease. In the meantime though, I needed to see the desert again, with further exploration, beyond where I'd already been. To the places the tourists would flock to.

They call it a Super Bloom. They call it the Valley of Death. Had that been my only incursion, I would have called them liars. Both of them. The bloom, though comprised of glorious, but small sections, and quite aesthetically pleasing, from both far and near, it did not seem 'super' in the slightest. And how, I wondered as I drove from end to end across that vast expanse of desert, could a *death valley* harbor so much life in bloom? The answer to both was a once-in-every-several-years event. Now likely even more distant between phenomena in the future, as the desert itself slowly creeps north.

But I didn't get to the salt plains on that excursion. And, for perhaps the only time in my life, following my mind over my heart was likely the correct decision. Many detours were to follow. But those detours led me to where I am now. Back again in the Emerald Realm, so close to turning the Silence into adventure and love.

Scene Five: August the Twenty-Ninth
TO LOSE OR <u>FIND</u>

*Was that her today? I heard no Voice, so I kept my head
down. I couldn't allow myself to look up...*

From this point, life stopped being about moving on from where I didn't want to be, and became about going where I wanted to go. I came back from that desolate land that was full of life, ready to move on. The *Eternal Summer* had become too endless for me. I craved some semblance of varying weather. I also had come to realize that my thought of growing cannabis, as a means of escape, was more often creating a trap. I wish I had had the sense enough to sell or give away everything I wasn't taking with me then, but my escape from the White Curtain was still untenable. Still though, I limited what my car would carry for this northbound journey. It wasn't like the straight shot I took west, rarely venturing off the interstate.

I planned it out, not quite as meticulously as I had for my trip abroad; but there wasn't much room to leave random adventure to my whims. Eight days, zigzagging up and across the State of Gold's landscape. The Ocean Dunes, El Sur Grande, nearly due east to the Valley Wonderland, then nearly due west to The City of Fog. Over the Golden Bridge and passed Muir's Grove. Then along the winding coastal road, through the Redwood Forests. I stopped only a moment in some college city that seemed near deserted, and two moments in that city where I was imprisoned in the Underground.

But first, I returned to the High Desert of Yuccas. To bid them farewell. I was there for imagery, but also, to give my soul one last encounter with the desert, before moving to the Forest of Evergreens. For the first time I actually began to study the Sun. Its arch across the sky. Understanding its trajectory. Reading its movements to foresee, where on the horizon, it will make its final descent for the day. There was also the oasis, deeper in the park than I had yet to visit. And the back entrance roads of desolation. The northern route came from the interstate, onto well-traveled, well-populated highways. The southern route was a path of solitude.

But my desire for adventure far outweighed my concern. I chose risk over fear. My first true understanding, that to find myself, I must first get lost. I also came to realize, getting lost doesn't necessarily mean that I don't know where I am, or where I plan to go. A lesson that had become habit in the comfort of the urban expanses I'd lived. But in the wild, the fear of being stranded often weighs heavy on the conscious mind.

I made it back to my house with no issues. Readied my car for the trip north. Some minor adjustments to how things were situated, in order to optimize room, and position everything so the least amount of moving stuff around would be necessary.

My first night was to be spent parked on the beach between the Pacific and the Ocean Dunes. A six-hour drive took ten, I barely made it for sunset. The Moon rose over the dunes behind me; more than enough light to explore under the stars.

With morning, I set out farther into the surrounding land-scape, and perhaps for a bit too long. It was only a three-hour drive to the winding coastal road, where the Northern Territory starts. But with all the random stops I made en route, I again arrived at my day's destination later than intended. The camp-grounds were all full. I had already spent plenty of days in that region on previous trips, so I wasn't all too upset to need to continue heading north. As I saw it, every mile I traveled away from where I had planned to spend that night, it put me a mile closer to my destination for the next two nights.

As I wrote earlier, it is the destination that's the journey. Everything in-between are just points of rest. There was a camp-ground at the winding road's northern entrance, just before my compass was to turn east. Thirty dollars. Basically just to park my car for the night, and to close my eyes for a few hours. Twenty dollars more, and I could've found a cheap motel for the night. But I decided to spend nothing. There was a truck stop in the

Central Valley, halfway between where I was, and where I was going. Half of my next day's drive conquered in the darkness.

I had rested at truck stops and rest areas many times before in my travels, but I had never purposefully utilized one as a place to sleep for the night. A restaurant. A toilet and sink. A convenience store. And I could fuel up before heading toward the rolling hills and pastures that border the western slopes of the Golden Range. I wasn't feeling exactly secure staying there for the night, the stories you hear; but that night changed how I would travel for the remainder of the time I had Aether, my Element.

Then I saw the Mighty Merced! The drive into the Valley Wonderland was born from a fairy tale, compared to everywhere else I'd previously ventured to on four wheels. The clouds were gathered, but with plenty of holes for the Sun to occasionally break through. The refraction of light sparkling in the raging white waters of Spring were dazzling, mesmerizing.

The rest of the drive toward camp was arduous, pedantic. The tourist hordes the cause. This time, mostly in their cars. The few others, humans acting like clueless, frightened animals crossing the road. Some greatly offended that they had to be cognizant of those of us traveling on the same asphalt they had also come there by. The usual self-absorption of American tourists. But with my campsite already reserved, I knew I could veer off the congested route, and explore some of the slightly less traveled roads. At least on those roads, recreation vehicles were prohibited.

The Valley View; the Falls, El Capitan, and Half Dome, spanning out across the heart of that Valley Wonderland. I very well could have been standing upon the exact spot where John Muir convinced Teddy Roosevelt of the importance of preserving our natural landscapes.

It was wonderful to have a proper night's rest. Stretched out in my tent, knowing the next night was to be spent in the same location. Being able to cook food, rather than subsisting on granola bars and beef jerky, as I had mostly done the first two days.

The next day I set off for Nevada Falls, to capture a rainbow. The first photograph truly intended, and planned for, in use for my thesis project. The imagery I had preserved from the Valley of Death, the High Desert of Yuccas, and my swift venture through El Sur Grande, were all more happened upon, rather than sought out. That rainbow was premeditated.

The trail, at first, ate at my soul. Asphalt, and people hardly capable of walking up a flight of stairs, much less a mountain. There wasn't much congestion though, the path being more than wide enough for me to circumvent those who would've delayed me, were we on a much more rugged narrow trail. But then the paved trail ends, once you come to the bridge. Beyond, a slippery climb through mud and granite. I greatly welcomed these features that would prove as obstacles to most others.

But I had an obstacle of my own. One I was powerless against. The vapor shroud above. There is no rainbow without sunlight. I could see faint cracks of blue here and there. So there was hope. All that was needed was patience. I found the framing I wanted for the imagery. And I waited. It wasn't much, I can't say I could really even discern where exactly the Sun was. But its rays vaporized enough of the cloud cover to provide the arching color I needed to produce distinctiveness in the imagery I wanted to create.

My exit from the park was slightly different from my entrance, headed on the westward road with a marginally northbound inclination. There was snow, rather than the torrents caused by the melting snows. Nothing of concern really even happened that second night, or on the departure. Other than wishing I had more time for exploration on the few excursions I had had time for. Six years in that Land of Eternal Summer, a mere eight-hour drive to that Valley Wonderland, and I never went, until then. How likely was it I'd make the sixteen-hour journey from the Emerald Realm, once settled there?

I crossed similar landscapes heading back west to those I saw on my way toward the Valley Wonderland. But only after the pulse quickening descent from the mountains. The drive along the Merced on my way into the park hardly had any noticeable elevation change. I was quickly back in urban traffic. But I didn't stay in the City of Fog very long. That night, I spent a rare night of travel in a bed. A motel just across the Golden Bridge they had painted red.

I still had nearly half of the state to traverse, on its much longer south to north distance. I took the winding coastal road, rather than the multi-lane highway through the coastal mountain valleys and vineyards. The curving, cliff-side roads always feel much safer when heading north on the Western Coast. My stop for the night wasn't much different from the thirty dollar campsite I had passed up on the northern end of El Sur Grande. But there were no truck stops where I was, no rest areas along the coastal path. In hindsight, I probably should have found another cheap motel.

But travel that day still had plenty of adventure. The Mountain Redwoods and their Avenue of Giants, the Little Secluded Beach Community, and that random port town just north from there, of which the name escapes me. Then there was where I spent most of my night, before driving off back to the campground a few miles north of that town.

The drive through the Mountain Redwoods, along its Avenue of Giants. It was everything I had hoped it would be, when I veered off the main road on a whim. When you see a sign for a scenic route, take it. A leisurely detour. The pull-off spots that surround you in groves of ancient redwoods, the seclusion of the less traveled road; all worth the extra couple of hours it takes to travel through that inland portion of the Northern Coastal Route.

That Little Secluded Beach Community is worth mentioning if only for its personal draw. I should love to retire to a small picturesque town like that, so far from any major city, or major thruway. Yet, more than populated enough, with a fairly consistent influx of people traveling through. I wish I could have had the time and expense to stay there, rather than just up the road, north of that unnamed port town. But the night was somewhat of an adventure. The bar. The woman who sat next to me. The conversation. The invitation back to her motel room. Nothing much happened. It was awkward, and I quickly left. I see no point to lust, if there is no love. I've always been that way.

But earlier in the day. The harbor docks of that port town. The little fish and chips spot, with its large deck and oversized fire pit, crowded with locals. That spot was pure influence, pure magic. I loathe small talk, but with people like that, salt of the earth people, and a trip like the one I was undertaking, there is no small talk. The camaraderie, the community feeling, that was, is, what I crave when I'm searching for a place to call home.

The next day, my journey up the coast continued. From the Mountain Redwoods to those growing along the coast. Another campsite. But this time I stocked up at a local grocery store. Five different cheeses, all locally made. Including three from the creamery I had wanted to visit. Cypress Grove. They apparently do not open their doors to the public, but the store was within a few miles of their location. I doubt there is anywhere I could obtain their cheese more fresh (save perhaps a farmer's market in that region). Food is one of the best reasons to travel. Their Midnight Moon pairs remarkably well with Northwest cherries.

That night, at the campsite, was the most memorable of the trip. The Valley Wonderland was great and all, but the campground provided little solitude from other campers. Not to mention the vast difference in those who were camping at each location. Surely the difference between tourist and traveler. The campfire glowing off the redwoods surrounding me further added to the delight, along with the stars shining through the canopy three hundred feet above.

And then, by the next evening, I was in the Emerald Realm. The calendar just turning to May. I can't say much really happened during that month. I slept in my car, parked on the street next to a park. I lay out in the park daily, reading, writing, watching the people pass by. I eventually found a job, working at a cannabis dispensary. I worked for three days. I nearly signed a lease for an apartment. But I was gripped by fear. It didn't seem as if the income I was promised would suffice, and the hours they required wouldn't have allowed for me to obtain a second job.

So I left. I retreated back to the Land of Eternal Summer. The delivery service was still operating, and my friend was more than thankful to have me back, seeing as how he didn't want to work. But the drive south afforded me further adventure. First, a trip around the Olympians' Coastal Range. Waterfalls, rain forests, the glistening Crescent Lake, and the raging Pacific of the Northwest. Then off to the State of Gold's most northern snow-capped volcanic mountain. Waterfalls abound there too, regardless of the region's arid climate. The rest of the drive was a fast descent through the Central Valley, and a blur past the Angelic Kingdom.

I was lost. Uncertain what to do with my life, my future. Rent prices had skyrocketed in the couple of years since I had found the house with power. And my surplus from the photography degree loans was on its last semester.

So I entered the Palms Hotel. It sounds luxurious, I know. Nothing could be further from the truth though. But it was an experience beyond anything I had ever encountered in my life. A mix between a haunted hotel and halfway house. Monthly rentals in a European style hotel. The rooms were just rooms. Shared bathrooms down the hall. My room didn't even have a sink. I could have afforded something better, but I wanted to spend my money on travel, on adventure. Not trapping myself in a city I knew I didn't want to stay.

My first expedition upon my return to the Land of Eternal Summer was back up to the Valley Wonderland. The mountain roads were inaccessible when I first came through on my northbound voyage. For so long I had wanted to see the alpine meadows of the upper Golden Range blanketed in lupine flowers. August was a bit too late apparently. But the timing was perfect, as I had intended, for viewing of the Perseids streaking in the night sky. I gazed upward for hours, trying to capture the perfect photographs for the imagery I wanted to create. I had no idea anywhere in the State of Gold could be so cold in the dead of Summer. But I endured the frigid night on the shores of that alpine lake.

The first image I captured, gazing east across the icy, still waters of Tenaya Lake, featured Perseus cresting just over the mountain peaks. The second image, facing the opposite direction. The lodgepole pine spires slicing through the black, diamond-studded sky with their jagged edges. I was attempting to capture a meteor in motion. I had given up active attempts. Choosing instead to just set my camera to capture automatically in programmed intervals. I didn't even bother scanning through my cache once the sequence was finished, knowing I would want to stay longer in the plummeting temperatures, had I not caught one of Perseus's arrows slicing through the firmament. It was the next morning I saw it. The last image recorded. One fireball, cutting straight down the spine of the Milky Way.

In October, I again visited the Valley of Death. Far more confident in my exploration, and having missed the spectacle of the salt flat hexagons, I entered the park under cover of night. A dark dirt road, ten miles driving precariously slow along the border of the ancient lake bed; the definition of being in the middle of nowhere. Sleeping in my car had become quite comfortable, after the nearly two months I spent doing so in the Spring. But I was also able to experience the true nature of that desert landscape. I saw little signs of life. Some small cacti. And a lone coyote the next day on my exit.

A week later I was back in the High Desert of Yuccas. Looking toward the night sky again. This time for Orion and his celestial missiles. The last image I needed for my project. Two months later, as the White Curtain was plunged into turmoil, I was to see my last sunset on the West Coast for the foreseeable future.

Heading east, just crossing the imaginary line into a State of Lonely Stars, I was stopped at a 'border' checkpoint. Why there are border checkpoints traveling within the borders of the White Curtain, I can't say. But it's authoritarian through and through. Their dog smelled the small amount of cannabis I had taken with me. The last of what I had grown from nearly a year earlier. Luckily, they only found the tiny bit I had in my car, not asking me to open my rooftop cargo where the larger amount was stored, and let me go. I had wanted to enjoy the trip back east with detours and random exploration, but the incident unnerved me, and I just sped back to the Oaken Commonwealth without any unnecessary delays. I hardly even stopped for sleep, beyond the rest my body required.

So there I was. In full retreat. Back where I had first decided to journey west; just over seven years earlier. As I wrote, I was lost, looking for future direction. The plan was to live in a State of Sunshine, to help some people I knew start a dispensary. It was meant to be a springboard for my departure from the White Curtain. To leave for Europe with a one-way ticket. But they weren't to be ready until February, so I stayed with my friend in the Oaken Commonwealth. I had two months of leisure with nothing to do.

That two months turned to four, then six, then they backed out altogether. I had left the only place I had ever truly felt at home, for nothing. I had to return to work after the first two months. A job at a restaurant of course. My debt that was all but eliminated rose out of necessity for survival. But it wasn't all bad. I still found time for adventure.

Missing the grandeur of the West, I sought the only nearby landscape that could console me. The Little City in the Mountains, and all the nature that surrounds it. The initial plan was to just travel along those Mountain Ridges of the Deepest Blue. But as usual, once cost of travel was factored in, the trip length, both miles and days, had to be shorn. I stopped at a waterfall near Mount Mitchell, that parking lot mountain peak that first sent me journeying in solitude. Then the fog rolled in.

As I descended into the city below, I realized that it was not fog obscuring my vision, but the clouds themselves. A torrent in the late Spring evening flooding the road. It quickly passed though, and after finding a place for dinner, I returned up into the mountains to sleep on the roadside, overlooking the valley below.

The morning greeted me quite wonderfully. The timber-clad mountains all softly jutting out of the bluish-purple vapor that filled the lowlands. Once the Sun rose, the day cleared. The waterfall from the previous day was only inspiration for what followed. Instead of following the main road, I ventured off onto unknown trails, in search of more falling water. I found five cascades in all on my improvised route. Most quite far from the beaten path. And all quite unique from one another.

The first had many gradual tiers, easily climbed alongside, ascending on the granite on which it flowed down. The second was more humble, but wide and picturesque, with the watermill cottage that sat perched beside it. Third was a sheer roaring drop of sixty feet, reached from the second stop by traveling along a ten-mile drive through the unpaved forest roads. For the fourth waterfall, I had my first ever encounter with an overhanging flow, being able to stand behind the curtained deluge. The last was far less aesthetically pleasing; more of an amusement park slide than a waterfall, but the happiness of the children all enjoying the natural glissade was a delight itself.

That evening, sunset lit the sky ablaze, as I made my way back up to my roadside overlook for slumber. The next day was far less eventful, spending some time around the city, after the morning rain came to pass. I kept finding reasons to delay my drive back to the Oaken Commonwealth. I felt almost at home up in those mountains, in that city. Almost as I had among the Forest of Evergreens and the Emerald Realm for that singular month. I had to go west again.

But first, I went south. The Sun was to be eclipsed by the Moon, and the path of totality was only three hours away. The Palmetto Capitol. I knew the crowd the celestial event would draw, so I left at night, and slept a few hours parked on a side street. The temperature drop wasn't nearly as drastic as it had been in the desert a few years earlier, but I also didn't ingest psychedelics on this short journey. However, the rarefied celebration was far more extravagant to witness. Particularly the momentary ring of fire I was able to preserve for eternity.

I flew west first this time. To secure both employment and a room to live. I had barely saved enough for the journey west, and needed to ensure my return to the Emerald Realm would be permanent this time. I stayed with my friend for two weeks while I situated myself into my new job and home. Then I went back for Azzura and Aether, and the few belongings that had traveled back east with me.

I left the Oaken Commonwealth around noon on a Sunday. Just barely a day later, I was speeding toward the Setting Sun, crossing the nothingness of the prairie-lands that cut through the center of this country. Within thirty-two hours of my departure, I was a Mile High. The next day was spent traversing the snowy pastoral lands of the Cowboy Range, before crossing the Divide of the Continent and passing the Great Lake of Salt, on my way toward the Wooded Desert City at the base of the Cascade Slopes. It was very late. It was beyond cold. I knew I shouldn't have stopped. But I needed rest.

The frigid temperatures woke me in the middle of the night. So I had the thought to eclipse the mountains before the Sun's ascent behind me. It would have been a marvelous golden path to light the way toward my new home. But for the first time, in all of my travels crossing dirt and asphalt, west, north, south, and east, Aether failed me. The temperature gauge accelerated faster than the speedometer. Hours in wait for a tow truck, then more hours in wait for the repair. The quick rise of internal temperature, the air below freezing; the radiator hose simply slipped off. Easy enough to fix. And twelve hours after my roadside rescue, I was cruising along the streets of the Emerald Realm.

For six months I found myself truly feeling as if I was home. The way I did that first year of life in the Little Beach Town. My birthday came. My friend and I consumed those poisonous fungi, and we wandered the city. The greatest visuals I had ever had. There was the marble wall of the skyscraper. The ivy and brick in the Pioneer's Rectangle. The trail of the Sun creating a pathway of dazzling light across the Sound, leading toward the Olympians' Coastal Range I had sped around two years prior.

But nothing compared to the red light stairs. The first experience with that drug that I couldn't explain, and still can't. Waves of red flooded my eyes, ever increasing in magnitude and frequency. It was a very intense experience. My first meditative gaze quickly ended. The second was longer, but still, my eyes couldn't hold the vision. I slowed my breath. Third time's a charm. The waves flowed at me, more rapidly, larger and larger. Then, it was as if the ground had torn open. Like I was staring directly into the central fiery heat of the Earth. My search to *find* home seemed finally at an end.

PART THREE
FirmaMentality

Firmament: the vault or arch of the sky

Act IV: Year Three

Prelude: September the Sixth
FROM REWARD TO <u>RISK</u>

It seems as if the Silence is gone...

My friend was gone, he had moved back east. And that's when I met the Silence. The Silence is the firmament above. And I, the sea, in all its calm and madness. Us both flowing on our zodiacs, along the hardened immovable earth. The Atmosphere and the Ocean.

And this. This is where I realized I'm not *crazy*. Believe me or not, it doesn't matter. Without knowing all truths involved in a specific scenario, actuality is an impossibility, and individual reality reigns. Honestly, I don't even always *believe* myself. That's the trouble with having a strong imagination, you'll question your own reality.

I found what it is though, supposedly. Fires of identical lights. Two sparks born from the same star. A flickering dual of dancing candle flames. I don't believe in the singular eternity of such a thing. No. To me, it's a sixth sense; but there's nothing superstitious about it. Nothing formed from a spiritual or divine power.

As I've alluded to previously, it's a latent ability, mostly lost to humanity. While evolution and the development of language have certainly played a part in the suppression of our metaphysical sense(s), it seems that with the technological advancements since humanity's escape from the Dark Ages, and the birth of science with its demand for temporal certainty, our abilities have been greatly subdued. Not just to believe in the unverifiable, but to conceive of anything that doesn't exist as physical material.

But we know of light spectrums unseeable to the human eye. Sound waves not discernible to our sense of hearing. Sensations like the wind that we can feel, but not touch. Tastes that will forever be unknown to humanity's refined palette. And scents that simply can't penetrate the mind through our olfactory senses. Why should there not be waves of energy we've lost the ability to sense internally, like those the insect's antenna send and receive?

It was the Voice, before it became the Silence. And the Atmosphere before that. There's nothing to really speak of. It was only a few weeks. The Atmosphere darkened, and then the Voice abandoned me. I tried on multiple occasions, but even with the small whispers I received, the Silence still remained dominant. No matter the risks I took, the courage I showed in the face of the Silence, all remained quiet. But that's not really this story. This is my story of seeking escape from the White Curtain. I just believe that the Voice will rise again, to flow as the Atmosphere, and seek escape with the Ocean.

No. This story. This entry. It is about my vision, and my adventures. The things I did, the signs I followed. My intuition guiding me toward freedom. During these months, before the City that Imprisoned Me, before my room in the Underground, I kept a journal of my expeditions. As it was with my time on the Azure Riviera, the words I wrote in the moment will serve far better to tell my story than the current state of my hazy mind. This first entry, I wrote it in Year Zero, a few months before I was introduced to the Atmosphere. They seem relevant considering what was to follow...

Scene One: Freedom

The only way to deal with an unfree world is to become so absolutely free that your very existence is an act of rebellion...

-Albert Camus-

January One: Omens

We all walk this same planet, but the universe is beyond any scope we humans can comprehend. This is true for us all, regardless of our beliefs being based in theism or science, or some combination of the two (if such a thing can truly exist). But for the theologians, omens pose no existential crisis; they simply believe they are being guided by their god, or gods, or spirits of sorts acting on behalf of their god(s). However, for the atheist, the agnostic (perhaps even the Buddhist), the concept of an omen may also have a mystical foundation.

If you are the latter, as mentioned above, it is easy to dismiss any conscious influences from those not currently walking the Earth. But what of your subconscious? Do you not think your most base desires guide you? Or perhaps it is more mystical than that, perhaps the scientific fact that we are all made from the same ancient stardust means that the universe itself is capable of guiding us, if we would only listen.

I keep my belief in the Voice and its Silence because of what was said. Something about a connection. Something about never having had *this* with anyone. But I never held the Voice to fault, I only ever hoped for faith in me to return. But I had to go back to my life of solitude. Though, now with a spirit riding shotgun. As the leaves began to turn in that Year Zero, I was left in silence awaiting that first return. The Atmosphere had initially thought to come along, yet decided to venture elsewhere. So I set off from the Emerald Realm, to wander the Autumn desert alone, and to once again skim up the western coast of this land.

October Three: The Arches of Moab

I really have no idea what they are, the stars. I just trust what I'm told about them. I like sleeping in the car. It's uncomfortable, so you never really sleep. And you always wake up to a different view throughout the night. Enough of them, and you finally get the motivation to actually get up. It not being that cold out also helps. I love the desert.

Watching the color return to the sky from an unmoving car is a bit more enjoyable, though not nearly as pulse quickening, as when your eyelids shut for that uncontrollable moment, when your brain says, "fuck you, I'm tired." I think I was wrong, about where the Sun will rise. The early colors are deceiving. There's a mountain, covered by a mass of clouds. I thought it would be behind all that initially. After surveying for a bit more, taking in the balance of color and light off to the left and right, I discerned it might rise elsewhere. Just to the left of the curtains.

The return of color is amazing. But even more so, watching the black nothingness return to visible form. After this though, I don't know if I ever want to see new scenery unless I arrive at night. Seeing a landscape for the first time as the only true light 'turns on'. It's fucking marvelous. I'd never been here, to Arches. I'd only ever seen photos. Those are always just the arches. The landscape here, desert landscapes, all so invariably different. I wasn't that off with the Sun's position... Yea, not far off at all. I glanced up just as I wrote that last sentence. Ten minutes of glory. The Sun's rays dazzled with a starburst, cresting over the plateaus below the mountain. Temperance though. Someone parked next to me, they left their phone, their programmed alarm went off the entire time.

They all left. Lemmings. The sunrise. Then they left. There were about thirty people here moments ago. The Sun is still low, just behind a cloud. They'll all miss this second sunrise.

* * * * *

There's a fly right now. I found a more quiet spot along a dirt road. Less people, less noise, than all the coming and going in that vista parking lot. But the fly, as persistently annoying as the alarm from earlier. No matter. Adventure time. I hate how they get stuck in your teeth. Should make for a fun drive back through the park, and back down into Moab though.

* * * * *

Leaving Arches, everything seemed so invariably different from when I had come, mere hours ago, down the same stretch of road. Sure, I had a cap and a stem. But the light, it was different, no longer covered by the shrouded morning. Though thankful I am for that, as it provided a much grander rising Sun. But no. It all looks so different bathed in light. Especially the path down from where I watched the sunrise. I arrived under cover of dark. The landscape was hidden. A formless void. What I seek, it is found when looking at the in-between. The lines of cars coming in, as I go… It'll be the same at Zion, or

Capitol Reef, or wherever I go. I leaving, as everyone arrives. Or I coming, as everyone is leaving, or already gone. It beats sitting on the sidelines watching life pass by.

I'm back, kind of, maybe I never really left… I told myself I'd only smoke four from the pack on this trip. This is my third today. Found this sweet view pull-off, some amazing mesas. But no cliffs. An open expanse, prairie, field, or whatever. Threw Azzura's ball for a bit. I picked up a Rumi poetry book the other day. Some are good. But translated poetry, I don't know, I feel like something gets lost. Not just something, but the flow of the words. But the translated words, still pretty good. "Like the shadow, I am and I am not." I'm not out of Utah yet. So little sleep. So uncomfortable when it comes. I miss Aether, my Element. It's the 4th now. Six in the morning. Still in Utah. Rain. Dark roads, heavy eyelids, and rain don't mix. So I slept three hours.

October Four: The Arizona Border

In Arizona now, some little park, near some river. Just far enough from the freeway that you hear water instead of cars. I've been here too long already, but this road trip is meant to be enjoyed. Tomatoes, cheese, and salami for breakfast. I was just gonna be on my way. But I wanted coffee. So I set up my propane stove and made coffee with my Moka pot. Melted the handle a bit. The scenery is fantastic. Dried desert mountains, clouds floating above and between them. The Sun, dipping in and out.

I'm heading to Vegas next. Never been. In all my years living in San Diego, never went. Casinos and strip clubs are poisonous holes to nowhere. But this trip has been full of fate. I'll probably just drop $20 on black thirteen or something. Then be on my way with $20 less. No matter. About to leave, a cigarette with the rest of my coffee.

Three days on the road. I finally reorganized the car. Finally had time. I'm not sure how people road trip in anything but an Element. There's no room in this rental. I suppose I didn't need the camp chair, nor all the books I bring, yet never open. The thought of reading in open nature, in the quietness, it's always alluring. But there's always something else to do, or look at. My attention span is no good in nature. Especially on these trips where I bound from place to place so fast. It's been seventy-two hours since I departed on this journey, and I've just eclipsed 1,500 miles. I think I'm at fifteen hours of sleep.

October Eight: Avenue of the Giants

"If I die I die." Sure, I agree, but my recklessness, my wildness, it is spontaneously calculated, equations made to always be on the side of life. Not out of fear of death, but out of love for life. Out of the craving we should all have within, for that next unknown adventure. I live tempting death, but I will always cling to life, with all the strength my soul has. I lay here, around 5am. Once again watching the light return. Watching the spaces between this ancient canopy fill with something other than black. My camp neighbor said it would probably rain in the morning…

7:30 now, blue skies and pink clouds. I wonder, have you ever actually watched the Sun rise? It's day eight, I wish I had a day nine. I'd stay right here. But onward I must go. I see blue and clouds sailing by, but still no Sun. I was right on yesterday, in Napa. Sat in a tree scanning the desolate mountain ridges in the distance, across the acres of vineyards. What excitement, not a cloud in the sky, nothing could spoil this rise! The Sun's aura, a flat line when gazing at the spot I expected to see its crown peak over; while scanning though, in my periphery, a giant bubble full of every color within the spectrum of the human eye. No fucking doubt, that was where the Sun would come. Thirty minutes, sitting in a tree. Waiting for those golden spires to bathe the valley below in light. There might be too many clouds to see the sunrise today. But my shadow has faintly shown itself. The fire is pretty much out. Time to go.

October Nine: Cannon and Haystack

So, I'm in Northwest Oregon, just south of Cannon Beach. So many miles covered. I wasn't going to go this way, it's mostly been a blur because I was so intent on returning the rental car on time, but I overslept. I was always going to have to choose between finishing this route and being charged an extra day, or cutting east, back toward the freeway, and saving this all for another time. I thought I could split the difference, skip most of it, just cut straight for the famed Haystack Rock. But the allure to stop, even for just five minutes here, ten minutes there, it adds up. It's cool though, it's still all basically an unknown to me. I just noticed a sea cave.

* * * * *

It's around 6pm now, watching the sunset in Cannon Beach, a panorama with Haystack Rock off to the south. I only really saw one sunset on this trip, out near Joshua Tree. But I was driving, my photos, rushed. The last three days, just missed them as I arrived at the respective viewpoints. I wasn't going to watch today's but this journey needs an epilogue. Still so many miles to go, yet I sit here, so still. The Sun is hanging today. It's not really setting, no, instead it is being enveloped by the clouds, which in turn, are being consumed by the ocean. "Beauty of the human perception." I suppose I should go. All that's left are remnants of the Sun's light.

* * * * *

Another stop. Astoria. I saw nothing of interest driving through town. Then, the Rogue Public House. Out on some pier. Outskirts of town. Hidden behind hotels I'd never bother to stay at. I thought at first that the public house was one of the mundane hotel's restaurants. It wasn't. It's out on some pier. You'd fucjing love it! They have some interesting ciders here. My drink, marionberry sour. I don't even really know what a marionberry is. I'll have to try the Dead Guy whiskey. I left some mark all over the West, all over this twisted triangle route. My poetic anarchy.

I still have a distaste for crude 'tagging' and unnecessary property destruction. But artistic intent is everything. A rock in Moab. I left a *Moab* quote, along with some artwork. In the California desert, a print, left for the next person to stay at the yurt. Another print in Joshua Tree, the start of my 'returning' project. I was gonna bury the box of prints. I found a spot. But when I pulled out the box, I had the thought of burying just a single print. A 'return to the earth' concept of sorts. But the print looked so beautiful, lit by the brilliance of the desert Sun.

Mussels Frites with Andouille Sausage and a Rogue hard cider broth. He asked if I wanted fries. Funny… They brought me ketchup, not funny. I decided instead to leave the print on a rock, on the dirt road where I was going to bury my artwork. Either someone will find it, or the desert will reclaim the image. You know a place is cool when they don't have any televisions. And the frites, the broth is great for dipping them in. I could have so easily died so many times on this trip.

I returned to the Emerald Realm. The Voice, a month or so later, came back with whispers. Uncertainty sent me spiraling. I hardly felt the weight of the connection at that point though, so I once again began planning my escape in solitude. I would move to the City that Imprisoned Me. But that chapter wasn't quite ready yet. I was to be back and forth between the two cities for work. Why pay rent I thought… I could just travel, my car as conveyance and cradle.

I decided to keep a more detailed documentation of my adventures. With photography of course. But also, using a grade school composition book, instead of the more expensive journals I generally write in. I had recently met an old man named Richard. He was what inspired the grade school composition book; that's what he wrote in. So, in playing off the school schedule in the front, I made Richard my first instructor. Music Theory, the subject. He had sent me a text message, "Hello, hope you enjoy the music." Finding new music to enjoy became the assignment. To listen to it, not with my ears, but through my heart. This is what I believe he truly meant. A wise man's gift to a foolish boy. So began my six-month journey, as the calendar turned from Year Zero to Year One.

MUSIC THEORY: RICHARD MAGNOLIA

January Four

Olympic National Park, Beach One. The mighty Pacific, it makes the Puget Sound look like a small duck pond. I'd say I learned my lesson, the real issue though, I had forgotten past lessons. Years with my eyes trained on the oceans flanking this country, watching their swells, the patterns, the timing. I knew full well of the danger, that's why I called Zura back behind the driftwood. She barely escaped a wave. I just planned on taking a few photos, nothing spectacular, just imagery to write poems on.

The ebb and flow, the waves being sucked back out, the remaining water flowing down the smooth stones lining this shoreline. Click. And at that moment. The image frozen in my right eye, I saw the depths of that flow, enough to know to turn and run. I jumped up over the driftwood for cover, like diving into a foxhole. I don't know if I slipped first, or if the wave just swept out my feet, but I was on the ground, drenched in frigid water. My camera was soaked, but that's why

I bought the one with weatherproofing. My pants created just enough of a barrier to spare my phone. All in all, I just have some wet clothes. Nothing to fear. Just a simple mistake, a lack of proper observation. I'm dry, and alive, onward…

* * * * *

Beach Two. Much less eventful, though I did hear the roar of a wave as I was peering through my viewfinder. Scared me a bit. I got some fantastic shots to use for poetry. And I found a stone, a new collection. I got a really rad street shot also; you know, the empty long road, wet from rain, with Sun rays piercing through the clouds and mist. Stopped at the Kalaloch Lodge. Coffee and a cookie. Great views, cool little cabins perched on the bluffs. I'd like to stay a night or two there one day.

* * * * *

Sitting at the campground day area now. The Sun is pouring through in random spots. The beach here seems a bit unsafe to explore. I write this as I stand on deteriorated wood pilings, just as likely to give way as a sandstone cliff. That misty aura of light along shrouded rocky coasts, it's mesmerizing. I don't think anything similar can be seen along the Atlantic Coast, unless you're up in Maine. I'm hungry, and a bit cold; I could make some oatmeal, but then I'd have to clean the pot. Onward.

* * * * *

Beach Three. I may not get to Rialto at this pace. I do need food though. I'm out of bread. I could make oatmeal I suppose. I'm glad I came down here prepared. Camera, journal, both in my bag, coffee, and a spliff. Should've brought my flask though. It's good I left Zura behind in Aether. The foam reaches the cliffs. I'm sitting perched on a small one. There would've been nowhere for her to lay down. The foam is telling, a non-verbal barrier of Mother Nature's warnings. Been watching the Sun shine through all the holes where the atmosphere reflects the ocean, finally its rays struck me. I thought this coast would be much colder in January. The foam looks like molten snow when being pushed around by the tidal waters. It's stunning. I almost didn't stop here, there was no pull-off spot on the northbound side of the road. But I pulled a quick U-turn and stopped.

* * * * *

Beach Four. There's a parking lot. I need to document this stop, but my phone is almost dead. At least it seems to be finally charging. It's empty here. I feel safe enough to leave Aether unlocked with the keys in the ignition. I did not expect so much Sun today. The bluff will do here. No full panoramic, but the view from above makes up for it. I think I twisted my knee earlier, the Beach One incident. The waves look so slow from up here, like giant mounds of foam. I need to learn more about nature. What bird is it? What plant, what tree? I think Zura was just brushing up against a poisonous oak. It's half dead though, and I'm fairly certain of my immunity to such plants. Seeing as how I've never been poisoned by them. Some quick photographs, documentation with my phone, something for the collection, and onward. I'd like to find some mussels to boil for dinner.

* * * * *

Ruby Beach. I thought there was a Beach Five, maybe there still is. The seastacks here a quite beautiful. They remind me of the ones I saw at Arcadia Beach in Oregon, that first stop just before Cannon last year. The beach here is much safer from the raging ocean, so Zura came along. As did my flask and sketchbook. Photos first though, while the Sun still pours through the clouds.

* * * * *

Apparently there is no Beach Five, unless I missed it. The weather started turning as I captured my photographs. No time to sketch the seastacks as I hoped. Hopefully Forks has a decent store.

* * * * *

Thriftway will have to do. It started raining pretty hard. Trying to wait it out. I seem to be sidetracked sitting here in Aether whenever it slows. Like now, I finished rolling a few spliffs, and like that, it's heavy again. Fuck it. I was way more wet earlier than I'll be walking through the parking lot to the store entrance.

* * * * *

The good, they had mussels. The bad, they are farm-raised. I got a pear, salami, a loaf of bread, and some snacks. Boiled the mussels at the Third Beach parking area, dumped out most of the water, and sliced some pear to throw in for a broth. Better than plain water. It all went together just fine. Hardly my most gourmet road trip meal, but that butane burner is far better for my needs than the two-burner propane camp stove I've always used. I can just operate it safely on my hatch tailgate. I'm not certain I should sleep here though. Then again, it's dark already, finding a better spot to pull off and sleep will be hard. I was planning on spending the night at Rialto Beach, but the road was closed. So I went down into La Push, saw the seastacks with the last remnants of light quickly fading behind the clouds that were floating over the Pacific. It's early still, I'm sure the traffic will quiet. And it's only three or four hours back to Seattle. I'd like to be closer though, to be sure I'm there on time.

January Five

I woke up along the roadside, mist rising from Lake Crescent. Twenty miles outside of Port Angeles. If I had another hour, the morning Sun may have given me better photographs. I wandered around town here for a bit, stopped in some bookstores, bought a book on clairvoyance; then a cortado and ham, egg, and cheese croissant at Bada NW. Got an Americano for the road. It's a cool little spot, the rustic decor, on par with something you'd find in Ballard.

* * * * *

On the Edmond's ferry. I've taken three now, this one, the first time going east. I had hoped for a better shot of the mountains as we pulled away from Kingston, but only the low-lying mountains were visible. The tallest peaks are enshrouded, quite

densely. I was so close to those mountains, yet saw so little
of them.

Just after this first journey though, the Atmosphere whispered. "I didn't think you'd come." She was leaving the Emerald Realm, to return to a State of Sunshine. So I wandered alone, and the Voice flowed away into the Silence...

January Six

King Solomon's Reef. The diner is cool and all, but the back
bar, way better. Except for this country music someone picked.
Poutine, drenched in Dijon, and an Olympia draught. It just
seems wrong to drink anything else in this city. That was a fun
trip. Still so much to see though.

January Nine

At King Solomon's again. It's a good midway point between the
two cities, roughly, for the weekly trips back and forth. I got
the last piece of pie. Bacon pecan, with a scoop of vanilla
and an Irish coffee. It's a bit weird, frequenting a bar in a
city I don't live. The music coming from the bar in the back is
beyond awful. It sounds like a haunted house theme park ride.

January Thirteen

Aren't we always surviving something, be it nature, society, others, or ourselves? What's a secret? Ah, a thought for another place. Learn which moments you should stay in. Zura hasn't played much yet.

* * * * *

I had to write those thoughts at Long Beach, but didn't want to stay there too long. I brought a spliff down here with me. To the lighthouse at Cape Disappointment. I wish I had brought whiskey or coffee instead. The grass in the hills is too dry to smoke. Fire safety kids. I'm on another trip, this one to the Oregon Coast. I have two extra days for this excursion though, so I decided on a short detour to the southern end of the Washington Coast. My short detours always turn into long ones. Spoke with my oldest friend for about an hour parked on the beach in Long Beach. Got a coffee and some pastries at a pretty good bakery. Like one I was hoping to find in Leavenworth. Or that one I lived down the street from for over a year, yet only went to twice.

The lighthouse is closed, would've been cool to explore. But it's in a state of disrepair, so the photos I could get are rather unique. Or they will be in the scope of history. Ah, they come, they go. The bench opened up, better view of the Pacific. I should go. So long, Astoria is next.

* * * * *

I got here around 2:30. Made another short stop before crossing the Columbia River. Fort Columbia. The bunkers were fucking cool. Most places like that aren't so open to explore. I want to go back with some paint markers.

First order of business, as it usually is, ice cream. Frite and scoop, chocolate milk and cookies; like cookies and cream, but with ice cream that tastes like chocolate milk. They do a great job on the cookies too, large chunks, some almost whole cookies. None of that shitty crumbled dust you'd get from a corporate ice cream shop. Wandered about town a bit, the used bookstore had little in the way of used books. Made my way over to the Buoy Beer Co. Chowder and two oyster shooters, paired with an IPA. This little dog was crying outside for twenty minutes; they have a patio, the Sun is out. People can be so cruel. I put Zura next to the dog to keep it company. It worked for a little bit. It was funny though, hearing people wrongly, unknowingly judging me as a person who left their dog outside in the cold.

* * * * *

I stopped in Seaside for a pretty epic sunset. I'd say I got one of those 'once in a lifetime' shots, but my camera does not perform well in conditions with low lighting. Even on the tripod, it's hardly worth it. Plus the seagrass in the dunes would be wavy with a long exposure.

Cannon Beach now. No idea where I am. The sign said "Bistro" fairly large. Underneath, "live music". I could get a drink at the very least. *Winter Manhattan*. Bulleit Rye, cranberry bitters, sweet vermouth. Paired that with the pork belly served over a sweet potato puree. I have two bottles of wine in Aether. Rye bread from the bakery in Long Beach, and smoked salmon from Astoria. But my addiction, being out. Exploring the civilized world. Finding my nomadic roots. "Freedom's just another word for nothing left to lose." Words heard from the live band. Of course they'd be playing that song.

I wouldn't be here. I wouldn't have seen any of what I saw today if I was still paying rent. I wouldn't be able to afford these meals. Zura and I are far better off living this way, rather than cramped into that micro-studio we were in. This isn't a forever thing, and other than the cold nights, this is how I want to live at this moment. The cold isn't even so bad. That winter sleeping bag I have is great. And Zura, she stays warm just fine. My only worry is thieves. Especially when I leave her in Aether. She played a lot today, rest is good.

January Fourteen

I'm parked at a pull-off spot for the night, just south of
Cannon Beach. Fitting, that name, the reason I'm awake and
writing at two in the morning. The rest area I planned on is
only about another thirty miles, and it wasn't that late when
I stopped. Sleeping here, I'll have daylight for driving.
Not for safety, but to see the things I pass, so I won't
miss anything of interest. Then there's the view. A cliff
straight down to the Pacific. The ocean thrashing hundreds
of feet below.

A poem…

Bombardment Overlook

The waves below batter the coast
thunderous cracks
like artillery shells
crashing down on a battlefield
instead of smoke
there's darkness
instead of screams and sounds of war
there's silence between bombardments
only broken by the random passing engines
the stars above though
they shine all the same
no matter who we are
no matter if our home is near or far

* * * * *

Manhattan Beach, eleven in the morning. I haven't made it
very far. Stopped at the beach in Manzanita, let Zura run for a
while. My partial insomnia last night, I woke up later than I
thought I would. I finally pulled myself out of Aether when I
saw the sunrise looking just as magical as the sunset yesterday.
The people at the coffee shop seemed oddly passive aggressive,
but still friendly. Maybe I was just stoned. It was windy and

cold earlier at the other beach. Now it feels like early Summer along the Central California Coast.

* * * * *

Tillamook now. Just past six in the evening. Pelican Brewery, pretzels and mustard, with a cherry Belgian dubbel. There were a lot of detours today. Never made it to the cheese factory. I'm sleeping near here, I'll go tomorrow. After Manhattan Beach though… Heading south, I had my windows down. The weather is great. But clearly there's an issue with the climate. Pulled off at a viewpoint just outside of Garibaldi. Crossed some railroad tracks, and wandered the shores of Tillamook Bay.

I tried heading down to Cape Lookout, but didn't see the need to pay a fee when there's so much to explore for free. Stopped along Netarts Bay on the way out. Tried to clam, just dug sand. But those seastacks to the north, surely a worthy detour. Oceanside Beach. I parked far back. There was a place to stop, the seastacks well in view. It was roughly a twenty-minute walk. Longer with taking photos on the way toward the cliff. There was an opening, a tunnel. I came through to the other side. Got some great images of the Sun beginning its final approach.

After that, I sped my way to Cape Meares. I didn't see the lighthouse though. It was that or the view of the seastacks while facing south, with the Sun setting off to the right. They sat perfectly framed in my wide-angle lens. Two days in a row, I watched that last sliver of Sun disappear into the Pacific. I think I'll head south. Find a bar in Lincoln City. It's not yet seven, and ten in the morning would be too early for sampling cheese and wine. I do want to camp near Cannon Beach tomorrow. We'll see how that goes though…

January Fifteen

I paid the $5 for Cape Lookout today. It was worth it. Of all the spots I visited so far, this area is the most rugged. Towering cliffs with trees towering above them. A fairly easy venture as well. It's like La Jolla on steroids, and Big Sur with accessibility to the beach. I didn't do anything in Lincoln

City. I didn't feel up for anything. But there was nowhere to really park for the night around there. There was an overlook I had passed, about twenty minutes back north. So I slept there. Windy, but quiet and safe. A cloudy sunrise when I woke up. First stop, Cape Kiwanda. Well, actually it was some State Park and small town just south of there, when I first spotted the massive seastack.

I parked, thought to bring Zura along. She kept walking into the street, so I brought her back to Aether. Good thing I did, my exploration would have been too dangerous for her. There was a fence, and multiple signs warning of danger, but the reward of seeing that seastack from up high, on that tiny peninsula jutting out from the massive dune wall, worth the risk. It wasn't that dangerous at all, but I'd definitely recommend only doing it if you are sure-footed and in decent shape. Some people obviously made their way under the fence, that was clear by the beer bottles left behind. I would guess most don't though. Most listen to the sign. Most miss out on one of the best views the Northern Coast likely has to offer. But it's good most listen. Surely the barrier would have been harder to cross if more people didn't listen to the sign.

After my descent from the danger zone, I went and got coffee, threw a stick on the beach with Zura while it cooled. Smoked a spliff while I watched the waves for a bit. Then onward to Cape Lookout. Ah, but first, "I should make a U-turn" I thought.

Whalen Island. Maybe twenty acres. Safeguarded by barrier dunes across the Sand Lake. It was low-tide, assumably. Zura had a run with it, showing off her agility, not to impress anyone, she just seems to find it fun to run so freely. I'll need some clamming equipment for my next excursion here. I've been wearing the same pants for two weeks. Been brushing my teeth every day and a half or so. I've never felt cleaner. Been seven days since my last shower too.

* * * * *

I'm at the Tillamook Creamery now. Had the grilled cheese. Absolutely worth it. Ice cream next for sure. I'll have to come back with a cooler next time. Some of the cheeses here, I have to eat them, and they're only available to purchase here. I'm thinking, this is what I'll do until I decide to pay rent again. Right here, the Oregon Coast. Why deal with snow and cold? This is accessible, and fairly close to both cities I work in. There's so much to explore. And I know where to sleep, where to eat, where and when I can wash up. I just hope that Aether's engine can take it.

Cape Lookout though, where I started today's entry. As I wrote, worth it. There was only one way down to the beach. Across a watershed. About eight feet wide, a few inches deep. I crossed with the help of some non-submerged rocks and downed trees. Zura was scared though. She just sees the flow, not the depth. But she's clever. Jumped on a log about five feet long that lay across perfectly perpendicular. I thought of doing the same thing, but with only two feet, a higher center of gravity, and shoes I don't completely trust, I knew I'd likely slip. She can always find her own route to keep up. We then explored a sea cave, but it wasn't very deep. Probably bordering on the definition between cave and overhang. Up and over a sandstone cliff that split the beach, momentarily stopping to smoke a spliff.

Unsure of how often the surf came up high on the beach below, we raced across the sand for two hundred yards or so, toward the small coastal waterfall I spotted from the cliff while smoking. There was a little cove there. That's where the La Jolla/Big Sur comparison thought came from. The tide was rising fast again. As it did last evening when I came to the tunnel. We made it back to the cliff, where I began today's entry, then again forded the small rush of water feeding the ocean. I, a slightly different route, Zura the same, though with much more angst, as the log was about a foot farther away approaching from the south.

* * * * *

Cannon Beach is my kind of town. At a pub, playing French jazz. I loved the first spot I went to the other night. It's classy, but unpretentious. The Oregon Coast is probably my favorite place I've visited in this country. It's rugged and rustic, yet cultured with enough modern necessities. If I ever buy property in this country, I might opt for here over Northern California's Coast, Mendocino to be exact. This coast is far more accessible, both to get to, and the beachfront.

As mentioned, I stopped at the Tillamook Creamery. I was pushing my time, to reach Cannon Beach for sunset. Were it not for the clouds off on the horizon, I would have had plenty of time. The color was still wonderful. The sky reflecting with unimaginable hues in the wet sand, as the ocean momentarily retreated west. There are fairly noticeable indentations in my fingers from all the writing I've been doing. I plan to sleep at the same overlook as from the other night. Unless the lot here allows overnight parking. It likely doesn't though. I'll be back here tomorrow regardless. I want to wander this place in the daylight. Three times I've been here now, though the last two with only a day between. But three times I've arrived after all the shops had closed. There's a bookstore I want to go to.

January Sixteen

I was about a half mile away from a once-in-a-lifetime photograph. A full arching rainbow, sprouting from the ocean and touching the coast. Some of the deepest full color I've ever seen too. I got a decent photograph, but that would've been a great frame with Haystack Rock if I were that half mile farther south. Story of my life though, my timing is always so terrible. Still, I ran toward the rainbow with the excitement of a child. Fuck getting old. It's just a state of mind. Life only truly beats you down if you let it. Sometimes though, the reward for the risk, it's worth letting it happen.

I thought I heard live music last night, coming from Driftwood. No live music. Just really good outdoor speakers. I went to Bill's Tavern. Good burger, better beer. At Cheri's now. Bread pudding and coffee. Sat at the bar, a random tide chart in front of me. I was wondering when low tide was today. 2:50. Two and a half hours away. Good to know. Maybe I'll get a second rainbow with the sunset. The weather seems to have stayed the same through the morning. I found some new music last night, at both spots; not live, but at least it sticks with the theme from these past few days. Music. I'll be working by myself at the grow facility, so I'll be blasting music. Edgefield, at the winery, there's always live music there.

More jazz here. I really love this town. The Sun looks like it's breaking through again. The bookstore is closed on Wednesday. Sleepy Monk Coffee is closed until February. I'll be back. A random sign in the bar. "Without music life would be a mistake," Nietzsche. Poignant. I had just texted Richard. Two hours to low tide, I should head back to Aether soon.

EXISTENTIALISM: ALBERT CAMUS

January Twenty-Two

It's already the twenty-second. Camus. The author who is an existentialist, as opposed to Sartre, the existentialist who is an author. I enjoy Sartre just fine, it was his work I was first introduced to when I was in high school. Not at high school though, they don't teach minds to be free there. Sartre though, he's a bit dry. Camus, he writes with flair, with pageantry. It's the difference between writing for an audience, rather than to them. It's allowing those you write for to find your words, to find meaning in them, rather than writing to them, telling them what it is you mean. An artist, as opposed to an artisan. Flow instead of formula. A truer existentialism in my view, the reader is left to discern meaning for the self.

I had only really known of Camus through his novel, *The Outsider*. Required school reading, with no background on the author, no understanding of his short life. I didn't even know that history considered him a philosopher. I found a book at the San Diego Library when I was living there two and a half years ago. *The Thought and Art of Albert Camus* by Thomas Hanna. There are few books I've read faster. Camus's major works, *The Myth of Sisyphus*, *The Outsider*, *The Rebel*, *The Fall*, *The Plague*, they were all well broken down. The book, Thomas Hanna's writing, it was like a lecture hall for one. Yet for many, for anyone who picks up his book, for anyone interested in Albert Camus.

The Outsider, it made far more sense on my last reread of the book, after reading Hanna, and at his recommendation, reading *The Myth* first. I wrote three short excerpts, influenced, inspired, by Camus's *Sisyphus*, *Outsider*, and *Rebel*.

<u>Pushing a Boulder</u>

I've had a long-standing inquiry into the concept of suicide; more contemplating the contemplation than interest in committing the act. This inquiry can be best explained as nihilistic despondency, rather than the suffering of depression. The sort of inquiry led by Albert Camus in his essays within *The Myth of Sisyphus*. Suicide is not a joke, nor something to be taken lightly, but I feel it must be explored truthfully when one is of right mind in order to avoid ever succumbing to it. The most base question that leads to suicide is "what is the point of living?" Again, this isn't suicide out of a distraught life, or moment in life; it's the question of "what purpose is there in continuing a life of unchanging routine?"

<u>Understanding Camus</u>

I've often read others' thoughts on the most famous line of Camus's; but until recently, it was without proper context, and perhaps, with too much influence from the over-inflated egos of literary critics, along with oversimplified translations. "Mother died today. Or yesterday maybe, I don't know." Some will say this implies an uncaring man, someone who isn't inclined to care about his mother's death. But as the translator Matthew Ward patently states, the word Camus used was "Maman", a child's word. He then goes on, "I got a telegraph from the home: 'Mother deceased. Funeral tomorrow. Faithfully yours.' That doesn't mean anything. Maybe it was yesterday." With the proper context it is clear he is distraught, or at the very least, quite sad. He just is commenting that there is essentially no way for him to know when she passed.

The Absurd Rebel

When I speak of suicide, I aim to leave out those who succumb to it due to prescribed medications that alter the brain chemistry, though it is not entirely left out of the equation. Suicide is simply a knowledgeable realization of the inevitable order of nature. Whether one realizes it or not, the mind is always choosing whether to go on with life or end it. When you plan a trip, or a wedding, or to retire at fifty-five, you are choosing life over suicide. You know the outcome will eventually, essentially be the same, yet you choose life. Clearly, this argument doesn't pertain to the theists who believe in another life, but for the secular individual, we always look to answer the questions of purpose and meaning. Choosing to live life, knowing of eventual death, is an act of rebellion against the logic of the human mind. Through the essence of knowledge we become aware of the absurdity of the essence of nature.

January Twenty-Three

Whatcom Falls Park. We took the muddy trails that followed close to the river. It's a bit cold, so writing while walking will have to do. This park is a bit weird. You feel as if you're out in nature, but there's an abundance of suburbanites taking their afternoon walks. Zura is wet and muddy. I need to figure out a way to keep Aether's inside clean when she's not. Surely we won't have the same luck with the lack of rain we did on the Oregon Coast last week, with everywhere we'll venture to over these next five weeks. Saw what looked like a pretty awesome bridge from far away. Turned out to be what was left of a bridge. I could have risked crossing it on my own, but it would have been impossible for Zura to cross.

* * * * *

Made it around to the other side. An old railroad crossing. I assumed as much from the structure of it when we were down below before finding a safe spot to cross. I didn't quite get the photograph I wanted. I'd have had to climb a bit. It's too wet. Calculated risks…

I fell elsewhere, not the bridge. A hill, I tried skidding down it. My back foot slid faster than my front foot. Vertical enough that I bounced right back up. I thought for sure my pants would be covered in mud. They weren't, the only wet spot was from where I stupidly wiped my mud covered glove, trying to wipe off the mud I was sure would be on my pants.

I was there for three hours. Much longer than I thought I'd be. Headed to downtown Bellingham. First stop, Henderson's Books. I could really go for some ice cream. Henderson's has more books than most local neighborhood libraries. The poetry section is as big as most used bookstores have for literature. I picked up a first English edition of *Resistance Rebellion and Death* by Camus. Good find for sure.

Sitting here now, at Caffe Adagio, "Fine Italian Coffee". Universal talk, first book I picked up today in the store, first page I turned to, *Preparations for Italy*. I'm going eventually; *with* or *without you*. The coffee is good. I'm actually more impressed by the proper temperature. In Italy, I could drink my Americano the second it was handed to me. America fucks so many things up.

I'll be heading to the Florida Keys in March. A short road trip from Miami. I could go elsewhere, but I have a secondary, well, primary reason for going. It's the road trip that's secondary. I'll leave my main motivation for another time, should that time come to be.

I got to thinking last night, what motivates me? I'm sure others see me as wandering aimlessly. A vagabond with no motivation, no goals. The thing of it is though, my motivation, my goals, they simply just don't meet the societal standards forced upon us. I'm not motivated by money, not on any high level at least. I'm only motivated to acquire money so I can eat, and afford to continue my adventures. Power, I seek no such thing. I'm not corruptible, so I'd likely wind up dead if I sought power, because my goal would be to give that power to the people. Fame, I don't desire to be famous. Should my writing or art gain fame, I would surely find excitement and pride in that. But I don't want the spotlight to be placed on me, I want it placed upon my creations. Fame is a prison.

* * * * *

Still no ice cream, cash only at the place down the street. I did find delicious beer though. Structures Brewing. I was going to go to Aslan. I'd been there before though, and it was mighty crowded. At the Local Public House now. Needed food. A poutine burger. Heart of Stone sour, from Urban Family. Why do I refuse to cut my burgers in half? Learned behavior I suppose.

I should have added bacon. Then again, I don't want my heart to stop. This freedom I seek, I should mention, the heart condition I have; I recently came to understand how much it affected my life decisions. My existentialist nature, before I educated myself on what existentialism is. Modern Times Berliner superweisse. So many good sour beers tonight. I basically sat on the sidelines before my reparative surgery when I was eight. I tried to keep up with my brothers and friends, my body just couldn't produce oxygen fast enough. At least that's the conclusion I've come to. Still though, I always tried to keep up. I didn't have any outward physical limitations. It just didn't make sense to my young mind why I struggled so much. Then, the reparative surgery. I grew, caught up a bit to where I should have been. I could keep up now. I wasn't the fastest. But I had endurance. My fucking endurance. I still have it.

I was always fed such fear though. Fear of my impending death, if I wasn't careful with my *fragile little heart*. I was a bit of a test subject. They had done cadaver valve surgeries for adults. But they required medications to thin the blood, so any amount of alcohol was unsafe for them. And they generally failed after a decade or so. They assumed I would need another repair at eighteen. Eighteen came, and nothing seemed even remotely urgent. This is why I'm convinced with the capabilities of stem cells. I was young enough, my body still developing, cells rapidly multiplying. My body accepted the cadaver valve as its own. Reverse of the stem cell theory I guess.

I'm loving this life I created for myself. Other than the solitude of it. I'm used to it. But that doesn't mean I'm okay with it. Nor that it's what I want. But it is fun, all these new places. No one here seems interested in talking though. Not like in Seattle.

January Twenty-Four

Cama Beach State Park. Been here for around four hours, maybe a bit longer. I thought of taking the route through Deception Pass, taking the ferry to Mukilteo. I had already passed the exit though. And I'd never been to Camano Island. I took an early exit, the country road that runs parallel to the interstate down into Stanwood. Got my coffee and half-priced day-olds from Camano Island Coffee Roasters. They're smart with their day olds sign, "we baked too much yesterday" is much more appealing to the masses.

This is what motivates me. Days like yesterday and today. Constantly seeing something new. Sure, the view might look similar in Everett, or Edmonds even. And it might be more grand from Golden Gardens. But there's no one here. A few people, but I could count them with my fingers. It's chilly, cloudy. But no wind, no rain. Not bad for entering into the second month of Winter. We've yet to reach the true depths of these frozen months though. The nights are going to get colder, even as the days grow longer. That's one of my favorite parts with this adventure though, the cold. It brings peace. Seclusion from the tourist hordes that would plague all these towns and shorelines, with their clutter, and their mindless chatter, and their aversion to decency.

I get why they act as such. It's the programming. It's their desperation to be free. Work fifty weeks, get two weeks free. Right now, I'm getting a surplus. Work three days, get four free. Maybe it's not quite that good, and it certainly lacks the comfortable aspects the two-to-five ratio had back in San

Diego. But those comfortable aspects, they made me stationary. Including the weather in San Diego. It's cold here, gotta keep moving. Camano Island State Park next.

* * * * *

I mostly sat in Aether at the second stop today, Camano Island State Park. Took one of my *Da Vinci* style twenty minute naps. Read Camus's first letter to a German friend. It astounds me how many of his thoughts I have in my own head. It's not agreement of what he's saying, like it is with Sartre. It's my thoughts, just a half-century older, by a man who grew up in much different circumstances. "For it is not much to be able to do violence when you have been simply preparing for it for years and when violence is more natural to you than thinking." I've long had this thought, that anyone willing to pick up arms against strangers, without a weapon being pointed at them is an enemy to humanity.

He was writing to his friend. A man he no longer considered a friend. A Nazi. But his words speak universally. There's no pettiness in his attrition. It's not a hate for his friend, it's disdain for a broken ideology that has spanned and crippled humanity for ten thousand years. But the combating ideology, the one of morality, it has been there all the same, leading humanity toward progress. The problem, throughout history, both sides, the good and evil, they were needed for progress to take place. Resistance, rebellion, they will always take their course. And win or lose, that ideology, that, in its truest sense, seeks true freedom for all. It will eternally endure. That ideology will forever be a guiding light in the darkest of times.

February Eighteen

I've been stagnantly busy. Other projects taking up my free time. When I do go out, I've been with friends, or short on time. At Alchemy Wine Bar. Kept it simple. House French red blend and a caprese. Took the ferry from Mukilteo to Whidbey Island, then crossed to here, Port Townsend. I almost just continued on my way like everyone else turning left toward the 101. But I followed the signs to the right, for the main street area. It was early enough to at least explore a little. Almost went to the winery tasting room I parked in front of. $10 for five, one-ounce pours. $3.50 more, and I got an extra ounce of wine, and the caprese. Surely a better environment as well. Though I can't hear the live music coming from the dining room, with where I'm seated at the bar.

I've been starved of adventure after having taken so many in such a short period. Heading toward the Olympic Coast again. Hopefully Rialto Beach is open this time. Regardless, I'll have more time in general than I did on my first excursion. I'm unprepared, but prepared enough. I have bread. I have a sleeping bag. And I have my dog, Azzura.

Sangiovese now. $3.50 just turned into $12.50. Damn. Good wine though. I've got two half bottles in Aether. Zura is there resting. Big day playing on the beach for her tomorrow. On to the Gros Petit Manseng. Left over from Valentine's Day. Bartender gave me a taste. It's a Bordeaux blend. Earthy. I had to have it. I would've got a bottle, but it's cheaper by the glass. Whatever, I have those bottles in Aether.

February Nineteen

At First Beach, the Sun is gone. I'll sleep for a bit at the Third Beach parking area, then move on to the Forks rest area in the early morning. Been here since five or so, it's twenty to eight. Took a nap for a bit, with the hatch open. Reread Camus's first letter before that. It's a bit cold, wind gusting quite fierce. I woke up this morning at the rest area outside of Port Angeles. An easy drive at night, in the winter, hardly another car on the way from Port Townsend. And those three glasses of wine were spaced out well enough. A couple at the bar, the guy wanted me to try his pen. It flowed well. But the ink needs time to dry. My thoughts can't wait for drying time. They recommended researching different pens and paper, drying times of the combinations, etc. I'm a bit too simple to get into all that, but interesting conversation regardless. We discussed wines with the bartender. Then we talked of travel. I truly enjoy conversing with strangers, so long as we speak on something of substance.

I was leaving, a few last things were said, ideas for where to travel to. I told them to check out Henderson's Books in Bellingham. I was on my way toward the restroom as the conversation was finishing. The woman turned back toward me. "Barcelona," she said. "If you're gonna go anywhere, go there." "You didn't just say Barcelona did you?" My response. Rhetorical. I asked them what they believed with regard to clairvoyance, omens and such. I told them of one of my last exchanges with you. Barcelona was mentioned. But Key West first. Barcelona will be there for us.

Stopped in Port Angeles for a bit in the morning. Bada NW for coffee again. And I knew they allowed dogs inside from having seen one last time I was there. At least Zura could greet everyone with her smiling face as they came in, even if she was restless.

Picked up some salami and parmigiana, and peanut butter for the trip. The recent snow seemed to limit side excursions, but I figured the road to the Northwestern Point would be clear. Cape Flattery. I was in an odd haze, a bit of a trance driving up there. I think it was just the cars I was behind. My brain switched to autopilot. I stopped for some seastacks, smoked a spliff. It was raining fairly heavily by the time I parked at the trailhead. The trees caught most of the rain, but being coastal terrain, the density of the canopy didn't shield us for most of the hike. Still, it was a blast, and the trail itself was amazing, with about one-third of it being foot bridges, made of smoothed worn wood. The hike didn't take much time, maybe two hours from when I parked till when I pulled away. The most northwest point in the continental United States. Not much up that way, other than *windows to the soul*.

Back on the 101, I went past the turn for La Push, stopped in Forks. Fuel, bread, then backtracked three miles. Rialto Beach wasn't closed. The road past the ranger station is. I knew the parking area in La Push for First Beach was more what I wanted. An ocean view, without the drenching hike. So I came down here.

February Twenty

I'm parked back where I was last night. It feels colder today, even with the Sun fully out. The clouds, only visible far off on the horizon, or lingering below the treeline as fog. Slept in the Second Beach lot instead of Third Beach. I saw the Sun kissing the top of a tree. Just enough inspiration to pull me from my warm sleeping bag, and into the cold morning. That's why I came back down here, to use the Sun to heat Aether, instead of fuel. I gave the crows some sunflower seeds. I know, don't feed wild animals. But I have a thing with crows, they're my friends. And their intelligence restrains them from being wild in the rawest instinctual sense.

The seastacks that line this coast, a friend said to me of them, "It's amazing to think how they used to be part of this land." He's correct, but my interest here, it is purely aesthetic. Beauty, in any sense, it is far more important than what it formed from. This is not the sophomoric, superficial beauty of contemporary thought. This is eternal beauty, the raw instinctual draw of the subjective individual spirit. True personal freedom is understanding this concept of beauty, because true personal freedom, it is simply seeking to create the most beautiful life for one's self, and if applicable, for those we cherish and love.

* * * * *

I passed a sign on the way in toward this section of the coast. "Discovery Pass Required". I almost missed it on the way back out. Technically, I did, but I was looking for it, and saw the sign as I passed it. It was much more visible heading west. There were no other signs. Just a dirt road, and one that the State of Washington has set aside for us to enjoy. That was all that was known. Well, not entirely. I also know I've been driving around with blown struts. The mechanic told me there's no risk of damage driving with them. It's just bumpy. Like a pioneer on wooden wheels. The unknown, will Aether be able to handle the trail, or will I have to turn back, forever unsure of what greets the traveler at the end? Unknown, where the road ends, how long the road is. But that's exactly what keeps me going, what should keep us all going. The unknown.

I doubt the road was longer than two miles. I've driven city streets with more potholes. The road, it just ends. I suppose these are primitive campsites, for hunters, for kids in Forks to experience what they think is love. The treetops are calm, this area obviously protected from the thrashing coastal winds. A log to sit on. A place to make coffee.

I'm where the fog was, where some of it still remains. The Sun is doing its best to burn it off. To clear the haze. It's cold. But no wind. And the Sun keeps getting stronger. The best rays I've felt yet, striking me as the water in my Moka pot began to boil. The fog, it may be different from the clouds that bring storms, but it rains down on the earth all the same. It turns from vapor to liquid, and clings to the trees, collecting until gravity takes its toll on each water droplet and carries it to the ground.

A baby bird has been incessantly chirping for the twenty minutes I've been here. Far off, but still, I hear it. Did it fall from a nest, or are the parents late with breakfast? Will the parents even return? The drops of water are almost louder than the chirp.

The trees surrounding me, most of them, they're young, but tall enough to hide most of the devastation this area saw before they had even taken root. This coastline, it's littered with bare spots. Timber farms. There are signs all along the roadside. Feel good stories for those who pass all the destroyed habitats. Signs telling us of charity, and commerce for locals, and how this 'crop' of trees was replanted in such and such year.

Advertisement, all of it. And I almost bought it myself. "At least they're being responsible with harvesting this resource," was my thought. That's the programming, that's what they want the tourists to think when they pass by these scarred mountainsides. That's how they keep their industry alive, by refusing to evolve.

But what of that baby bird chirping away? What of all the animals that call a specific plot of land their home, when the machines come to tear it all down, to be consumed by us? For homes that will be left vacant, while we have people sleeping on the streets. No one can truly help the helpless, not in the face of this capitalistic imperialism at least.

February Twenty-One

It's noon, woke up about a quarter mile up the road. Kalaloch Campground. $22 for a night. Pricey, but worth it. The sunset, the warm soup for dinner. The assured undisturbed sleep. And the morning. The Sun kissing the treetops again. Went down to the beach with Zura. Low-tide, plenty of room to run. Below freezing though. Warm enough in the Sun. More than anything though, including making some oatmeal with my coffee; the frost on the driftwood, that alone was worth the $22. Crossing the field of it back out to the beach. Worth it. You never know how good your balance is until you try crossing driftwood covered in ice. It made for some spectacular imagery as well. And Zura. She's turning into quite the trail dog. We were wandering through the closed camp loop. I was drawn in by a large patch of sunshine. It appeared a dead end to me. But Zura found the trail. Then of course, I found one; that little yellow buttercup, braving the cold, all alone. It's below freezing here. Yet I feel so warm. Florida will surely set me free.

Yesterday. I went through Forks. Stopped at the info center, brought Zura in with me. The lady there, such wonderful stories she shared of her dog. She told me of the guy the dog always seemed suspicious of. I told her Zura doesn't have that sense. She thinks everyone is her friend.

I took a detour after that, into the Hoh Rainforest. Didn't do much, just let Zura run in the snow for a bit. I thought Sol Duc Falls was down that road. It wasn't. At least Zura got to play in the snow. I was worried. The cold, the cloud cover. The twisting wet roads. I had hit a small patch of black ice that morning. But the Sun came out, and beautifully at that.

The steam rising, the rays cutting through the canopy. I was treated to quite the light show on the drive out. One of those moments where you can understand how people with less exposure to scientific understanding, especially some centuries ago, how they could see such light as divine. It is divine though, isn't it?

Ruby Beach came next. I was able to walk right up to one of the small seastacks; one that was previously surrounded by the flow of the river rushing out to meet the Pacific, the last time I was there. Climbed around a bit on a much larger seastack. I saw another guy ford the river. Shoes off, pants cuffed. Zura wouldn't have crossed though, and I wanted to get to the campsite before sunset anyway. I should have offered those photos to the family as I passed them on my way down to the beach last night. Moments earlier, I had captured them walking on the path of the Sun. At one point, mom and dad knelt down on either side of their child, their shadows, forming a heart in the sand. Unknown silhouettes make the best subject matter. The imagery, it captures the experience, and the human spirit, without making the photograph about an individual. Shadows, backs, reflections, they can do so as well.

* * * * *

Hi-Tide now. I guess that's where I am. There's a sign that says "Thanks for Visiting". Off the 101, the sign said beaches, with an arrow pointing westward. Right turn. 70 MPH through empty forest roads. The sign said 50 MPH. Fuck that. Not sure what I'm doing. Or where I'll sleep for the night. Questions better solved before dark, but the Sun and the ocean are calling Zura and I.

* * * * *

Apparently you can drive on the beach here. Makes for a better hangout. Ate some bread and salami while playing fetch. I could go for a beer. Hopefully I can find a place that allows dogs inside. Digging holes now. That stick we found on the Oregon Coast beach last October is still with us. I don't lose things worth keeping.

I love the freedom on this coast. Freedom and desolation seem to go hand in hand in this country. I understand why people who live out here, or in the desert, or out on the Midwest plains, I understand why they hate 'big government'. What gets lost in this all, the small towns in those areas that think they should have the same freedom as those out on the open range, or those hidden among the trees.

These small towns though, they cater to the capitalist imperialism. Full towns taken over by corporations. When I say small town, I mean those places where the population is large enough that people generally don't know each other, unless they're from the same neighborhood, or work together, or share some other basic form of common ground. These other places, where everyone seems to know each other, most would call them 'small towns'; to me, they're villages. Places where it just wouldn't be financially profitable for McDonald's or Starbucks, for Walmart, for even Chevron, or Safe Way. Places where the only money you spend, it goes to the people living there. This is what Europe is to me. Local villages, existing on their own. But so intricately connected.

* * * * *

I'm in Seabrook now. This little village, it seems like it was constructed overnight. Everything is so uniform. Like an Old West town, with the pretentiousness of an 'upper-crust' New England community. The Stowaway, wine and cheese. The patio was open, the Sun is out. Normally I'd move on from a place like this, it's like a village wealthy people built for themselves to get away from the 'plebs'. But wine and cheese are pretty damn good no matter where you are. Some kind of bleu, some kind of red. I want to get going again before sunset.

* * * * *

Aberdeen now. Passed a .08 limit road sign. Mount Olympus Brewing right there. "Come as You Are" sang from the speakers as I walked in. Wheat IPA. Well balanced. They have a nice carpet for Zura to lay on. Could do without the hardcore music blasting from the back though. No matter. One beer, then off to Olympia. Truck stop near there. Good place for the night. I'll get going early to beat the traffic into Seattle. Get there around six, find a place to sleep in, at Golden Gardens most likely. I'll probably stop at King Solomon's before heading off to sleep tonight. Maybe not. Unnecessary expenditure. We'll see.

February Twenty-Two

It's 5:40am, left the rest area about an hour ago. Parked on the street in Ballard, waiting for 6am to arrive, to head over to Golden Gardens. Sleep a bit more... There shouldn't be that many cars on the road before 6am. I'd guess most of those people are there every day though. Maybe they get to leave early. 7-3 instead of 9-5, or something of the sort. Still, how were any of them convinced that that is life? It's funny, all the places I've lived, I always seem to end up knowing more about a region than the locals. Not facts and figures, but places to see, parks, villages, stores unaffiliated with the massive corporations. I seek to discover this world, most people seem content on just passing through it without really exploring beyond what they grew up around.

Scene Two: Revolt

One of the only coherent philosophical positions is thus revolt. It is a constant confrontation between man and his own obscurity. It is an insistence upon an impossible transparency. It challenges the world anew every second.
-Albert Camus-

My adventures around the Pacific Northwest needed a moment away. A risk I had to take. Off to that State of Sunshine, to try and break the Silence again. I planned everything to, what I thought was, clever perfection. Using every clue that I believed was left for me. A trail of digital breadcrumbs as I saw it. Even more so though, I was following what seemed some unmistakable universal call; like the omens and signs found in Paulo Coelho's novels. Unfortunately, my mind wasn't settled. I missed the meaning of the Atmosphere's whispered words, "You're still going?", and set off on a reckless solo adventure.

CLAIRVOYANCE: PAULO COELHO

March One

The Alchemist. The boy with his heeler. I'm following my omens. On the way to Florida. I've been shown enough to quell my insecurities. Some things, they are coincidence, some things, they only appear as coincidence. These omens, the signs I see, the universal guidance, I still question the fullness of it as reality, as opposed to my subconscious mind recognizing personal desire. Either way, whether following fate, or internal thoughts, it is a path of personal freedom.

<u>March Three</u>

I plan on drinking myself to near death today. Or at the very least, to incoherence. If this town wasn't where it is, it would be even more overrun with the tourists and the programmed crap that draws them in. The tourist trolleys, the little golf cart train that almost ran me over, the people wandering around like lost puppies, it's sad and hilarious at the same time.

White Tarpon. Live Bluegrass. A patio to smoke. The closest I've ever been to Jamaica, so Red Stripe seems fitting. And rum. They pour a stiff drink here. Four ounces. And to top it all off, poutine Benedict. I'm in a better mood after those first two drinks, but I still plan on being incoherent. I'll probably eat half of the mushrooms I have too. A lot of older people here though. And if they're not older, they're too young to have *real* fun. This still sucks though, on a certain level. Would have been better to have company.

* * * * *

Passed out for way too long after I checked in at the bed and breakfast I'm staying at. It's fine, late nights are more fun. Diplimatico rum at the Roost. Poignant. I had just sent off a photograph of Hemingway's rooster. Roosters in Key West, all supposedly descendants. The question of the hour though, do I start a new day in this journal in fifteen minutes, or will it still count as today? "We're in the moment, might as well stay in it." Gruby, the man sitting across from me at the bar. Link, another man sitting at the bar. He told me, "Back in the 60s and 70s, people wrote all the time. Everybody wrote letters in the past." He showed me his pen, "It's the sweetest pen I ever met." His mother's, now his, containers full of Hemingway's letters. He inherited these relics, he's been cataloging them with some philanthropic foundation.

<u>March Four</u>

I feel as if I should feel way worse. Maybe I'm still a little drunk. My heart, it feels like it's dead, and on fire at the same time. Someone wandering down the alley just now, just after I moved outside to enjoy my coffee in the Sun. "It's a pretty yellow flower, isn't it?" Fuck yea it is. The yellow cup, the blue napkin, the peach yogurt, yea, I consciously selected them. The blue plate with the yellow rim though, that was noticed after. Heron House Court. Just the cheapest place I found to stay at. The blue heron mural the other night, with the yellow, golden speckled flowers. Just stop. I need to get going, at least check out and wander this island a bit more. Stay in the moment.

* * * * *

Wandered a bit, should have left already, but I'm here still. I still haven't been to the beach. I tried, but there will be plenty of beach on the drive back. At Sloppy Joe's now. Apparently the bar Hemingway frequented. I just passed by Link's house, left a letter for him. I get why he wanted his personal information to remain personal. What a beautiful mansion. Found the Green Parrot before all that. Met two wonderful souls there, Booker and Jeff. "Great balls of fire," coming from the man playing piano here, at Sloppy Joe's. I never realized what that truly meant. "You're mine, mine, mine."

Back at Green Parrot, the conversation, it's what I crave. Sailboats, weed, life in general. I asked Jeff what he did for a living, but it had its place in the conversation, it wasn't the bullshit mundane surface level 'small talk' question. He cleaned the bar there. I was just wondering what he did, to allow for a sailboat, to allow for drinking at noon on a Monday. Booker was older, so I assumed he was retired. Sloppy Joe's is a bit of a tourist trap, but it's one of those traps that even the traveler must pass through. The live piano man is fantastic. *Here Comes the Sun.*

I should go, I can take my drink with me. "No one will bother you." I asked the bartender, that was her response. He didn't play it, the song, *Here Comes the Sun*. But he played the keys of it momentarily. Even more poignant, considering how observant one would need to be to notice it. This is why Coelho is the instructor, why Clairvoyance is the subject. I truly don't know where your mind is at, but I will never give up. Fate is fucking fate, even if it takes more time to become reality than one thinks they can endure.

<u>March Seven</u>

Regardless of things not going the way I had hoped, the trip was still worth it, especially the extended day. I think an understanding might have finally been reached. And the future isn't written. The drive was amazing, even with the heartache. The people I met along the way, such great conversation. Link, and Jeff and Booker, the man going to stay in Florence for a month at Eola Wine Bar, Nick, the bartender there. And Sean, who shared his wine with all of us at the other end of the bar.

Then there was Mike. A retired firefighter on a bicycle ride. I don't recall where he had started, the panhandle I think; I was in the middle of my mushroom trip, driving back from Key West. I had just crossed the Seven Mile Bridge. He was trying to hitch a ride across, going toward Key West. I was pretty focused on getting back to Miami. *Rebels of the Sacred Heart* by Flogging Molly was rocking me pretty hard crossing the bridge. I told myself I didn't have time. But my secondary subconscious… It was like out of nowhere, but I heard a voice clear as day cry out, "help him!" So I made a quick U-turn, added another fourteen miles, and twenty minutes to my trip. The Sun was starting to lower in the western sky. And with the mushrooms, the view I got, my kindness was fully rewarded. I was also able to capture that lone tree, growing halfway along the abandoned railroad track. I had missed it the first three times crossing that bridge.

"Changing one base in the genetic code can switch the light seen from, for example, blue to green." Venter, a biochemist. I could easily read into it, but maybe it's just commentary on that blue doesn't need yellow to change to green. Regardless, that wasn't my point. My soul is blue, and will remain so. But it's a sky blue, a turquoise sea blue. My sadness isn't deep. I'll always find the light.

I'm done now, with Coelho, with Clairvoyance. Within these pages at least. They'll always intrigue me. Like the fact I got held up waiting for my bag to be checked going through security. While waiting for the TSA to slowly do their 'job'; the first thing I noticed, a bin, marked S56. The reason my bag was held up, the Key Lime gluten-free rum cake that was refused. As I wrote earlier, the future is unwritten.

After returning from my failed victory (or was it a victorious failure), the Silence was momentarily broken, though it came from across the continent. And so I returned to traveling between the two northwestern cities, driving figure eights along the coastal and mountain routes, with that spirit again riding shotgun.

NATURE: SAN FRANCESCO D'ASSISI

March Eleven

The subject of Nature isn't just something to contemplate within the Natural World, there too are us beings, and our Human Nature. My mind right now, it rests on love and lies. My influence, helping me to constantly discover the truth, both outward, and within myself. It's that inner calling we all have, for personal freedom.

Is there a difference between withholding the truth and lying? On the surface it doesn't seem so, but look deeper. Why does one lie? A simple answer, to hide the truth, purposefully. But it isn't always that simple. And hiding the truth isn't always the purpose of a lie, is it? The lie of Santa Claus. Harmless enough, but there may be years, in-between when you've broken the trust of your child, and when that child realizes the actual harmlessness of that lie. But this lie of merriment, it is an *honest lie*. It's the *deceptive lie* that causes the most damage.

Deception Pass State Park, seems fitting I'm here today, considering the daily topic, not to mention the new subject, *Nature*. The picnic shelter is great for blocking the wind. I wish I brought some firewood. No matter, whiskey works too. I'd say it's fitting, considering the last subject as well, but it was a conscious decision to come here. I'd been here twice before, both times finding love. The first time, it was the landscape here, the allure of the islands of the Puget Sound. The last time, a kindred spirit.

* * * * *

I've mostly staved off my addiction to civilization today, passing through all these little towns. Two cups of coffee, a day-old scone. But I did spend quite a bit on books. Good finds though for sure. And poignant. The books, I'll run through them quick. Dante's *Divine Comedia*, John Muir *Wilderness Essays*,

Lucretius *On the Nature of Things*, a book on Saint Francis, *Wildflowers of North America*, *A Textbook of Botany*, and some writings of Democritus.

Sitting in Aether now, the hatch open. I ate what was left of the mushroom sandwich, the one I brought to Florida to share. After eating my meal of bread, meat, cheese, and tomato, being unsuccessful at starting my fire before the rain came, a shower, and now settling into Aether for the night with the hatch open, it appears those mushrooms are finally starting to come through with their intended effect.

It's a shame this campsite overlooking the pond is so near, and facing toward the roadway. The wet pavement is amplifying the sounds of the cars. It's been a while since I wrote on mushrooms. But my mind is empty, or elsewhere at the moment, and I feel my thoughts for within these pages are somewhat exhausted for the day. The earth shattering sounds from the planes at the nearby military base don't exactly help with my intended seclusion into nature either.

...these fucking planes. I miss the sound of the cars on the wet pavement. I sure wish I could fly one of those planes though. I bet it's a fucking blast! For about forty minutes now, every time I think stillness has returned, like a Harley rider revving the engine, the peaceful night is decimated. Maddening, and a lesson on patience in one. The sound of the rain would be nice to hear for more than two seconds though.

Ah, the training exercise seems to be complete. Hopefully for the night. The cars on the wet pavement are so soothing now. A lesson on comfort for sure. And one on endurance. And as mentioned, one on patience. I need some wine. And I have that large macaroon that I only took two bites of. It's fucking delicious. It's funny, I could sleep through all these sounds, save the loudest rumblings from the planes. But the nearby humming, it breaks my concentration, all the same as the planes. Well, maybe not the same. Those planes were fucking loud.

<u>March Twelve</u>

Camped the night at Quarry Pond. Once the planes stopped it was peaceful. The rain eventually became a steady downpour. My firewood got wet, now it's slowly burning in the fireplace of the picnic shelter, the same one as yesterday. Hardly giving off the warmth I hoped for. At least I can make coffee. I was hoping the fire would be warm enough that I could sit with my back to it, and take in the scenery facing west as I write, rather than huddled and hunched over with my journal on my lap. At least it's quiet up here in the cold. And Zura can roam free. It looks like the Sun might break through too. There is some clear blue sky out on the Sound.

* * * * *

A day trip turned adventure. The silhouette of the mountains, slightly enshrouded by clouds. The promised land. I wish I brought my camera up here to the deck. The shot with my phone came out decent enough. Damn it's windy out there. Not quite raging waters, but there are a few peaks of brackish white caps. Certainly the most movement I've felt on a ferry, granted the Port Townsend ferry that I'm currently on is smaller than the others. I'm not sure where I'm headed, but I figure a glass of wine in the Sun would be nice. The Sun is dropping though.

* * * * *

Port Townsend. I'd love to spend two weeks here, that would be long enough to feel at home. Alchemy Wine Bar again. Same bartender, he remembered me. It's nice to be remembered. And to get drink pours that reflect that recognition. Gonna try this nature immersion again. East side of the Olympics. Haven't gone that way yet. And I'm sure there are plenty of spots to pull off and sleep in the National Forest. Or just a grocery store parking lot for a few hours even. Some guy at the fountain just busted out a violin. Were it five degrees warmer I might stay. But the Natural World is calling, I spend too much time in civilization.

* * * * *

All the areas I thought would be good to sleep for the night were closed. No matter. It would have been colder up in the mountains. I found a pull-off spot along the 101. Nothing here, but it's a place to park for the night. At least I'll get to drive and witness the Hood Canal during daylight. I'm a fucking idiot by the way. Took out $20 with the cash back at the self-checkout line. Left the $20 just sitting there. I was looking forward to getting a few joints out this way.

March Thirteen

About three miles down the road from where I slept was a small open public shoreline, with a campfire ring made from the rocks in the creek right there. No signs of any kind. A quarter mile farther, Triton Cove, no gate, no sign forbidding camping overnight. But a spot to sleep is of little matter, I'm just always wary of signs forbidding overnight parking. I get it, we as a society don't want people just camping out in parks continuously, because eventually it draws the worst kinds of people; and their concept of anarchy as freedom, it takes away from the freedom of others, those who have decided, in some sense, to be a contributing member of society.

I've realized, we seem to have a government structure that has wholly forgotten the concept of discretionary enforcement. For instance, noticing the difference between a person traveling through, and a person looking to take advantage of every free resource a locality has to offer. What I mean by this, have your rules in place, but learn who they should be enforced upon. Equal enforcement is not about fairness or freedom, it's about ultimate control. It's about power, "...the only people at liberty will be prison guards who will then have to lock up one another. When only one remains, he will be called the 'supreme guard' and that will be the ideal society in which problems of opposition will be settled once and for all," Camus, *Bread and Freedom*.

Farther down the road was the Hamma Hamma Wilderness, but again, it ascended into the mountains, and would have been much colder up there overnight. The point, you can study every inch of a map, digital or analog, but you won't really know anything about the area until you see it for yourself. It's the same with photographs. There are probably millions of images from this shoreline at Potlatch State Park, but how many of them captured empty picnic tables with the fog so dense that you can hardly see the water? There are a few people here though, enduring the thirty-degree morning, the icy breeze coming off the mountains.

It's oyster season. Eighteen oyster limit. By the shoreline, you'd think there's far more than eighteen per person to go around. Birds are crafty fuckers. The oysters though, such difference in size, obvious signs of age on the larger ones. But what I marvel at most, the purplish hue on some of them; the effervescence even more so. Yet they all seem to have the cleanest white inside. I suppose my insides are likely clean as well. The Sun is doing its best to shake off the fog. It'll warm.

* * * * *

The Sun is out now, here in the mountains. Vance Creek Wilderness. Overlooking the Vance Creek Trestle. They've made the bridge inaccessible from the north. The south entrance is on private land. I'm not concerned with the trespassing, it's only a logging plot. It's just that the snow is a bit too much. This adventure seems better suited for late Spring, or more so, early Autumn. I figure there's not much need to hike farther, just to see under the bridge, especially with the snow. All or nothing for me. It would be nice to have a camera set here though, for when my feet are dangling from the center of the bridge.

* * * * *

Westport now. Zigzagging, as I'm prone to do. Went back up, northwest slightly, after a short detour to the *steel bridge*, or something of the sort, while coming down out of the mountains. Surely not the trestle above Vance Creek, but pulse quickening heights regardless. Not certain of the name of the body of water that ran below it though. After that, I stopped at Hunter Farms. Pistachio and Bordeaux cherry ice cream, salmon jerky sticks, and some hot and sweet pickles. Cruised along route 106, finding some fairly interesting things to photograph, before stopping momentarily at Twanoh State Park. I would have stayed there longer to write, but I forgot to hang my Discovery Pass Tag. And I wasn't exactly near Aether where I was thinking of writing, with the clouds held so perfectly calm in the waters of the Hood Canal's southeastern portion. I passed through Allyn, thought of stopping there, but I wanted more nature. Found a Discovery Pass pull-off spot.

* * * * *

The Sun has gone behind the clouds, though sunset isn't technically for another twenty minutes. I'll wait to see if there are any remnants of color. Grayland Beach State Park. I just wanted to drive on the beach with the sunset. Got here just in time I suppose. I got some clam strips and fries from somewhere in Westport. They do you right with the tartar sauce. Mixed one with hot sauce, the other with mustard. I'm fairly drunk. A few shots of whiskey coming out of the mountains, a pour of wine at that pull-off spot, another for the drive, and a beer when the wine was gone. No remaining color in the sky, so I'm gone. Need to find a place to sleep for the night. I thought about a room, but I might save that for Cannon Beach tomorrow night, or maybe next week. Onward.

March Fourteen

I'm somewhere south of where I was, and north of where I'm going. This stretch of land I'm sleeping on tonight was the last outcrop of the Washington Coast for me to discover. That's not to say I've seen it all, but simply there are, by my count, six distinctly separate areas to pass through. It's nearing 1:00am, been awake since 10:00pm, passed out around 8. I'm parked somewhere right near a beach. The spot is on a slant, but it's not too bad, I've slept on more uneven surfaces before. The constant calling of the ocean, the waves up here don't stop like they do back east or in Southern California. I suppose they don't technically stop anywhere. But here, there is no recess between waves. It's dark here, and quiet. No cell service. I wish I had known of this spot last August. Hopefully the weather is clear, and the Moon hidden for Perseus's show this year.

* * * * *

I had some personal thoughts that seemed relatable to Human Nature as I lay in the darkness for three hours, hoping the ocean would lull me back to sleep. Relationships. Of course there's the family relationship, but we're born into that, and so those hold a different dynamic. My thoughts, they are about friendships and romantic relationships. Too many people have this idea that the two should be separate. But that's like eating one slice of bread with only peanut butter, and the other with only jam. Sure, they're both delicious, but they're better together. It's the yin and the yang. I can sit and eat cheese and drink wine with anyone. But what layers are there within our conversation, our silent observations, both of each other, and everything around us? How do we communicate about those silent observations?

I re-awoke around 6:30am, then again at 8. It was a cool little spot for the night, just the sounds of the ocean. I'd try to camp there one night, if what I thought was a river outlet was actually from a river. It wasn't. It's a runoff from the farms. Zura eats sand like she eats snow, so she'd end up eating the sand soaked with that runoff. Weird day. The sky was just a blanket of gray, the Sun playing its game from yesterday. At least the clouds have definition now. Hanging on the Long Beach Peninsula. Probably head to Astoria later. I have some things to attend to near Portland tomorrow, so heading down to Cannon Beach will have to wait for next week. I'd be more inclined to do something if the Sun would just burn off the clouds. It's powering through them, just not fully.

* * * * *

Cape Disappointment again. Went to the area I skipped last time. Awesome secluded little beach, with what would be a little island were the tide higher. Heading up toward the lighthouse now. Apparently there are two here. This one less accessible to most visitors. The trail started off easy enough, but the path down to this beach, I slipped in one spot; didn't fall, but a slip nonetheless. Then there was the cliff Zura almost went straight down. There was a long root to grab, so a human could easily go that way. But Zura would've face-planted into rocks and driftwood had I not called her back.

* * * * *

Great views from the lighthouse as one would expect. Well, the base area surrounding the lighthouse. Yet another one closed off. I did get to climb up a small tower lookout though. The Sun isn't quite as warm as I hoped it would be sitting out here. The breeze overpowers any warmth it's trying to impart on me, before disappearing below the horizon in two hours or so. Where is my mind right now? I just want to keep doing this. Road trips, travel.

* * * * *

I'm at the Rogue Public House in Astoria. Bought five half-gram joints, and a quarter of flower for $30. Some random sale. Then made my way up to the Astoria Column. I conquered my fear of heights long ago, but heights seemed to be a theme on this trip. Bellingham to Astoria, through the Hood Canal. I used to think adventuring to places that have long been discovered couldn't truly count as adventuring. How wrong I was. I'm not very hopeful for a colorful sunset. Too many clouds off on the horizon.

I got the Paradise Pucker, a sour beer, a Dead Guy whiskey, pretzels, and sweet potato lettuce wraps. This is how I prefer my meals, much cleaner. Those fried clam strips were a mistake, too greasy. Again, five degrees warmer would be nice. My server saw my dog as I came in, asked if I wanted to sit inside or outside. I figured he meant my dog could sit inside with me. No, he simply meant people leave their dogs outside in the cold, alone, while they get drunk in the heated interior.

* * * * *

I rarely backtrack, but it was only a mile back into town. Zura is resting in Aether. I walked toward the water, smoked what was left of a joint I started up near the Column, where I sat under a burial canoe and finished reading Camus's *Bread and*

Freedom. "No, the doves of peace do not perch on gallows! No, the forces of freedom cannot mingle the sons of the victims with the executioners of Madrid or elsewhere!...as we shall be sure that freedom is not a gift received from a state or a leader but a possession to be won every day by the effort of each and the union of all." *Bread and Freedom* was a speech Camus gave at the Labor Exchange of Saint-Etienne in May of 1953.

I'm at Baked Alaska. A great view out the window. Even the perspective of the cargo ships lined up has a distinct beauty to it. My new Camus book, it doesn't look so new anymore. A book printed in 1961 should not look so pristine. I'm glad it is, but I aim to make it look used. These words feel biblical to me, or rather, I read them, and feel them as a universal truth. Burnside rye. A bit sugary. Maybe he poured the bourbon and I wasn't paying attention. I chose the bar, even though the dining room has the better view. But I only wanted a few oysters. I just feel more comfortable sitting at the bar alone than in a dining room, especially when I'm only ordering a whiskey and some oysters. That's why I came in. Been wanting oysters a few days now. Two on the half-shell with ginger beer ice, and an odd serving of five for the Rockefeller. Speaking of the bourgeois society, "They often say that they are defending freedom, but they are defending first of all the privileges freedom gives to them, and to them alone," Camus.

Painted Lady gin, more spice than floral, but herbaceous. And no, I'm not pretentious, I know what the fuck I'm talking about. Look up the definition of pretentious, it's self-aggrandized ignorance. Perhaps I'm a bit inwardly snobbish with my palate, it's just perplexing what people find to taste good. It's programming. I was programmed once, but I learned. I haven't just worked at a lot of restaurants, I worked at places with good food, generally, and all different styles. An upscale bar, a four-star steakhouse, American 'Italian', Greek, and several undefinable places that opened me up to all sorts of flavors, not to mention the education I received on alcohol.

* * * * *

This place is tight on space, Astoria Bistro, but it's pretty cool. The 'starter menu' prices are a bit high. There are several entree options that cost less than most of the appetizers. This is another one of those two-week towns. In two weeks I'd know all the best spots. Next time I'm here I need to try the Japanese takeout window next door. Busu. He's not claiming to serve Japanese though, just Japanese influence. Respect for understanding the difference. Fifteen globes, fifteen of them used for mere decoration in this bar. No child can spin them in wonder. Influence, not inspiration. I truly understand the difference now. Inspiration must come from a tangible source. Still, this fortnight, it's in hopes that an understanding will be met.

March Fifteen

Stopped out on Route 30 for a bit. 10pm till 3am or so. Just slept across the front seats instead of moving everything around. I'm a bit out from Portland, but the stars are already faint from the city lights. I can drive tired on dark roads for hours, but throw in any other factor, other than cannabis and coffee, and, well... I know my limits. The six drinks I had in Astoria finally caught up to me. So I stopped.

* * * * *

It's 4:30am now. Blew through Portland. Stopped for gas in Troutdale, my destination. But I have nothing to do until 10am. I'd never been to Multnomah Falls. All the times down here, visiting or working, never been. It's only twenty minutes away from where I stay with my friend. Parked down the road a bit at Wahkeena Falls. I figure a hike with the rising Sun is in order. It'll help keep me warm with the cold mountain morning. All that nature I passed through, no waterfalls. It's only a mile hike up to Fairy Falls from where I'm parked, but I'm uncertain of the trail conditions. There's snow on the ground along the road.

But the stars, oh how they shine out here, especially looking east. And the nearby sound of cascading water, it's just enough to drown out most of the sounds coming from the interstate below. I had some thoughts on Human Nature while driving out this way, mostly coming from my speeding along at 70 MPH on a 55 MPH road. Trust has something to do with it, but my thoughts, they were generally contemplating expectations and hope. I expect that the engineers who planned out a 55 MPH road are expecting people to go at least 70 MPH on it. The speed limit is 55 MPH so people won't go 80-90 MPH, as they would if the signs read 70 MPH.

But what can we expect, what expectations of others can we have? If any? Or is trust in another human merely about hope? In and out of sleep over the past two or so hours. The dreams I had were odd, but relevant. I watched as the stars and black faded to blue, then there was a sheet of gray. The blue has returned, as dull as it is. The mountain ridge, across the Columbia, in Washington, it has a slight blanketing of light. That, and the northeastern sky showing depth instead of dullness, they are the only things that changed my hopes for a sunny day into an expectation.

Our Human Nature, it is based on knowledge. Knowledge of what we are shown. The littlest thing, it can turn hope into expectations. The problem, when more than the individual and personal knowledge are involved, some people will put forth false expectations. Regardless of their reasoning, they turn hope into expectation, perhaps even unknowingly. And while expectations can be small to large, or weak to strong, the moment we are shown something tangible, it becomes knowledge. Hope, it is simply walking blind through silence. Hope is the unknown. Hope makes us stronger.

* * * * *

This seems a fitting way to end this journey. Multnomah Falls Lodge for breakfast. Smoked salmon hash with a biscuit and two eggs over easy. Fireplace or waterfall view? It's surprisingly moderately priced as well, $17 with the coffee. Plus tip of course. This was a much better decision than sleeping at a truck stop in Troutdale. That hike this morning was invigorating. The switchbacks really got the blood flowing. Not sure if I made it to Fairy Falls; the spot I turned around at had a small cascade. But the trail turned from dirt to ice quickly. It wasn't the ascent that would have been the issue. It's the same with climbing a tree. How precarious is the way back down?

This lodge is great. And I apparently arrived just in time. The empty restaurant is now crowding. And I got the front-row seat for viewing the waterfall from the dining room. The portion size is what you would hope for too. But I'm learning, with places like this, you can expect something amazing, instead of hoping for it. Even the egg yolks show the quality. Not quite orange, but a deep yellow nonetheless. And the music. Not live, but classical piano. I wonder how many people pass through here, take their pictures, and then head off to McDonald's?

* * * * *

Cascade Locks now. The Bridge of the Gods. No pedestrian pathway, but you can cross on foot. Not for the faint of heart, even driving over it is probably a bit more pulse quickening than a typical bridge. As I wrote, heights seem to be a theme on this trip. I decided to save the Vista House for my next venture this way.

March Seventeen

Astoria now, I should have left work earlier. Missed my chance for a drink in the Sun. Surprisingly there aren't a lot of patios here with their seating on the west side of the city blocks. It's funny, I was literally just here three days ago. But it was a different trip, it could easily have been a month. Work though, the wealthy elite celebrity tour is lame as fuck and all. But what really crushes my soul, the packages we sell. Pre-ordered roses delivered by the captain, or rose petals to scatter on the table. And the balloons, fuck the balloons. It's all commodified waste.

* * * * *

Sitting parked south of Cannon Beach. Everything was closing by the time I arrived. And instead of writing in a bar, I decided to head to Bombardment Overlook. But I passed this single car spot near there, I remembered it from the last time. A VW bus was parked here. It's my spot tonight. And close enough to head back into Cannon Beach for some Sleepy Monk Coffee when the Sun rejoins me, if the cafe is open on Mondays. Then there's that bookstore. I've managed to only spend $4 on an Americano today. That was coming through Astoria.

I stopped in Seaside. Parked outside what looked like it could be a decent dive bar to drink in for a bit. Walked to the beach first. The end of the Louis and Clark Trail. I thought to stop for ice cream, but the only place open served Dryer's. If I don't buy it at the grocery store, I sure as hell don't want it from an ice cream shop.

Dropped Zura in Aether after the beach and went into the bar ready to write. Four people. I ordered a shot of well whiskey, $3.75, then I left. So I guess I spent $10 today with tip. That's how fast I left that bar, it was nearly already void from my memory. Speaking of which. I'm not certain how much this relates to memory, but since this month started, I left an unopened pack of batteries in a bag I threw out in Florida. I left that already mentioned $20 back at the self-checkout stand just outside of Port Townsend. And most recently, I crumbled up a bag with two of the five joints I purchased on Thursday, and threw those out on accident with some trash I had in Aether. The point, I'm a bit of a fucking idiot sometimes. A bit spacey, always have been. As a child, my parents always got on me for it. That, coupled with my solitude, I've become hyper-aware. But that spaciness will always be a part of me.

This spot though. Hatch open, enjoying some Rogue rye, with Irish soda bread from Edgefield, and some ham I got from work. I plan on waking up early. Sunrise from Haystack Rock. And I think there's a trail right here leading to a cliff with a tree. After I left Seaside, and after being too late to get anything in Cannon Beach, Zura and I headed to Haystack Rock. The brilliance of the Moon. It lit up the beach quite well. Passed several fire pits, had to make my way across a water outlet by using the glimmer of the Moon off the rushing water to know which spots to avoid getting my shoes wet.

The moonlight creates wonderful lighting for long-exposure photographs. I wish I still had my full-frame camera. The incoming tide chased us twice, the first time my noticing within a second of what would have been soaking wet shoes, and by extension, socks and feet. But I was aware just enough.

March Eighteen

"What a lovely day to be lonely." Broken Bells, *Holding on for Life*. This plot of earth is finally warming. Last night, the first night where the day's heat somewhat remained. Even with the gusting winds on the beach this morning, standing in the shade, waiting for the Sun's rays to engulf Haystack Rock, it wasn't the least bit cold. Slightly chilly after a half hour of motionlessness though. I captured some great photographs, to match those from last night.

Finally got into Sleepy Monk Cafe. They bake all of what they sell in house. The bagels look great, but the maple bar drew me in. It's an excellent spot to hang out, but the Sun is fully out now, and Zura is waiting to play. The coffee though, exactly what I would expect. No hope needed here. Bookstore, then nature.

* * * * *

Rockaway Beach now. About to head farther south, just a bit. *The Twins* seastacks. Other than being next to each other, I see no reason why they would be called twins. The bookstore was closed. Next time. Filled the pages of the first composition book. Two and a half months. It's warm today, almost too warm for my hat and fingerless wool gloves. Almost warm enough to wear just a t-shirt. But the breeze, even as warm as it is compared to what I've felt these past 74 days, it's still just cool enough. And I'm more comfortable being slightly warm than slightly cold.

* * * * *

Probably would have been closer if I walked from where I was parked in Rockaway, but then I would have missed the driftwood pile. But yea, they look nothing like twins, even from this angle. I need some new sketch pens, mine are out of ink, so I'm using a uni-ball that bleeds too much for writing. It's a decent sketch pen, but even still, it bleeds too much.

* * * * *

Stopped along Tillamook Bay, the Three Graces and Crab Rock seastacks. Took some photos while standing on the road barrier that drops down to the train tracks. Some asshole yelled, another beeped their horn. I have nothing but scorn for people like that. Honestly, what kind of asshole passes by a stranger and actively tries to cause harm, even if done in a passive way? But the seastacks, they're calming. The herons all perched, motionless, while the occasional gull swoops around the tiny islands, they bring peace.

At Cape Kiwanda now, Pelican Brewery, these are the prices I expect. But the view is worth it. The smoked salmon flatbread and Hazy Rock IPA, worth it too. The Brute Lupes is even better, like an IPA farmhouse sour. I also was gifted the best table again, as I was at Multnomah Falls. The view here, straight on to Chief Kiwanda Rock. Might as well stay here for sunset, might even be able to capture the Sun through the keyhole. The angle might not be right though, maybe a month or so earlier.

Instead of the 'off limits' area I explored in January, I took Zura with me, we climbed the dunes hill which still provided a spectacular panoramic view. I stopped in Garibaldi, got some clams and oysters from a little fish market right on the bay. Had two of the oysters at a park table there, one with a pickle from Hunter Farms I got the other day, the other just straight. My ridiculous 'Rambo' knife finally came in handy. Birds are crafty mother fuckers. Those oysters really don't want to be eaten.

I sped along just fine from there to Tillamook, but after getting through town, there were far too many cars in front of me, with the lead car going 45 MPH in a 55 MPH zone. No one else took the right turn toward Kiwanda, so I did. It was a much quicker drive than I thought it would be too. A great mix of nature and culture, of the Natural World and Human Nature. The Sun almost definitely won't be dropping through the grand seastack's keyhole. It's far too small, and the Sun's arc has already led it too far north for that possibility. I'm sure it has its dates, like the *Firefall* at Yosemite. There hasn't been a cloud in the sky all day. The hat and gloves are gone. T-shirt, pants cuffed, sandals. Who said "fuck the comfortable"? Comfort should be strived for, but only in the form of personal comfort. Comfort is subjective. But fuck conforming to the programmed comfort they tell us we want.

A third beer, surely one too many, but I still have an hour or so before sunset. The Pink Panther pilsner. Eight percent ABV, doesn't taste much like a pilsner, but tasty still. I'm glad I said yes to the ice for the clams and oysters I bought. Probably have the oysters for breakfast, the clams for lunch. I'll stop at the store here in town for items to make a broth for the clams. The Sun has dropped low enough, and the wind returned, I need my long-sleeve shirt at the very least. That keyhole shot would have a tight window, and it might be farther than a month back. A cloudless day in the heart of Winter is unlikely. I'll take the whale though, breaching and spouting just off-shore. I'm uncertain where to sleep for the night, but I know there are rest areas south of here. And I'd like to explore the dunes region. So I'll head toward Florence, before coming back this way and going up through Tillamook State Forest on Highway 6 toward Portland. I'm sure there will be dispersed camping somewhere through there where I can spend two nights truly immersed in nature.

March Nineteen

Lincoln City, Roads End. Watching the swells come in. Perfectly formed waves. Center break, left or right, barrels big enough to stand in. The waves were similar at Kiwanda last night. Actually saw someone get *barreled*. This water is far too cold for me to surf in. Hell, San Diego was almost always too cold.

I woke up at a viewpoint, same one I stayed at last time, coming back up from Lincoln City toward Tillamook, just outside of Neskowin. Stopped at the beach there. Proposal Rock. Took a few photos, but my camera batteries are failing. So the extra one I took with me only captured about ten images. Made coffee back in the parking lot with the Sun rising over the tree-covered mountains.

* * * * *

I never really found that spot to sit and write today. Too much to see, too much ground to cover to get to the dunes. I made it, with just enough remnant light to cook dinner and get the fire started. Though I did have to eat under the light of my lantern. Found a spot to camp. Honeyman State Park Forest, and the ocean dunes. Not enough time to get to them tonight, though the full Moon would make exploring the dunes easy. But I'm not certain where the dunes are, or how far through the forest the trail leads before getting to the sand.

From Lincoln City, I drove to the Yaquina Head Lighthouse, on the northern end of Newport. I wasn't really planning on stopping anywhere, but seeing the lighthouse from up the road, I decided on a short detour. If anything, it would be a good place for lunch. I put my knife into my palm. The first oyster was easy. The second one, it was a fighter. The knife slipped. I attended to it quickly, the blood didn't even have time to breach the surface. A layer of super glue does wonders; in this case, several layers.

Patched up, I went back to work on the remaining three oysters, including my vendetta against that second one. That one, I ate as is, to enjoy the raw taste of my victory. The other three, an oyster sandwich, mustard and pickles on French bread. I then wandered about the lighthouse area, shortly leaving to then explore the tide pools (the lighthouse itself of course being closed). High tide, or in-between, so not much to see. Other than the end of the world.

Stopped in Newport for a little bit. I bought a mountain huckleberry and Oregon strawberry ice cream milkshake for the road. My next stopping point, Thor's Well. Thankfully low tide had arrived by then. Judging from all the tide pools, that feature of nature is likely inaccessible during high tide.

__March Twenty__

It's almost 5pm. That makes me want to drive instead of write.
But the bookstore would be closed anyway by the time I arrived
back in Newport. Sidetracked three times, add in a late start,
and a longer dunes walk than I had planned, and it's almost
5pm. There is that fish spot in Yachats my friend told me of.
But with no cell service, here at Thor's Well again, I have no
way of checking how late they're open. I suppose I'll drive…

* * * * *

South Beach, just south of Newport. I'll figure out my night
after sunset. Enough clouds to make the sky interesting, but the
Sun is dominant tonight. A little wine with the fading light.
The fish spot in Yachats looked great, from the menu, but no one
seemed to be working there, and there was construction happening
on the patio. So I decided to continue on. Stopped at Seal Rock
overlook again, finished my panorama of sketches, then played
with my camera and the light down on the beach. Low-tide is so
wonderful. A beautiful sunset. Another family walking the path
of light. Captured them kneeling down again, huddled, another
heart.

* * * * *

Yesterday. Thor's Well yesterday. A warning. Watch, witness,
observe, before standing on the edge of a hole in the earth
that fills with water from the raging ocean. I didn't get wet
yesterday, but had I not heeded that warning, the next one
could have very likely taken me in. Then there were the rock
formations. The best one by far, a natural path of stone leading
directly to the Nordic God's Chasm.

I suppose I skipped ahead last night. I forgot to mention
my brief stop to sketch Seal Rock from the overlook. Did two
sketches. After Thor's Well though, the descent into Florence,
into the dunes region. Quite the epic view. The first place
I stopped to camp didn't quite seem like a campground for
travelers. I decided to get into the heart of the dunes, south
of Florence. I'm glad I did. Honeyman State Park was a perfect

location. Both for the night, and for the future. They have yurts to camp in. The bathrooms have showers. They were free, so I was a bit apprehensive, thinking they wouldn't have hot water. But they did. Which is good, because I needed a shower, and I sure as hell wasn't taking a cold one with the chill this morning.

Dinner last night. I made the clams. They boiled open pretty fast. But it was the broth that made them. A little water, some pickle juice, mustard, and chopped ginger and garlic. Along with French bread to dip in the broth. I was parked alongside the fire ring, and with the 'suicide doors' of Aether open, I had a great spot to lie next to the fire while I drifted off to sleep. I had intended to put out the fire and close the doors before my eyes fully closed, but I was tired from the day. I slept about twelve hours, from 9-9, with some intermittent waking; including the cool breeze that woke me to an extinguished fire and open car doors. I opened the hatch around 7, to let Zura out. She hopped right back in to fall back asleep. Such a good dog.

Took the morning slow, but we were walking on dune sand by 10:30. The easy way, or the steep way? Let's see that view. That wall of sand when you get to the top of what you thought was a wall of sand… Humbling to say the least. We conquered that wall too though. ATVs; shit looks like fun. I'd probably break something, somehow. Still, future plan for sure. Tried taking a different route back, after realizing we headed south for an hour, not west. And that even still, the ocean was way too far to hike to. Not to mention we'd need to cross the ATV area. But that different route, I wasn't sure it led me back to where we parked. Probably added 30-45 minutes. Desert dunes are easy, there's no dense forest in the way from point B back to A.

I keep expecting the superglue on my palm to break down and blood to come gushing out from the wound. 36 hours though, even with the sliver of inside on the outside, it should be sealed and healing. At Newport Cafe. Oyster sandwich with a cup of clam chowder. I was actually at a place that was serving New York clam chowder earlier today. Fuck that style. The chowder here is stupid good. Like, brain shutdown good. They oyster sandwich. One half with mustard and malt vinegar, the other, the Pepper Plant chunky garlic hot pepper sauce. Mirror Pond pale while I waited to order. Hop Valley Citrus Mistress grapefruit IPA with my meal. The fact that I seem to be the only person not getting good service, it makes everything all that much better. I'm in no rush, and I'm no one here anyway. I hate service where they kiss your ass. "Fuck the fake", who said that? Cause that shit should be universal. "To thine own self be true…" That doesn't mean *only* "thine own self", because then, you're not being true to yourself, if you don't allow others to be true to themselves. The mustard and malt side was better.

We made it back above the parking lot, by the lake sitting at the eastern base of that section of the dunes. Zura took a good bath, dried off with the Sun and sand. A detour to the South Jetty next, to see the dunes along the ocean shoreline. Found two cool pieces of driftwood. A stick with the head of a snake, and a footprint.

Another detour, Heceta Head Lighthouse. I didn't make the hike, as it was yet another closed lighthouse I could only walk around the base of. Instead, I sketched the seastacks there. The shepherd and the buffalo, at least that's what I saw. Then the cliffs, with the house in the foreground, and the lighthouse perched higher, mostly hidden by the trees. A few photographs, and we were off again. Driving, pretty stoned, I thought I had already passed Thor's Well. I hadn't though. I stopped, left Zura to rest in Aether.

I suppose it wasn't the Devil's Churn, as I thought while photographing it. But the back-splash wave was fierce and frightening. I felt somewhat unsafe being so close; one big wave while looking through the camera viewfinder, I could be thrashed quite easily. This wasn't some driftwood and rocks, as dangerous as that was back when I started this all. Regardless, the backsplash, when large enough, created a rainbow in its mist. Patience is a virtue for sure. Fifteen minutes watching the patterns as the Pacific rushed in toward this channel in the earth. I miss-timed the first attempt, my camera not quite at the ready. Then after my successful attempt, I decided to tempt fate a second day, standing on the edge of Thor's Well. My legs got a bit wet, but I got my image. Far better than the one from yesterday.

<u>March Twenty-One</u>

The Moon was there, in full, slight haze covering its blemishes, but it was there. Perfectly framed with Chief Kiwanda. Dead camera battery. Unsure what to do or where to sleep last night, I had the thought to be here for the setting full Moon. Still got some pretty good images. And the full Moon setting behind the Chief, hardly a once-in-a-lifetime chance. But it did look amazing with the streaking clouds just becoming more defined from the earliest fragments of light. It doesn't look as if I'll get to watch the Sun's rays slowly illuminate the seastack either, far too many clouds to the east.

What a fantastic morning though. Even with the missed photo opportunity, and the more typical PNW weather. Rested without fully succumbing to sleep for about an hour. Then I started a fire, just dug a hole in the sand to block the wind, and I had a solid fire for about two hours. The heat from the coals and the large, already charred log I found lasted another hour. Made two cups of coffee, rolled four joints, smoked two of them. People passed me by, my hatch open, and some semblance of a life clearly packed into Aether, but no noticeable judgment. This coast is freedom. Though I can tell just from experiencing January to March, some of the freedom will greatly diminish with the warmer months. I'm sure cops become a little more active as well, keeping people from sleeping on the roadside. And I'd assume the areas to park and sleep become a bit more crowded. It's fine, I'll probably spend most of the warmer weather months in the mountains.

* * * * *

The Three Arch Rocks. I had a sketch of them, but I was unsure of where it was from. I'm at Netarts Bay. The view I sketched was from Oceanside. I think that's where the tunnel was. The Sun isn't fully out, but it's shining brightly on those seastacks. I had a thought to sketch them from this angle, so you can see the arch opening of the middle rock. But there is land much closer to them. The Netarts spit, a 5.5 mile peninsula that juts out from Cape Lookout, and separates the Pacific from Netarts Bay. 11 miles out and back, an expedition for another time. Camp for a night at Cape Lookout, make the hike in the morning, maybe hang out until sunset, get the golden hour light going both ways. And in-between, just get drunk, smoke spliffs, read, write, sketch, nap, pass out, get drunk again. All while playing fetch with Zura of course.

Just as we did this morning. Playing fetch with the epic background of Cape Kiwanda, and the Chief Rock. Zura finally broke the piece of driftwood we found along this coast back in October. It's her birthday today. She got to play on the beach all morning. Heading into the mountains now. Tillamook State Forest. She loves the forest trails too, especially the rivers. Not a fan of waterfalls though. I'm sure, as with everything, she just needs to get used to them. She used to be terrified of the ocean. Now she meets it without hesitation or fear. That driftwood fetch stick, I let it return to the earth with its kin this morning, in the form of ash. Dust to dust, it was a good stick.

* * * * *

Birds calling. Rushing water nearby. The soft snaps of the fire. Lyda camp. ATV trails, so not much for hiking. Found a small trail on the side of this dirt road out near nowhere. Slipped on my way down, crushed my flask a bit, tore a few holes in my back left pocket, where the flask was. And no, the flask had nothing to do with the slip. Same way I fell last time, at Whatcom Falls Park. Moved the flask to my right pocket. No real damage, except to my pride. Continued on exploring.

Found a neat little river bend. About a four-foot drop from the grass overhang to the river. A swimming pool that would be perfect on a hot Summer day. I wanted the best angle to capture the rushing water with the pool's stillness. The first two rocks along the edge were sturdy, the third, I tested it.

It too seemed sturdy, so I planted my left foot, took a peek through my viewfinder.

Next thing I knew, I'm horizontal. I released the camera from my right hand, more concerned with falling without harm over saving my camera. My left hand landing on the edge of the river. A wet glove, but it braced me well. My camera bounced off the second rock, and my right hand quickly regained control of it in mid-air before it fell into the river. A bruise on my right hip, and some scrapes near my left ankle. So close to remaining unscathed. The hip? My flask, now in my right back pocket. The ankle? That third rock that gave way, somehow it fell slower than I did.

The problem with wet wood. It just burns. It never really catches fire. The stack design I made did look beautiful though. It's cheating, I know, but on cold nights, a quick start log can be a lifesaver. Well, maybe it's not that cold. But still, it's not worth the fight to get a real fire started if it's under sixty degrees and you're exhausted from travel.

March Twenty-Eight

Quinault Rainforest, Merriman Falls. It's 1pm. Woke up in the Aberdeen Walmart parking lot at 7am. This was my destination, though that may change with the campgrounds all being closed still. There's some dispersed camping off the road passed the coastal beaches. There's that dirt road to nowhere where I watched the fog lift. It's dispersed camping. Rialto Beach in the morning. It's a plan I suppose. I'll see how sidetracked I get.

The sign this morning, "Ocean Shores". Had I been there? The road seemed unfamiliar. Ah yes, my excursion back in February. I was reminded I'd been there, once I arrived there, by the large archway sign for greeting visitors to Ocean Shores. It was a good detour anyway. Zura got to play on the beach. I discovered that the market in Seabrook, that town that seemed to spring up all at once, that market does not have fresh baguettes. So I don't know what I saw that man carrying out of the market last time I was there. And, indeed, that little bourgeois village, it was established only fifteen years ago.

Hi-Tide, it's not a town. It's a resort in Moclips, the furthest northern town on that stretch of the Washington Coast, other than the Quinault tribe village of Taholah. What a sad state colonialism has permanently created for the Native population in this country. There's a small campground just before the village, up on a bluff overlooking the crashing waves and coastline littered with seastacks. But being on tribal land, I'm not certain where, or if, I can register to camp.

Waterfalls though, they're the only natural water feature that can draw me in and hold me as the ocean can. Rivers and lakes are pleasing, sure, but they just don't have the same power over me. I was looking for shoreline along Quinault Lake to write. Ended up driving farther along the road, to the river that feeds the lake. This waterfall is better. The question though, do I continue around the loop on the unpaved road? Of course I will, the terrain can't be that bad…

* * * * *

90 miles, one hour and thirty minutes. Backtracking. I made it to Rialto Beach. I was correct the first time, the road was closed, and it's a decent hike from the Mora Campground, so driving in is certainly preferred. Parked at the day use area, made a sandwich; heirloom tomato, avocado, and mustard on French bread. Fed Zura. 40 minutes to sunset. Perfect timing. "It's a bit chilly," I thought, "better grab my jacket. Where is my jacket?" The memory of me laying it down on smoothed rocks along a shoreline came flooding back. My first thought was Ruby Beach, surely my jacket would be gone with the tide. But no, it was before that. Ah, right, the Quinault River, just after the second waterfall. I took it off to skim rocks, wandered a bit upstream with Zura. The day had already warmed.

The good news, it was still there. Being a river, I knew I'd have no tidal issues. And with how remote that spot was, I gathered it would have been unlikely anyone else even stopped to wander there today. The bad news, Aether has a new sound. But it didn't seem to get any worse as I sped along my route from earlier, in reverse, at 70 MPH. It's only 9pm, I could easily drive back towards where I intended to be for the night, but with that noise, I think it's best I stay put until the world once again awakens.

Parked alongside the South Shore road at Bunch Falls, the cascading water will be pleasant to sleep to. With the morning detour, and backtracking for my jacket, I'm only an hour or so from that Walmart parking lot I woke up in fourteen hours ago. Still, it was an enjoyable day. Far better than being stuck working in an office, or laying around an apartment watching the fake lives of other people.

And regardless, the initial plan was to camp around here for the night anyway. I'm tempted to head back along the coast, the setting crescent Moon paired with Saturn should be visible on the horizon just before sunrise. But the forecast calls for clouds, and a photograph isn't worth getting stranded on one of the farthest areas on this peninsula to reach from Seattle. At least it's peaceful here. And I did have the thought to get breakfast at the Quinault Lodge this morning before the ocean called me.

March Twenty-Nine

Beach Four. Making coffee. After a bit of research, coupled with knowing my tires needed to be rotated and balanced, knowing the state of my suspension, knowing I need new tires in general, I'm assuming the noise is related to all that. So I decided to come back this way. It'll be fine, it always is for me. My timing should match up pretty well for low tide at Rialto Beach too. And the Sun is out, hardly a cloud. Hopefully it stays that way.

Yesterday though, as much as the day seemed to be uneventful, until having to backtrack for my jacket, there were two events that certainly made the day worth all the lost miles. Heading back toward the 101 from Taholah, a bald eagle perched just off the road on a large piece of driftwood. There were a few actually, but only one adult, with the well-known appearance of a white head and brown body. And upon further inspection of a photograph I captured, I realized the eagle, when I caught it in flight, was soaring toward several eagles all bunched together at the river inlet about two hundred yards north of where I stopped.

The other instance, driving along between Ruby Beach and Forks. Sun showers. I was thinking how wonderful it would be to see a rainbow arching over the seastacks once I arrived at Rialto Beach. I came around a curve, and though it was only partial, the color was deep. A rainbow coming up from the Bogachel River, and disappearing into the blue sky.

* * * * *

At the Bear Creek Campground for the night. Beach 4, Rialto Beach, First Beach in La Push, they all made leaving my jacket behind worth the backtrack. It's like I was meant to stay in Quinault last night. My only regret from this two-day excursion, not staying for sunset last night at Rialto. Granted, I likely wouldn't have returned there today if I had. So maybe it shouldn't be a regret.

Beach Four. I only observed it from the overlook last time, well, two times ago. In January, when this all started. (I didn't stop at Beach Four last time I passed through here.) The tide was very high then, so no wonder I had no clue what I truly missed. Beaches One, Two, and Three, along with Kalaloch Campground Beach, there are no seastacks. Beach Four, there are plenty. With tide pools and Pacific waves crashing below as you stand peering over the edge of the earth. Scientifically speaking of course…

Zura kept herself entertained on the beach chewing sticks, soaking up the early Sun. I hopped around and climbed on those last portions of earth before the vast Pacific takes full hold of the crust. I've stopped using a camera strap. I trust my two legs and one arm, with the other firmly holding my camera, far more than the pendulum created by my camera strap that throws off my balance.

Out of nowhere I noticed a woman in black, bounding about, snapping photos of the tide pools and waves, just as I was. We glanced at each other and smiled. I returned down to the beach to play with Zura a bit, and then to leave everything I was carrying behind, except my camera. Pants cuffed, boots off, I waited for the perfect moment to cross the thigh-deep water, where the waves swirled around the largest seastack there, to then rejoin as one. After the swells died down, with the water retreating west, I made my move. One rock, then the next, the third, and a jump to a slightly submerged plot of sand. The water started rushing back in from both directions. I splashed through the shallow pools, just below the knees. Deep enough for the cuffed-up portion of my pants to get wet, but far better than the waist high soaking I would have received had I not noticed the split wave about the clash back into itself right where I stood. I climbed about a bit, exploring that not-always-accessible piece of land. Then I found the path to the top.

The morning had been chilly, but with the expedition, my black jacket and boots were removed; still, I was wearing a dark gray sweater. I get why Johnny Cash wore black. Sure there's the theatrics of it, being *The Man in Black*, but also, black looks clean, even when dirty. I looked down from my tower. And there was Zura. Running to greet the woman in black as she descended from the seastack where we had exchanged glances earlier. She threw a stick for Zura a few times, then returned to her camera, now removing her black shoes as well. I once again climbed down, wandering back toward my belongings. I had words in my head for a new poem. Then, like that, the woman in black wandered off. Zura ran after her. I called out that she wants to say goodbye. She murmured something, petted Zura, then started down the beach again. I figured she probably wasn't in the mood for conversing. The black angels that seemed to be flocking around us that hour though, they make me wonder if I should have tried to converse, regardless of her seeming disinterest. Perhaps she's just shy… What a grand projectionist I am. No matter. My interest lies elsewhere anyway, it just would've been nice to talk to someone.

Instead of settling with the denial of the road being closed on my first two excursions, and the glimpse I allowed myself last night while eating my sandwich, I decided on a fourth attempt to visit Rialto Beach, and was rewarded with the full glory that coastal wilderness offers. A three-mile out-and-back hike to *Hole-in-the-Wall*. Zura had a good morning at Beach 4, and she needed to rest before we headed over to First Beach down in La Push. Dogs aren't allowed past a certain point on Rialto Beach, and there were too many people for her to be off leash. Beach 4 was different, there was hardly a soul there. She bothered no one, regardless of the guy with the blue jeans and a cowboy hat yelling toward me from 100 yards away that dogs are supposed to be on a leash. Fuck laws, all I care about is civility. I also cared about me being able to wander that area I had so longed to see, without the worry of looking after Zura. Or the restriction, for both of us, of her being leashed. The best spots are where we can both wander wild, alone, but together.

It's getting late though, and the stars are asking for my attention. Thinking just now, had I seen that sunset yesterday, I'd likely be where I am right now anyway. I probably would have had a fire, and I'd likely be sleeping in my tent tonight, but at this moment, regardless of the events that delayed my arrival, right now, at 10:45pm, I would have been right here, 40 miles west of Port Angeles.

<u>March Thirty</u>

Sitting in the ferry line at Kingston. I could have crossed two hours earlier, it'll be another two by the time I reach Edmonds. Maybe three. It's a cool little village, I doubt I'd need more than a few days here though. A week at most. Too much of society passing through here. Not like Port Townsend. There, those passing through, they never see the main street area. Here, the ferry line goes straight through the heart.

I decided to park and relax for a bit before getting on the ferry. Let Zura stretch her legs, get a coffee, finish some inking on my unfinished sketches. Break into that John Muir book I bought earlier this month. But getting coffee, man, some people… It's a Saturday, late morning; there's a kite festival today.

There was a long line for coffee. An 'in' door, an 'out' door at the small cafe near the ferry terminal. I guess someone started the line going inside through the 'out' door before the line grew larger. There are no signs specifying which direction to enter though. The locals, or the regulars, whichever they are, they kept entering through the 'in' door, as they were used to. But they all seemed to graciously understand that the flow was different today, or at least at that moment, and they proceeded to the back of the line. One woman though, you'd think we all cursed her out. The lady behind me kindly pointed out that the line was going the other way. "Yea, well this way is shorter," the woman said with contempt. The lady, she retorted that we had all been waiting. The woman then responded by telling us that the line always goes the other way. So I peeked my head out of the door, asking her if there was a sign pointing this out to those of us unfamiliar with the usual way. She screamed "fuck it" and stormed off. I guess some people really do need their morning coffee. Of course, I also know there was no sign, so I guess I'm guilty too.

* * * * *

Crossing the Sound, leaving the Olympic Range behind. That's the view I was hoping for when I crossed here last time, on my first excursion, in much more of a hurry than I am today. Sitting out on the back deck. Not as comfortable as it sounds, at least not to the average person. Sitting on the ground is comfortable to me. So long as I have something to lean back against. The front may be a smoother ride. But the back has the view, and the Sun. And it's blocked from the headwinds. I'm tired, I don't feel much like working today. But it is what it is I suppose. Adventure doesn't pay for itself, at least not yet. I need a sailboat. Ground transportation is easy enough to come by.

To yesterday though, I began my trek along Rialto Beach…

<u>March Thirty-One</u>

I thought I would have had time to finish that thought yesterday. Such as it is when you don't pay attention to the time, when you have somewhere to be. I pulled into work two hours before my shift. I still clocked in late. Same as this morning. I slept in the parking lot. I took a five minute walk. Late again. Mind you, no more than three minutes late each time.

Rialto Beach. I was determined to see *Hole-in-the-Wall*. But I was determined to enjoy the hike to it. I began by playing 'don't touch the lava' while crossing along the driftwood. Slipped once. Had a piece break on me once. Straight lost my balance and fell off once. Not down, just off. The only time I actually touched sand, until sand was the only option. What interesting geology though. The rocks, pebbles, and pellets nearer to the shore, all still grinding against each other to become rough grains of sand. And the waves there, along the whole coast (but Rialto especially), they seem to be coming from all directions. Like multiple swells rolling in at different intervals, with different paths.

I almost captured what would have been the best in my crow side series. The Sun crowning the first tall seastack I passed, a crow swooping down from that spot. Unfortunately, I only caught half the crow. Fitting I suppose, with the events of this month. And the photograph I did capture with the crow perched, it's hard to discern it's a crow. The next large seastacks, walking toward them, they appear as one. So I resumed my driftwood bounding, but for a better angle to photograph the optical illusion; the fun was secondary.

Next, I found myself staring through a gigantic hole in a fairly large mass of land, jutting out in a crescent shape. I passed through, something only to be done at low tide. A pool of water, reflecting the hole, and the Pacific beyond it. Perfect timing. It would have been high tide at sunset the day before. I then wandered to the exposed seastack with a mass of some of the best tide pools I'd ever seen. Three starfish. And a green, heart-shaped anemone. Not to mention the flows of the tidal water.

As always, unaware of the time that had passed, I began to feel a need to get back. I checked the time later on, based on a photo I took around when I first arrived. I was only fifteen minutes longer than I had planned. Time eventually becomes instinctual. I stopped to snap a shot of the water flow cascading down the rocks and pebbles from a large receding wave. My boots got a little wet when the next wave quickly came in. It was weird though, I consciously chose to stay in for the shot, and get wet, knowing the parking lot was close. Yet I still jumped back even after the water infiltrated my boots. Silly human instincts.

Back at Aether, we headed out, but I promised Zura more beach time at La Push, First Beach, where I knew she could run free. And the beach is sand there, instead of rocks and pebbles. I decided to rest for a bit after she had played enough. I captured a few photographs that struck me, rather amateurishly, while waiting for that first moment when the colors in the sky start to show something other than hues of blue.

I eventually pulled myself out of my cozy state to set up my camera on the tripod, with the 10x Neutral Density filter attached. Silk water. The Sun eventually dropping behind the clouds far off on the horizon. The clouds that far off usually block the show of color once the Sun is gone. Usually… I disassembled my camera setup. My back to the scenery. I looked over my shoulder, sensing no one else returning to their cars. The Sun had reemerged. That horizon shroud, not as dense as I thought it to be, as I had seen it those earlier months.

I only took snapshots, as my equipment was already put away, and the regular lens set back up. But still, I witnessed that last sliver of light being consumed by the ocean. Then, looking again, over my shoulder, eastward this time. That pink color in the clouds starting to show. And suddenly, all the colors and hues I had hoped to see. We drove on from there to the Bear Creek Campground, where we waited for the light to return. The Sun-kissed trees again being my cue to get going once morning came. Driving through Lake Crescent was a blast. 55-60 MPH on a marked 35 MPH winding road. That road, all these roads, they'll be even more fun once Aether is fully dependable again.

Scene Three: Passion

*From the moment absurdity is recognized, it becomes a
passion, the most harrowing of all. But whether or not
one can live with one's passions, whether or not one
can accept their law, which is to burn the heart they
simultaneously exalt – that is the whole question...*

-Albert Camus-

<u>April Third</u>

It's 8:30pm, been here since just after 3. I was lying in my tent by 4, the Sun pouring through a gap in the trees. I woke up at 6:30 this morning, far less disoriented than one would assume, waking up along an interstate. I've been traveling around for three months now. This is my first night in the tent. And only the fourth overall since I bought it, late Spring or early Summer of last year. Lake Annette, where I met the *Lady of the Lake*. Humboldt Redwoods, where the Sun was hidden. Mount Baker National Forest, along that lonesome river. And now here, Dugan Creek Campground, just a place I'd never been to, near to where I'm going.

Up until about 6:30, maybe 7, I heard nothing but the rush of water, and the crows. The crows are gone. The water still flows. I'm sure the crows will wake me, as they so often do, calling in the early hours. My rooster call, wild instead of domestic. Regardless of how little I've used this tent, considering how I am currently living, this will be the first time of consecutive nights sleeping in the same spot while on the road since the start of the year. Honestly, I can't remember the last time I spent consecutive nights in a single location while on a trip, since I decided to abandon the life I had in San Diego. Well, that's not true, there were those two times in Yosemite. I've likely covered over 20,000 miles since then. Including these past few months; obviously adding considerably more to the days than the miles. I've certainly eclipsed one hundred nights where I would claim myself as being 'on the road'.

The stars are starting to show their force. The pale blue, then the brightest, dimly glowing. Now they shine. I didn't feel much up for exploring the area once we got here. Something I may regret tomorrow, if the Sun doesn't repeat its showing. In the mountains though, even the most powerful Sun fades away early, and rises late. The Appalachian 'mountains' of my youth, mainly the Catskills of New York and the Poconos of Pennsylvania, they hardly knew a cold mountain morning in the Summer. I'm assuming it'll be around 10am by the time the earth warms enough, to think about getting up, should the Sun even be present. In Appalachia, the mosquitoes are your rooster.

Urban Family, in the Magnolia neighborhood of Seattle, they do a great job on sour beers. Had the Oracle tonight, instead of wine. Something I may regret tomorrow if the weather is warm. That creek looks inviting, even if to just let the snow melt pass over my legs as the Sun cascades down through the river's cut in the canopy. Ah, dreams. The wine would do just fine if I could get even a moment of warmth tomorrow. Just to sit in the Sun, on a rock, or log, reading John Muir, as the water flows around me. Composing poems, and sketching, as the rocks and water combine to sing.

April Four

The crows started at 6:50 today. I was partially awake for twenty minutes or so before that. 8:10 now, a light drizzle just started before I pulled myself from the tent about ten minutes ago. Certainly not enough to deter me from exploring, but this morning has a 'rainy day at home' feel to it. I grabbed our breakfast from Aether. Zura's dried compact crunchy stuff; bread, peanut butter, and honey for me, and we returned to the tent.

I closed my eyes last night after reading the first few pages of *Discovery of Glacier Bay*. I could have continued on reading, but I wanted to include a quote in here, and I was too comfortable and warm, to sit up and write. But at 41 years old, in the mid-Autumn weather of Alaska, weather that would make almost everything I've encountered look like a day on a sunny tropical beach, Muir had this to say. "After crouching cramped and benumbed in the canoe, poulticed in wet clothes and blankets night and day, my limbs had been long asleep. This day they were awake, and in the hour of trial proved that they had not lost the cunning learned on many a mountain peak of the high Sierra."

I did wake up at some point in the middle of the night. I don't know what time it was, but I know I couldn't see. When I awoke again, just before 7, my tent seemed full of light, yet the Sun was still an hour from rising, two here in the forested mountains. That constantly amazes me, how light it can be on the fringe shadows of this world. The morning mountain skies are a mystery to me, I can never tell if I'm seeing an early pale blue sky, or just a faint shroud in the atmosphere. The light drizzle and the echo of the planes answer that for me though. As remote feeling as this area is, it's still fairly close in vicinity to the Portland airport.

. . .

Almost noon now. Thankfully the morning spatters never turned to full rain. The pale, blue-gray sky is starting to shimmer white in some of the gaps in the canopy. Usually a sign that the Sun will make an appearance. Still, the weather is fine enough, the day so still and quiet. I think sixteen hours of rest is sufficient, ten of them sleeping. Yet, my pillow still calls for my head.

* * * * *

The pillow won out, for another hour or so. But with coffee made, we headed for Dugan Falls. The gray blanket above doesn't seem like it's going to even partially disperse. But I did have the same thought yesterday. This place is far from true wilderness, with the graffiti covered rocks, the litter, the unsightly slab bridge and its logging trucks that cross the falls, the two homes thirty feet above the riverside cliff. Still, the water rushes all the same as it would in an area more remote, more untouched and unspoiled. The large jagged rock I'm sitting on leaves something to be desired for comfort. But the blue of the water cascading down, Zura learning to wander, building confidence with the deafening noise of water crashing on rocks, this place is wild enough. And if the Sun were out, I would even contemplate going for a swim in the various pools protected from the rush downstream. As it is though, my feet can hardly stand more than five seconds submerged in the icy flow.

Two dogs led us here, not that we couldn't have found our way. I'm assuming they came from the camp host, who, by the look of their site, permanently call this place home. An enticing thought initially, but far too stationary for me. I'd guess, with its vicinity to society, Summers likely bring more disturbance than peace. Though being a 'working forest', I doubt the logging trucks ever allow for peace during the day. The same for the aforementioned airplanes. Sitting this close to the falls though, the trucks and planes seem to combine with the sounds of nature. If only the Sun would show itself…

* * * * *

The forest had quieted about a half hour ago from the call of the crows, and the infrequent songs of another bird. Then just before I began to write, the crows began their calls again, but almost in unison. I thought it a communal goodnight, until I heard the shriek of a hawk, and the chirps of forest rodents all sounding off in alarm, as the crows had continued with theirs'. It appears the threat is gone now, with only the sound of the water flowing over wood and stone left.

With the weather never turning pleasant, I decided on burning a longer fire, starting it in the early gloaming, rather than spending the waning hours of light by the creek. Still, I needed to wash my face. Leaving Zura behind, as I didn't want her getting wet before climbing into the tent, I headed down the short path that leads to the creek's edge alone. We explored it last night, but tonight I was able to take in its full beauty. Just before I began the descent, while remarking to myself about the dog hut someone recently fashioned out of pine fronds for a second time, I caught sight of a bird entering my periphery from the left, gliding through the ravine of trees above the creek. I noticed the white tail first, then a flash of the white head, finally through a gap in the trees, its brown body in-between. I'd curse myself for not having my camera, but it likely would have been comparable to a photo of Bigfoot. I never truly understood the majesty of the bald eagle, as it has been over-romanticized through programming. But I see it now, experiencing it, rather than merely being told about it in brief from the words of a textbook. We were all doomed from the moment education became about book sales.

Textbooks have their place as introductory information for early ages, but by ages 10-13, study should be direct. Textbooks, beyond the elementary age, they should only serve as detailed encyclopedias. Reading through Muir's *Discovery of Glacier Bay* I was unfamiliar with far too many words. In high school, we should be reading Muir, and Camus, and Dante, and only using our textbooks to enhance our understanding of what it was Muir was describing, or Camus was expressing, or what Dante's true meaning was, behind his cryptic alliteration.

<u>April Five</u>

Multnomah Falls. Sitting in the massive parking lot that they squeezed between the eastbound and westbound lanes of this interstate roadway. It's been raining fairly hard since 10pm last night. It's almost 1pm now. The people here, watching them park, put on their jackets, take out their umbrellas, and they're back at their cars in fifteen minutes, more or less. I doubt it would be much different if the Sun were out. Likely just more people, snapping their photos, and then moving on to wherever their travel guidebooks tell them to go next.

* * * * *

Horsetail Falls now. I had meant to stop momentarily at the Multnomah freeway island, and to just head on down to Troutdale, to start trimming; but my body, my mind, my spirit, they just aren't up for it today. Same thing here though, as it was at Multnomah; park, snapshot, leave. Some people are at least hiking the trail. I decided on making coffee here, the wall in the parking lot is situated perfectly with a view of the falls, my tailgate to sit on. The Sun is even peaking through, as it did for a few minutes as I climbed the pedestrian pathway to the famous bridge that overlooks Multnomah. There are supposedly 77 waterfalls along the Columbia Gorge; I should like to see them all. I'd even consider lying in Aether with the hatch open, gazing at this torrent, were it not for the mess I created in the back from fleeing the torrents that hindered my camping experience.

I'm uncertain what to do from here, with life. A quarter of a year, spent bounding around. I don't think the mountains are quite ready to receive me, and the coast, I know not where to roam without spending money that should be used to fix Aether. Perhaps I'll just stay in Seattle, though I need to avoid overspending if I do. I'll certainly spend less on fuel, and Aether will be saved from a potential breakdown in the middle of nowhere. If Aether were not a concern, everyone I'm in contact with in this region might not ever see me again. I had a thought to just keep driving until the engine gives out, and live in whatever town is nearest, until the wind carries me away again. My soul is too old for this modern world.

* * * * *

I'm parked back in front of Multnomah Falls. Off the scenic highway though, not the interstate. I thought I'd just check if there was a spot. Maybe sketch. The first spot was open. I could sit here for hours and watch all these people pass. Most people, I think they go places now just to say they were there. Most of the places I've seen these past three months, I sought out with purpose for me alone; well, and for the future adventures I hope occur The Sun is pouring through nicely right now, slightly blotted, but welcomed nonetheless.

People don't read John Muir because they want to know about
his personal life, they read because they want to experience
his adventures, and be inspired to find adventures of their
own. Muir exists as a legend because civilization decided, and
continues to decide, that his words are worthy of legendary
status. Muir didn't constantly try to convince the populace of
how great he was, or how wonderful nature is. No, instead he
did what all great artists do, he inspired. He may have been
modest, but he was confident in himself, and what he knew and
didn't.

The Sun is fully out now, its light creeping along the eastern
cliff of the Falls. Certainly makes for a reason to stay. And
like that, a cloud blocks my rays. Intermittent though, I just
hope it's back before the first strike of the Falls would occur.
It was supposed to rain all day today. The rain stopped right
about when I made my coffee. The Sun appearing with force with
my first smoke of the day. These clouds though, they linger
now. Any glimpse of hope seems to send me whirling. It's fine
though, I learned long ago that hope is just that.

Expectations are what matter, they're tangible. And to this
point in my life, I've learned to expect nothing from anything I
don't have direct control over. Whether it's people, the tides,
or if the clouds will cover the Sun. If I expected the Sun to
show itself, I might be disappointed. But I've learned to expect
no such things from the Sun, especially with an atmosphere like
the one that surrounds this Pacific Northwest. The clouds have
won out this hour. It's supposed to rain all week. Until then,
I'll just keep hoping that my vision and the Sun will align for
that one perfect chance to preserve light.

* * * * *

A downpour now, I pulled over at Shepperd's Dell. I saw
something magical looking about a quarter mile back. I'm hoping
the rain subsides, if only for safety reasons, walking along
this winding narrow road. And hello Sun, even with the rain
still pelting down. Maybe I should have been more patient at
the Falls, but I only have this one life, as far as I know… As
hail starts berating Aether's exterior.

.   .   .

They'll be plenty of time to get Multnomah lit by the late day's Sun. That experience was far better. The hail, the Sun, the water flows, the light striking through on the freshly wet earth and flora. The wildflowers clinging to the cliffs of the Dell. The thought that picking wildflowers from a cliff would be a grand way to die.

Then I headed down the road, probably closer to a tenth of a mile back; I'm no good with distances though. The scene I thought I saw, it was far more magical than the single glance could have ever led me to believe. A small cascading fall, dropping some hundred feet into a chute made by humans when craftsmanship mattered, with the moss clinging to the stone, and a beautiful plant, with stems of the purest green, and tiny pink flowers blooming from a bell into a star. Then the Sun struck the scene, and I was hit with the confidence of my balance to capture my photographs of the ravine, ignoring the thirty-foot fall into the abyss below jammed with logs. That confidence stayed on the walk back to Aether, as I balanced across the stone railing that separates the road from the cliff, rather than trusting other drivers speeding along the narrow twisting asphalt to see me. I *expect* I won't lose my balance. I can only *hope* that others will see me.

April Sixteen

There's a man vacuuming the sidewalk. I was going to start this entry with, "It's interesting how people choose to spend their time," but that had to be noted. The man vacuuming the sidewalk. I did at least just overhear him remark to a lady, "I know it's weird, but…"

But to the point. A man carrying a homemade sign, "Jesus Saves". He didn't have the appearance of a beggar, he seemed more on a mission. Assumably going to stand at a crowded intersection to hold his sign, in hope. Surely he can't expect his message to actually influence someone's thoughts toward *finding* Jesus, or god, or whatever his intent is in holding a sign, for likely hours. Maybe he's a preacher, and this is what he does on Tuesdays. No matter what though, if he was truly interested in sharing his passion for Jesus with others, he should be doing such through action. Jesus didn't preach to convince others to preach, he did it as a call to action. To live by his word. If the man with the sign truly cared, he should be helping those less fortunate; volunteer this free time to others. Blessings are universal, they don't solely belong to Christianity. Too many religious people do 'good' for their religion, rather than for the message of it. I'm a humanist, I don't tell people about how great humanism is every time I do something *good*. I don't tell the beggar that humanism 'saves' when I hand him a loaf of bread.

* * * * *

Anacortes now. Pelican Bay Books. I was thinking of taking the Guemes Island ferry, but their web page says the reason to go there is because most people haven't. Hardly convincing reasoning. The bookstore has a good little cafe in it, comfortable chairs, and a great selection of used books. Zura is curled up on the floor next to me.

There hasn't been much to write of up until yesterday, except for the glorious views that greeted me at the Vista House moments after the last words I wrote eleven days ago. My drive, well, general return back to Seattle was notable, wandering the arboretum and Green Lake, then Gas Works Park before work. *The city misses your light.* But the days are growing longer, the Sun, returning to these Northwest skies.

I finally purchased a rooftop box yesterday, to free up room in Aether. Saving money up to fix the engine. Decided on maybe getting a gym membership. Showers almost anywhere. Life is better on the road. Might try to find a good dog daycare for Zura for when I work. It'll all be cheaper than rent.

There's a mom and her son sitting at a table behind me. He's about four, and as with any child around that age, his enunciation isn't quite developed yet. Then his mom said something about nucleic acid. He then repeated it with such clarity it surpassed the pronunciation voiced by the mother. I thought of not writing about this, it seeming quite trivial, but then I listened to her speak to him as any adult would speak to another adult. Earlier today, I remarked to myself about just that, passing a mother talking to her toddler as if she were speaking to a puppy. It's important for the development of a child to speak to the child as a developing person, not an animal that forever remains in the cognitive state of responding best to tonal approval.

Aether's engine wasn't doing so well. I noticed the change in its sound immediately. My nomadic plan had to be abandoned. And so I spent two months stationed in the parking lot of work. I was no longer living as a traveler. I was by all accounts, a bum. But I love this Emerald Realm, especially in the late Spring. Still, after two months, I nearly went insane. Likely the same nihilism from my room in the Underground. I made one last adventure of my time in the Emerald Realm, before my final drive down to the City that Imprisoned Me.

April Twenty-Four

Honestly, why are there so many people living on the streets? Why is Amazon, and Google, and Microsoft not doing more to help this struggling city? And it's not just the homeless, there are plenty of destitute people grimly walking these streets, taking hour-long bus rides to work minimum wage jobs. I know people will say Bezos earned his money, but he would be nothing without his underpaid distribution staff. A staff that collectively feel they have no other choice for employment. A staff that likely consists of a majority that are working at least one other job. And if they're not, and they have children, they are likely being provided some sort of much needed assistance from government programs or elsewhere.

Then there's the food. The cheap processed poisonous food. It's not bad in small quantities, eaten infrequently. But as a consistent diet…

Diabetes, heart disease, sleep apnea, muscle and joint problems, liver disease. They all mostly stem from obesity. I saw how my grandparents ate, my grandfather may have had a 'pasta gut', but he was nowhere near obese. It's a drastic pendulum swing from Orwell's time, but his words ring true all the same. "The evil of poverty is not so much that it makes a man suffer as it rots him physically and spiritually." Is atrophy from malnutrition really any different than from overeating? The only difference is the malnourished of Orwell's time, they weren't actively choosing degeneration.

I realize that processed foods don't always cause obesity; genes, and the amount you consume obviously play a part. But the correlation between poverty and obesity is undeniable. And it's not just obesity from these processed foods that cause such higher healthcare costs. There's also the issue of allergies, food allergies to be exact.

I'll get back to all that later, maybe, probably not. I'm too drunk, and a bit too high for statistics. At Buckley's. High West Campfire rye for $10. I thought I'd be okay with just the ketchup. But then it sat on my tongue, sugary shit. I found the Dijon. I asked for a second Campfire with my tab. Bartender basically gave me a third along with it. Good pour. But to my adventures.

Last Tuesday. Not this past Tuesday, last Tuesday. Two Tuesdays ago. Skagit Valley. I was sitting at the rest area that morning, uncertain of what to do. Mount Vernon always looked so enticing. A small downtown pressed right up against the interstate. Looking at the map. (Yes, Google Maps. A good product is no reason to not contribute to the welfare of the city that your company is headquartered in.) The Tulip Festival Foundation building showed up on the map. Useful algorithms. (As opposed to the ones that try to sell us the product we just purchased.)

I wandered about town for a bit. The mural on the side of the coffee shop was far more impressive than the coffee shop itself. They didn't even serve drip coffee, so no Cafe au Lait. How does a coffee shop not have drip coffee? But the cappuccino I had was delicious. Provisions after all that, at the co-op grocery store. Some cheese, a baguette of course, pepperoni, and some dried tortellini. I had already decided, with the tulips leading me west, I'd venture through Fidalgo Island to Deception Pass. I figured the wildflowers would be quite choice at this time of year as well. My instinct for the Natural World, at least regionally, it's coming along quite well.

May Twelve

I wrote nearly every day in March. April started with a strong five days, yet I only wrote eight days in total. This is my first entry for May… It's interesting how stagnation in life leads to stagnation in creation. I went to the Tulip Festival. It was quite interesting, the theme park style entrance, and crowd. Entire families wandering like lost puppies, or sheep. I, alone, flowing through them, waiting patiently for them to move so I could photograph the scene. The Sun was out though, the weather warming; patience comes much easier on days when you can think past the cold. I just drove some country roads from there, only pulling off to the roadside for a few photos, once sliding out the of window for a shot over Aether's roof. I made my way toward Fidalgo Island. With nothing to do, I went to Anacortes first. Provisions of course. Then I remembered about Pelican Bay Books. That, I wrote of.

But after that. I went toward the San Juan ferry terminal, just to walk around. But there was nowhere to park without paying. So I turned back, found a spot to ponder what to do next. Washington Park. There was a campground. So I stayed. Deception Pass could wait another day. It was quiet there, wandered about with Zura until it was dark. I had a thought to take the ferry to Friday Harbor early in the day. The downtown is easily accessible to the ferry landing, and I could return on the same day. It was also much cheaper on foot than by taking Aether. I planned to leave around noon.

Noon came the next day, after a slow morning, reorganizing Aether, moving things into the rooftop box. The ferry runs fairly often, but I found out the departures I was looking at weren't all to Friday Harbor. 2:30 was the next departure, and I'd have to leave to return from the island by 9:30. Six hours didn't seem worth it, so I decided it was an adventure for another time. We explored Washington Park a bit more in-depth, with a lot more light. West Beach and the view of Burrows Channel, where I buried some treasure, being the main highlights.

I was looking for campsites at Deception Pass by the late afternoon. Zura and I then made our way down to the beach by the bridge, it being too late for a hike. I read some of Muir's Alaskan expeditions while listening to the lapping shore speak to me of closeness. Zura was busy chasing ghosts of her own, the shadows and sounds of the small Puget Sound waves.

May Thirteen

We woke up the next day, just taking the morning slow. Just before 11am I moved Aether to the day-use parking area nearest to the bridge. I hadn't explored around the north side of the pass since my first time to the park 4 or 5 years ago. I was more than ready for the hike, with a solid night of rest, and the first true meal I'd cooked on the road (I'd made only soup and oatmeal up until that point). Dried tortellini. Not ideal. But a fresh heirloom tomato, diced, and simmered in wine and garlic, adding pepperoni and grated Parmigiana I bought at the co-op in Mount Vernon.

Zura wasn't fond of the bridge crossing. It wasn't the height, it was the passing cars. I know it wasn't the height, she was peering over every cliff along the Lighthouse Point Trail. Aside from the view that always amazes, and the constant noise of the military jets disturbing the solitude of an otherwise tranquil place, it was the wildflowers that enthralled me the most. The yellow buttercups were plentiful. But it was Venus's slipper I found most fascinating. The Calypso Orchid or the Calypso Bulbosa if you wanna be scientific about it. It looked like a dragon head to me.

We returned to Aether around 6pm, leaving for the Mukilteo ferry, only stopping for a beer momentarily at Penn Cove Brewing Company in Coupeville. I was surprised to not see any beers of their own. But I sat there drinking a beer I don't recall, while reading Camus and listening to the mundane chatter of the four locals seated at the bar.

June Sixteen

Two weeks of freedom; I quit my job, oddly on the night of one of the most enjoyable shifts I've had there since they fired all the cool people. My two-week notice had already been placed anyway, and I was able to get my shifts covered…

I kinda get bird watching. Interesting creatures. Though I'm far more interested in their flight games and social interactions than watching, or rather looking for solitary birds out on nature trails. I guess what I mean is I don't aim to seek out birds to watch, but tend to become mesmerized by them. I'm starting full-time work in Oregon in July. Might as well actually take a vacation.

An earlier thought in these pages, this project. It is not comfort that should be avoided, it's conformity. Why bring it up again? A thought I had the other day. Can conformity be individualized? Sure, people can conform to social norms, or the norms of a group. More simply said though, it's 'fitting in'. Fitting in with others by adhering to what a certain society or group expects of their citizens. As opposed to finding a society or group in which you feel you truly belong. But can we conform to our own individual expectations? I don't mean what we expect of others, I mean what we expect of ourselves… I'm rambling. The point. We should all strive to conform to our own self-beliefs. What we as individuals believe is right. This is why morals, they are subjective to the individual, but they're objective in the society or group setting. This is what I believe it means, "To thine own self be true." Most see it with the selfish eyes of individualism.

June Twenty-Three

Been in Queen Anne, since Tuesday night I think. Yea, that's right. Left for a few hours on Friday, something I would normally avoid doing, not wanting to lose my spot along the park wall. But the Solstice sunset, I wanted to see it, and it did not disappoint. I left again yesterday, but by bus. Went to the Fremont Solstice Parade. Then a friend invited me over to her boss's house. She was house-sitting. It was fun playing rich person for a few hours. A wonderful reminder of what I don't need, and why I'm doing what I've been doing since January.

I was passing the time cracking peanut shells and eating their insides, unsure what to do with the relatively young night. Fifty pages into the novel I'm writing, *Prometheus's Flame*, a solid concept laid out in my memory for the rest of it. It's a concise rebuttal to Ayn Rand's *Atlas Shrugged*. Tonight was a good night for a break from writing. But I decided to write about cracking peanut shells to pass the time. No need to look so insane at the bar. Mindlessly eating peanuts and staring at nothing, it's nice for a few minutes, but my brain gets easily restless. It's almost 11 now. I'll get going soon. Another Olympia, another spliff.

I went camping at one point, I don't remember exactly when. Late April, early May. Not important really. I found a great empty spot along the river. Two nights. Cooked some food. A good change from the usual staple of bread, cheese, salami, tomatoes, and granola bars. We camped right near where the road was still closed from the lasting Winter conditions of the mountains in mid-Spring. Found an amazing spot just passed there for Zura and me to chase each other through the lush verdant forest. The best part of the trip though, the Lake 22 hike, on our way back. I only intended to climb up to a waterfall I knew of, to enjoy my breakfast and coffee. But it was a longer hike to that point than I remembered, I figured we might as well hike to the top. Glad we did, most of the alpine lake was still covered in ice, the mountain peak walls surrounding the lake, still blanketed in snow. Other than that, life has been stagnant until recent events. I'm moving to Oregon next Sunday, I'll need to find a place. I wish I didn't have to. I won't sign a lease though.

September Nineteen

It's ridiculous that I filled one of these composition books in just two and a half months, and six months later, in mid-September, I still have roughly a third of the pages left in this second one. Of course, that's what happens without adventure. Routine. And routine is fucking boring. I mean, I drove to San Diego and back, and I feel like I have nothing to write about from all those miles. Including the Oregon Coast detour. I need to go on a trip. I was initially thinking of something for two. But something for two takes two to plan. So I'll be going somewhere new. I thought of Kyoto for a week, but it would be too expensive. Iceland, too expensive. I'd love to go to Alaska, but I think I'd need two weeks at least.

One thing I've always wanted to do. Dia de los Muertos in Mexico. Oaxaca was too expensive. GDL. I saw it on a license plate. Guadalajara. The home of tequila. What better place could there be to raise a toast to the dead?

DREAMS: JUNG AND FREUD

September Twenty- Four

Perhaps this seems an abrupt change of subject, but I've spent enough time on nature. Dreams. Daydreams, sleeping dreams, and dreams of aspiration. But what of my aspirations? I wanted to play hockey as a kid. Then, with nothing of interest, I thought to become a psychologist. That quickly passed, and I was left with only the idea of art. That's why I went to design school. I thought to commodify my love for art. The true way for an artist to make money is to let the art become a commodity on its own.

The daydreams. A mixture of hope and wandering aspiration, moments of want or desire, moments of fear or anxiety. The things we think about when our minds can't focus, or when we don't want to concentrate.

Then there are the dreams. I'll be trying the psychological approach, like those of Freud and Jung. But I'll also be delving into my dreams from a spiritual approach. I don't usually recall much from dreams, especially lately. So I suppose I'll start with past dreams. Whatever I can remember.

September Twenty-Six

The Sun keeps popping in and out. I had a thought about dreams a few months back. Most people believe dreams are subconscious desire, nightmares, subconscious fears. But what if there is no fear in the dream world? What if dreams are only made of desire, and nightmares are truly our subconscious desire to face and overcome our fears? When the clouds hide the Sun, we don't fear that the Sun won't return. Dreams of fear, they are not an intrusion on our safety in the world of dream, they are a reminder that our fears can be overcome.

So where are my aspirations now? Europe. Ideally well off enough to just kick it on a sailboat in the Mediterranean and Adriatic ports. But realistically, whatever works best. It could be just spending two or three months there each year. My novel, that needs more focus, of which I'm sure it'll get plenty as the days become darker and wetter. A desk would be a good investment. A decent one costing no more than my typical day out drinking twelve dollar cocktails and fifteen dollar ryes.

Then there are my daydreams. When they're not of, or including my immediate concerns, I'm off exploring temples in Kyoto, or taking a train across Alaska. Touring around this West Coast in a capable car, or sailing through the Strait of Gibraltar after crossing the Atlantic Ocean. I don't daydream of a house with the white picket fence, though some property along the Oregon Coast, with a small house and manageable farm, that would be a great home base. I'd even like to get a sheep or two for Zura to play with. We'll see what dreams may come…

October Thirty

Well, I'm here in Guadalajara. It's a mix of beauty and dilapidation. I really thought I'd have company on this trip. Yet I never let my hopes rise too high. It doesn't really hurt, I'm used to it by now. I'm just fucking tired of solo travel I guess. It's fine on road trips, when I have Zura with me. I guess I'm just numb at this point. How do you walk away from something you don't want to?

I haven't eaten all day, woke up at 3:30 from a nap. I can't remember, but I think it was around 2 that I decided to lay down. Fuck me. Guy playing music at the bar just played *With or Without You*. This bar has an amazing view, but it's a bit too American. I mean, it's cool because it's not intended to cater to American tourists. It's basically the equivalence of a good Mexican restaurant in the US.

Anyway, I almost fell back asleep before my flight. I didn't, but I had to take a $24 ride to PDX. Probably for the best. I didn't really want to walk fifteen minutes to the train station in thirty degrees at 4am anyway. I figured I'd eat something at LAX, but fuck airport pricing. I should have prepared better for this trip. Brushed up on my Spanish, at least the basics; beyond *gracias* and *por favor*. And the conversion rate, I think I understand it, but it's far more complicated than Europe was. The exchange rate was damn near one-to-one when I was there.

I'm at Cuaganga. It sits on the southwest corner of Plaza Guadalajara, with both the Cathedral and Municipal Palace in view spectacularly. The view from this terrace restaurant though, I spotted my restaurant for tomorrow. Restaurant Las Sombrillas. It reminds me of the patio I sat at in Milan.

Papas a la Francesa. I think they're just regular fries. What an ass I am. Eating plain fries as my first meal in Mexico. I walked by countless taco spots, but I can't figure out how I'm supposed to order. Tomorrow will be different, I know I'll feel different. I also have zero spending cash at the moment. I transferred money to my account I use for travel. Stupidly I chose to transfer it instead of making a cash deposit before I left. Now I'm waiting for the transfer to complete. I need some cigarettes, and a bottle of tequila. Tomorrow will be better.

October Thirty-One

Tomorrow is always better. It's far easier to get what you need with cash around here. That bar last night, fries, two beers, and a 3-ounce pour of some damn good tequila… $11.65. Wandered quite a bit today. It's not even 1pm. It's funny, how correct my assessment of American culture is, with regard to shopping and dining. The server last night, he just stood at attention until someone needed him. Not once did he stop to ask if I needed anything, and I love that. The same can't be said for those selling merchandise around here. Pushy sales tactics are the worst.

I stopped in numerous churches, just for admiration of the architecture and art. Saw the first three los Muertos figures placed in the Plaza de Armas. And inside the Palacio de Gobierno, aside from the wonderful architecture, the mural of Miguel Hidalgo by Jose Clemente Orozco, fucking fantastic. My mood had already shifted. Seeing this though, I was revitalized. I then wandered over to Plaza Tapatia, thought of going into the Instituto Cultural Cabanas. Seventy pesos to enter, damn near free. But I'll go tomorrow, there's stuff north of there I want to explore. Right now I'm about to head west, check some things that way. Here's the real issue though. I forgot to pack my swim shorts, so I need to buy a pair. What the fuck is the point of booking a hotel with a pool if you don't use the pool.

November Four

There was too much to do and see to bury my head in here. Not to mention the poetry that was flowing. I'm far too exhausted to properly write of the past three days. I took more than enough photos to refresh me when that time comes. For now, I'll just say that city is beautiful. If you're not looking for pristine.

December Eleven

I've missed a lot. Right now, I'm returning from a trip to Florida. Nothing special, just did a favor for a friend. I had hoped for this trip, though not this exact one. I had hoped to be in Miami for Christmas, meeting family. Fuck, I can't believe that was August. Yet that trip to San Diego, it's still so painfully fresh in my mind. There's just been this void of nothingness since then, like I've been suspended in time. Even Guadalajara seems a distant memory.

With Year One ending, I began to regret so much. The loss of hope to ever reach the Atmosphere, the change of employment and location, the new car I bought for my commute constantly needing repairs, the Bungalow I was renting a room in being sold out from under me at the start of the year the world closed. And so I settled into my room in the Underground. I've already told you that part of this story. But I'm now back in the Emerald Realm. I had to leave that City that Imprisoned Me, there was no future for me there. Life was stale. I was no longer a rebel. I was failing to live by the absurd, and was instead succumbing to it, as all of Camus, Sartre, and Dostoevsky's anti-heroes have.

Those stories are not mine though. My heart, mind, and soul, they are *The Pilgrim*, *The Alchemist*, and *The Aleph* of Coelho. Fate doesn't dictate me, it is I who controls my own fate. I returned to this Emerald Realm to break the Silence. And to prepare for escape from this White Curtain. Risking it all to capture both love and adventure. Or in the mind of Camus's absurd rebel, revolting against society to seek passion and freedom. To me though, it's liberation I seek, by way of revolution and adoration.

PART FOUR
AttainMentality

Attainment: the condition of being accomplished

Act V: Year Four

Prelude: January the Sixth
To <u>Adventure</u> *with* <u>Love</u>

I still feel it, as intensely as always...

I have some thoughts on that, but I have to go. I can't allow myself to be *The Outsider*, Meursault, passing through life without honest concern for anything, even myself. I won't allow myself to be Antoine Roquentin, Sartre's anti-hero from *Nausea*, wandering the cold, rain-soaked streets, alone with only my thoughts. And I've already escaped from Dostoevsky's place in the Underground, in that City that Imprisoned Me.

I've told you, no one really dies in this story. But more so, this story, it is the story of my escape from the White Curtain. Plus I have my dog, Azzura, and Halcyon has been running smooth. I won't give up on love. But adventure calls me. I'll head south first, then east. All the way east, across the ocean. May the fair Atmosphere follow. I'll stay here until the weather warms, but then I'm gone.

It's Three Kings Day. The news today is only about what happened a year ago. They call it an anniversary. There should be a different word for the events that aren't worth celebrating. We don't adorn a funeral with balloons and streamers. I'm surprised though, with all the conspiracies surrounding this day, how is there not some conspiracy related to it being Three Kings Day, with all the religious zealots spread across this land? Oh yea, they know nothing of the religion they claim to follow.

It's been a few months since I wrote about all this. I've been waiting, thinking the Atmosphere would change. It's just drawn colder, and darker. I need the Sun. It's time to move on from here. The emeralds have dulled.

The Silence was broken, but not as I had hoped. Still, I believed the opportunity to properly break the Silence would present itself. Sure as the Sun will rise. I really thought it would happen with the Hunter Moon fully reflecting the Sun's radiance. I even heard whispers from the Atmosphere. What did I mean? I honestly don't know. I didn't recall it.

With a calm mind though, I'd say what it means, whether my original intent or not, it means this... Choices, second, first, these things should not be spoken of where we seek love. Love, it chooses us. Love, it is freedom, it is passion, it is revolt. When I speak of love though, I speak of a love born from revolution, cultivated with adoration, realized through liberation; a love beyond the simplicity of the platonic, and far deeper and layered than the programmed concept of a romantic love.

It was a thunderous crack in the Atmosphere. A fracturing of reality... I reminded myself though, reality is not actuality. Focus on what is known. Honesty can only exist in what's known. The unknown is best left for adventure.

All the great love stories, they are of an absurd revolt, spurred by passion and a desire for freedom. Cinderella and Prince Charming, Romeo and Juliet, Cleopatra and Marc Antony, Psyche and Eros, fictional or not, these stories are all tales of love. They are the fabled revolts of lovers against the worlds they knew, led by their shared hearts seeking the same freedom and passion.

But my world, it is not a fairy tale, nor is it controlled by feuds, or emperors, or gods. My world, it is one of self-determination. A world of personal freedom. All it takes is courage, and a little patience. A quiet mind, a calm soul, and an open heart, with this, love will find you. The mistake so many make is thinking everything will just fall perfectly into place. I'm always so focused on trying to part the clouds when there are so few cracks in the sky. But the clouds will only disperse when the Ocean is still.

For the wild animals, Autumn is the time of preparation, Winter, an extended moment of dormancy, and Spring brings the rebirth that leads to Summer activity. Most of the consumers, those who've conformed to life behind the White Curtain, they follow the same programmed life of instinct as the wild animals. A pattern of self-preservation.

But there are those of us who revolt against our instinctual nature. Instead, we live by reason and logic. Summer is for leisure, sure, but also, it is for exploration. Autumn is our time for rebirth, to ready ourselves for Winter, to keep the blood flowing when the cold snows descend. It is in the Spring when the rebel fortifies needed supplies, for the adventures that come during the longest of days. When those who conform return to the world from their slumber in Hades, that is when the rebel prepares for freedom.

Scene One: Revolution

Revolt begins first in the human heart. But there comes a time when revolt spreads from heart to spirit, when a feeling becomes an idea, when impulse leads to concerted action. This is the moment of revolution...
-Albert Camus-

<u>Fifteenth of January</u>

I think it's the same seagull. It followed me from the Market Downtown to the Space Fountain. Space... Fuck I'm stoned. I keep hoping, but the Atmosphere remains clouded, dampening my spirit. That song, my anthem, *Moab*, by Conor Oberst. "You can't escape a circle you didn't know you were in."

Escape. I had started thinking it would be more wise to stay here through the Summer rather than leaving with the thaw of Spring. The Summer months are lucrative where I work. I'm not certain my heart can endure it though, the hope my mind can't let go of. On second thought, it might be best for me to just leave now. The same route I was thinking the other day, south, then east; all the way east. But I'll leave February first. I want to be nowhere when Eros makes his commodified appearance, in some redwood forest grove, or gazing upon the stars of the Winter desert.

I mean, it definitely seems the more wise decision, leaving so soon, considering I think a seagull followed me for over a mile. Even waiting for me while I bought new fingerless gloves for the season, and when I stopped to get some joints. I've been thinking, if she's truly gone, if I'm really moving on from all this; I'm not sure I should be calling this year "Year Four". It seems more to be a *Year Zero*.

I had just finished smoking a joint before I bought another and struck it up for the rest of my walk in the drizzle. That's why I'm so stoned. I love this weather, you can walk for hours and never get wet, regardless of the sky's condensation. The fountain isn't active right now, with its towering jet bursts, but it is bubbling, flowing. The lights sparkling on the trees in my upper periphery are creating a pretty rad visual. I can get a near-mushroom effect when I'm this stoned if I concentrate hard enough. That's also when I feel *it* most. Why I still have hope.

I had once asked, "Does the metaphysical require tangibility to be known as a truth?" The response I received, "Is a feeling within your heart not tangible?" Ever the Socratic inquisitor.

Still, if our other senses require concrete evidence as proof, and if the metaphysical is not mystical, shouldn't they require such verifiable evidence as well? How can one verify a feeling though? This is why I think the metaphysical can't be blindly depended upon. Then again, perhaps I'm just blind...

But this brings me to my next inquiry, that of the metaphysical senses. I no longer believe them to be an 'extra sense' or a 'sixth sense' as I still believe *thought* to be. We have our temporal senses, and our clairesenses. The conscious and the subconscious senses. Though perhaps, upon further study, we should view them as the rational and instinctual senses. The clairesenses, as they're most widely identified as, are mirrors of our temporal senses; clairvoyance (sight), clairaudience (hearing), clairalience (scent), clairsentience (touch/feeling), and clairgustance (taste). But the clairesenses are not mystical, nor paranormal.

As there are those of us with temporal senses that are stronger or weaker than others, it would be logical to assume these 'clairesenses' to be just as varying in strength. The difference is that most people have no knowledge or belief in their instinctual senses. The heart, it is the doorway to the clairesenses, just as the mind is what allows us to navigate the physical world with our rational senses.

Seventeenth of January

Fourteen more days. I'll miss this city, but I'm going insane with hope. My parents live in the State of Lonely Stars, on some island on the Gulf. My uncles own a bar there. I can possibly work there for a bit. Only if it makes sense. I have no idea what kind of income I can make there. It might be the wiser decision to just stop for a few days to visit, then continue east. I could probably find work in that Western Key. It is peak tourist season at the moment.

I'm not certain I'll ever want to settle down anywhere. Frankly, there's just too much of this world to see. Too much to experience. My debts have been a hindrance of course, but for someone born to the laborer class, what choice do I really have but to work for survival, without betraying my ethics?

I have plenty of ideas with regard to not laboring for another's profits. But such an endeavor, it would likely require me to permanently stay in one city or another. Maybe when I'm older I'll feel differently, and the stationary life would make sense to me. Right now though, that type of life would only drive me further into madness, even here in this Emerald Realm I've come to love.

Perhaps I'll feel differently once I cross the East Ocean. A little cafe in some Romantic City with an apartment above, that might be just fine. Once again I find myself with the thought that I've always supposed a life of contentment would suffice. I'd be quite content in charge of my own little cafe, while having all those trains connecting me to all of those venerable cities scattered across that little continent. Zura still has some good years left, so maybe now is a better time to settle somewhere for a bit, if only to ensure she has a steady life of comfort. I'd love to be able to give her more, to have more to give her, more of my time... but I'm focused on our survival. And our escape.

It's a month into Winter, one of the coldest I've known as an adult. Certainly the coldest I've felt since leaving that northeast region I was born to. That's another reason I've decided to leave now. I don't want to wait for this portion of earth to warm again. I'd rather just go find the warmth of some region to the south.

...And yea, I just need to go. I thought I saw her passing by on the sidewalk below my towering bastille. The solitude of my local bars has become unbearable with the hope I still want to hold. I can't tell if it's my mind that's given up, and my heart that still hopes, or if it's the other way around. I know the soul is eternal though, that's why it's so hard to let go when I usually behave with such fleeting attachment to everything and everyone else. Fourteen more days.

<u>Nineteenth of January</u>

Still with these thoughts. I'm out at the French bistro. It's more like a French dive bar. I'm fairly certain it's not her, but maybe it is. It's not though, thoughts best left alone...

I need to be preparing for my escape, not holding onto the past. Especially one that never fully existed. I want to step out for a cigarette, but I'm waiting on some escargot. That's why I come here, to pretend I'm in France already. The American patrons are a dead giveaway that I'm not though. Most people are decent enough, but the expectancy of some, the sheer self-absorption, it's disheartening to say the least.

It's much better on the calmer nights. Not quite empty, but not so busy that I genuinely feel bad for the bartenders. Running a place like this would be great, a bit more cafe oriented though. An old style cafe, the kind of place where people drink coffee alongside their whiskeys and wines. The kind of place where writers and poets, artists and musicians gather, late into the night. That's not this place though.

Still, I don't feel at home here. Nor do I feel at home in my tower, as pleasant as that prison is compared to the cell I had in the Underground. Honestly, the problem is that I can't concentrate. The weight of the Silence. The torment of how it was broken. Even more so, my failure to lift my head on that day in late August. It's not just how certain I am that it was the Atmosphere at the table beside mine, at *that* coffee shop of all places. It's all that happened before I sat down on that sunny patio and turned mute.

I won't get into the specifics, but I was weighing the reality of what my heart felt against what had actually happened, what it was my eyes had seen. I was playing with Zura at the park, standing just near where I had seen that silhouette a few days earlier. I thought I saw a woman sitting on a nearby curb, hunched over and sobbing. I got closer, it was just a yellow fire hydrant. But then, on the walk over to the coffee shop; there was the numerology on a license plate, the poetry sticker telling me to be legendary, and the yellow flowers Zura had led me to.

I tried to garner attention, dropping my coffee mug on the table, allowing Zura off leash to wander near her table. But there was no response. How could I be certain it was her though without seeing her face? Without any indication that I should push harder for her attention?! I figured, if it was her, she clearly didn't seem interested in speaking with me, cause she damn well would have known it was me. So I kept my head down until she was gone. I figured I'd surely see her again, having seen her three times in less than a week. That was over four months ago now. Maybe it wasn't her...

I keep thinking I see her. So set in my mind that I finally have the right words ready, no matter the situation of our next encounter. But it's never her. Just as it was never her for those two years I spent in the City that Imprisoned Me, regardless of how often I thought she would make an appearance. So I've come to realize, my plan, to tell her where I end up, I can't do that to myself. To constantly live with a lie of hopeful expectancy is no different than living that life of routine I've so longed to avoid. I'll mention I'm leaving, that I'm heading all the way east. But should the Atmosphere wish to follow, it will need to ask for directions.

I think it'll just be nice to sit at bars where I'm not able to understand all the chatter from the other patrons. At least until I come to learn the language. I've lost my allegorical spirit if you couldn't tell. The reality of a situation I hoped wasn't actuality has become too much of a burden to keep up the flair. All that's left are the honest confessions. I'll save all that for another time though. My remaining days here need to be spent in celebration, not wallowing in what never was.

That's why I came out tonight from my prison tower. To drink and be merry. The escargot is fine and all, but with the cold weather, the French onion soup was certainly needed. Crème Brule and a French press coffee are coming, along with a rye. It's wonderful to order coffee in a restaurant and to then hear the coffee grinder. I can't wait to get to Europe. To once again feel comfort in being lost. Fucj, maybe it is her... I'll take that wager. A blue poker chip I found the other night, it'll be my message, "I didn't think you'd come."

Twenty-Third of January

It wasn't her, maybe it was. I really thought it was, but it was dark. Regardless, I don't think she was tall enough to be *her*... I didn't just come back here because of my hope to break the Silence. As I've wrote, I needed to escape that City that Imprisoned Me. Even in my solitude, I feel free in this Emerald Realm... Or I thought I would I suppose. I mean, I do, to an extent, but I trap myself with hope and expectation. I realize, the only way to free myself from it, is to *free myself* from it.

I think most would be able to give an accurate description of the conscious mind, but what of the subconscious, or even the unconscious mind? Can we learn to understand, or possibly even control our minds in their altered states of consciousness? I can do it on mushrooms, and cannabis seems to have a less potent, subtler effect.

Perhaps I was wrong, when I wrote that the past can't die until a new future is born. Maybe this makes sense with regard to the Natural World, but concerning Human Nature, a new future can't exist unless we let go of the past. So why do I still hold so tightly to all that happened that first Summer in Year Zero? Especially now, since that Year One August night on a mountaintop near the Land of Eternal Summer has been fully tainted; it now seeming more a reason to let go than believe.

I'm here in my prison tower, the light cascading through the open blinds is far better than the dungeon that was my room in the Underground. It's warmed up a bit, the clouds hovering over the city have mostly dispersed. It's funny, a day like today, with the Sun being out since it crested the eastern horizon, it being well past noon, and I've yet to leave my room. A day like today, four years ago, when I first came to the Emerald Realm, after so many days of frigid gray, I would have been out to greet those early rays. But that was then, when my soul felt free; when there was no heartache and my mind wasn't plagued with thinking about what could have been. That was when the Sun didn't hold any meaning to me beyond its heat and light. Before that long adventurous day... Still, I hate writing inside, and I need to get Zura out to enjoy the day.

* * * * *

I almost had no interest, the obliviousness displayed during that first picnic. But I quickly understood there was a difference in her oblivious nature, compared to the typical self-absorbed obliviousness I've so long witnessed from many residing behind this White Curtain. It wasn't a lack of decency (as it is with most), I realized, when I turned and saw her, just mesmerized by nature, carefully inspecting some plants and trees alongside the trail while hiking back from where we laid out in the grass enjoying some wine and cheese. An inquisitive mind is rare to find among the American populace.

She was aware enough later in the evening, as she elbowed her way in front of me to pay for our ice cream before I could. We then sat on a bench, near the bell tower, and shared a joint. I don't recall what we spoke of really (I never do), but I was enchanted far more than I'd ever been.

A few days later was the Seafood Festival in the neighborhood I lived in. What a *beautiful memory* that day was. The 24th Street dock, the garden and locks, the train bridge beach and the blue heart painted on the concrete arch; and the promise that never came. (Still haven't got that burger.) But I had never been so certain of my future as I was that night when we parted ways.

I'm back in that neighborhood now, at the spot where we met up those first two days together. All these places with their memories, it can be hard to bear at times. Especially with the memories of all the lonely months, when the Atmosphere first quieted. But this neighborhood taught me much, and it gave me a place to feel comfortable in my unwanted solitude. That's why I came here today, to say goodbye; to thank these streets for all the good they did for me. And to hopefully leave the memories that weigh me down behind.

<u>Twenty-Fourth of January</u>

This will probably be the last time I see this place. The Pass of Deception. I went up to that park where I buried treasure. The treasure was gone. I guess that doesn't really matter, it wasn't buried very deep, so it doesn't really mean anything. Went on a decent hike after that. Zura went running up to every cliff. It scares me a bit when she does that, but her freedom in these open expanses is what matters.

With the weather turning so rapidly to mild and dry, from the freezing temperatures, the rain-soaked days, and the snow, Spring seems to be awakening early. Not quite the abundance of wildflowers March and April bring, but far more than one would expect to see before the calendar even turns to February. Even the daffodils are breaking free from their bulbs early this year. And the little yellow buttercups, they are everywhere. It all gives me hope that I won't be leaving the Emerald Realm with only Zura, when that time comes, just a week from today.

I'm at a picnic shelter; not the same one from nearly three years ago, but it's the same structure, more or less, and the view is far better. I also have plenty of dry firewood this time. And Zura exhausted most of her energy earlier, so I can write without having to constantly be aware of her wanderings. Not that she would go far, this park is just extremely rigid with its off-leash rules. Not that it matters. I'm leaving.

As wonderful as the Seafood Festival day was, it was here that my certainty became absolute. Sure, the whole day was wonderful. The ferry, the fish and chips we ate while sitting in Aether on the ferry. The Inner Sound beach we stopped at, the drive up to this place. The beach here, the slight awkwardness I caused that was so softly comforted. It was all wonderful.

But really, it was after all that. The conversation, the questions asked and answered. Us both greatly appreciating how long the sky held its blue into the night this far north in Summer. The stars that began to show themselves, until the moment when it seemed all at once. Us both so sufficiently stoned at that point that neither of us could remember the word 'astrology'. All so *really* wonderful.

But *actually*, it was in those last moments, when the certainty became concrete. Aether was filled with smoke, quite obviously, as lights began flashing behind us where we were parked on the side of the road.

Anyone who has been pulled over knows the feeling, the heart beginning to race in dread, especially knowing you're doing something that could bring the law down on you. I had none of that. And it wasn't because I was stoned. If anything, that should have pushed me toward panic. But with the company I had, I somehow didn't panic.

It was a park ranger, that perhaps helped my calm demeanor, but there was no way of knowing that at first. Still, my heart didn't skip a beat as Aether's window lowered with cannabis smoke billowing out. He asked what we were doing. I told him the truth, "watching the stars appear." He just mentioned that they don't allow vehicle parking on the roadside overnight here. I assured him we'd be on our way soon. And that was it. He went back to his patrol car.

We then returned to the Emerald Realm. And for the first time in my life, I felt concern… No, not concern, concern has too negative of a connotation. Interest would better describe it. For the first time in my life, I felt interest in my future. A reason to not live moment to moment with fleeting attachment. My only regret from that day, not making a U-turn so we could stop at the Fairy Tent we passed on the way here, to this Pass of Deception. I'm just used to bounding from place to place so fast.

<u>Twenty-Sixth of January</u>

It was July the twenty-sixth of that Year Zero. Our day wandering the Emerald Realm. The day I realized her endurance matched mine, if not exceeding it. It was like any other adventure I'd planned, plenty of time for random whims, with only a general sense of which direction we'd flow. But the day didn't start with my plans.

Watching anything gracefully glide across the water is something that will always capture my aesthetic spirit. Once again though, it was the conversation that truly enthralled me. I suppose this is when she first became the Atmosphere, and I, the Ocean. Allegorical characterizations of the deep layers we see in each other.

Coffee after that. And the destruction of my art, to create art. It wasn't what she created, as lovely as that was. It was how open she was to the creation process, us sprawled out on the sidewalk like children playing in the hot Summer Sun. To me, showing her this part of myself was a huge risk; but those are the risks most worth taking.

From there we made our way to the Arboretum. I'd wandered so many similar places *alone* before, always wishing I had someone to discuss the flora with. *Together* though, I learned so much. Most importantly, at the pond, where she taught me how to allow Zura to be free. That's where I am now, writing this. No pink petals yet, but the cherry blossoms here seem to be budding early this year as well. She told me once, the pond was her favorite memory of that day. I also taught her, while reminding myself, that when you get the Death Card, *death* doesn't always me dying or the end; it can mean transformation, or be alluding to rebirth.

The bookstore was next, and then the stroll to the Market Downtown. That's where she taught me to gaze at the Sun, as we smoked a joint, overlooking the Sound and the Olympians' Range Helios was returning to. It was shortly after that, on the bus home, when I finally came to understand what it means to see that *sparkle in the eyes.*

Thirtieth of January

It's been over two years since I last heard live music, with the world having shut down the way it did. Nothing special tonight, just a neighborhood cafe, open-mic night. I couldn't revisit any more of the places where this story began, in that Year Zero. Well, I could, I just don't want to. The only place I thought to go was that overlook above the Sound, where we first went to watch the Perseids. But Halcyon wouldn't be able to climb that road anyway. Aether was hardly capable, but that had more to do with the deteriorated condition from all the miles that Element had covered.

Before that day, there wasn't much that happened after our long day of wandering. There was the third of August, when I was properly introduced to her wildness. Then the fifth, when I cooked dinner for her. She had made truffles, but left without eating them with me. Instead, she made some comment about not turning into a pumpkin and ran off like Cinderella at midnight.

I honestly didn't believe she'd come with me for the meteor shower. Too much chatter was directed at me from mutual friends, well, people I thought were my friends. Saboteurs, the lot of them. Their words still encroached on my conscious mind as we sat atop that overlook, just the two of us. I tried to brush them away, but she seemed distant, and her face, too often looking down, illuminated by artificial light. It wasn't to the level of rudeness, only occurring a handful of times, but it was 3am. It just seemed to me that she was uneasy with where I had brought her to watch the stars fall, and I have no interest in ever making anyone feel uncomfortable. So I kept myself at distance.

As much as I view that night as the moment of our downfall, that morning gave me reason to believe that we would one day rise together again. The clouds looked like giant waves rolling across the Sound. I tried gently waking her, but she didn't stir, having stayed awake almost until first light. Not that I didn't stay awake too, but my endurance... She needed to be back for work that night, so I started the engine to leave.

We were backed in on the far end of the lot, so Aether's tailgate was facing the view. But as I began to drive away, I caught a glimpse of the clouds again, even more alluring than they had appeared in the earlier light of day. It was a split-second decision, I think she saw it as reactionary anger toward her not waking. A hard turn into the first spot. We had plenty of time before she needed to be back in the Emerald Realm, and besides that, the drive down from the overlook would have woken her immediately. It was a rocky and craggy unpaved road. I figured I'd give her that view to wake up to, and just go for a short walk with Zura.

Upon returning to the parking lot, I saw her subtle waking movements from some distance. Yet, somehow I clearly heard her say, "Oh my gosh." Once I was nearer to Aether, I asked, "Oh my gosh, what?" She said she didn't say anything. I'm certain now though, that's when I was first introduced to the Voice. I kept telling myself I must've imagined it, having spent so much time with her. But my subconscious kept responding to me, that that last word, *gosh*, it is not a part of my personal vernacular.

And soon after that morning, I was left with only the Silence, unsure of the truth of the Voice, and no longer in the warm embrace of the Atmosphere during Summer. Then came my trip through the Autumn desert, and soon after, her return to the State of Sunshine. But that was all long ago at this point, and there have been plenty of moments since then that saw us both continue to falter and fall. So I'm leaving tomorrow, and leaving all these memories behind.

I've come to a realization though, with all these years of stagnation I've endured in hope of reaching the Atmosphere. There are times when we must listen to the mind over the heart; the heart is archaic, instinctual, and not capable of logic and reason. But it's following your heart that matters most, when we feel the rebel within has lost its flame. We should all strive to seek a life of personal freedom, not commodified lives of consumer conformity. Escape, it is subjective. To me though, escape is simply freedom from the White Curtain. That doesn't necessarily mean I have to leave this country. I just don't feel like there's anything for me here.

Still, I sit here wondering, is that her sitting across the room...

Scene Two: Adoration

*This passion which lifts the mind above the common-
places of a dispersed world from which it nevertheless
cannot free itself, is the passion for unity. It does not
result in mediocre efforts to escape, however, but in the
most obstinate demands. Religion or crime, every human
endeavor in fact, finally obeys this unreasonable desire
and claims to give life a form it does not have. The
same impulse which can lead to the adoration of the
heavens...*

-Albert Camus-

<u>Third of February</u>

T hat was her I saw my last night in the Emerald Realm,
along with the Cause of the Silence. She was alone when we
spoke, she told me to stay, and just enjoy the music. I know, I've
always known, my reactionary nature is the catalyst, the effect,
my solitude. But that's only from one perspective. To me, the
Cause of the Silence was the catalyst that set my reaction in
motion. That being caused by a question from long ago. "Are you
free?" And those shoes with the stars... they showed up again
and again.

The effect? The wind at my back. I saw her brush by the
Cause, followed by a glance in my direction; one I once again
misunderstood. She picked up her guitar and stepped on stage.
A warm smile, but this time, not in my direction. My left foot
was quickly out the door, and then I heard her voice over the
speakers. "I wrote this song for an old friend, it's called *Play and
Sing.*"

It wasn't me though, who walked out that night. The Cause of
the Silence was gone, as the Atmosphere cleared. I knew those

early yellow daffodils were worth mentioning. I told her I was planning to leave that next day, the thirty-first. But I also told her that I greatly enjoyed the music, and that I would most certainly like to stay. Her response, "Got room for one more? I'm probably gonna have to go collect my things off the sidewalk." She showed me a text, [come get your shit].

I went with her, we parked just down the road so as to not create the unnecessary possibility of an altercation. She went and gathered her things, no one else was in sight. I pulled up, she put what she wanted to bring in Halcyon, and off we went. *Alone together*, the Atmosphere and the Ocean, and of course, with my dog, Azzura.

We stayed in a hotel that night, everything I wasn't taking with me had already been moved out of my apartment, my mattress included. I was planning on a drunken night on the floor when I thought I'd be spending my last night in the Emerald Realm alone. It was a slow morning, breakfast just before noon, then we wandered the city, gathering provisions for the start of our journey.

We drove north first, just after sunset, to the City on its Bay, just near the Northland border. Another hotel that night, and then we left after another slow morning, on February first. She wanted to see the Pass of Deception a final time as I had just a week earlier, showing me the treasure she had unearthed; the one I had buried three years prior. We camped for the night, thankfully the military planes were fairly quiet. A hike in the morning, yesterday morning, along the shores of the Sound, before we began our southbound adventure.

Then last night, after a short ferry ride, Alchemy Wine Bar, in the Port Town at the End of the Peninsula. We stayed in a hotel there as well. Early to the road though today. We passed through the Angels Port around 9am. Gathering whatever other provisions we thought we'd need first, then I showed her around town.

I had intended our destination for the night to be camping somewhere around that most northwestern corner. The hike to where I found *windows to the soul* was far more enjoyable with the unseasonably mild weather, rather than the stinging cold Winter rain of three years ago. The water flows toward the ocean were marvelous too, with the, far too early, snow melt cascading down from the Olympians' Coastal Range that hovered above us, mostly hidden by all the trees. Then, we discovered the unfortunate circumstances of not being able to camp on the beach up that way with a dog.

We're at Rialto Beach right now, a few hours until sunset. We sped down this way after discovering we couldn't take Zura to the campsite I was planning on for the night. I figured there's more than enough of a gray area here with regard to dogs from my first actual expedition here. There are plenty of others strolling the shore with their dogs, unknowingly acting as anarchists. The beach camping area is just passed the imaginary line they say dogs aren't allowed beyond. I imagine the park rangers generally look the other way, as long as the dogs are well-behaved, considering the amount of dogs I've seen. I figure, worst case, I get a fine I'll never pay.

So, here we are. Well, Zura and I, sitting in the tent, watching the Sun ready itself for its nightly bath. She's off making the discoveries I made three years ago. It's weird, my heart feels like it's racing with fierce excitement as I sit here so still, with the calm lull of the waves. She should be arriving at *Hole-in-the-Wall* around now. That's what I'm assuming it is, her elation, not mine.

Thirteenth of February

There hasn't been very much to write of. I've just been showing her all that I've seen. But I never saw it this way, with love at my side. She's off with Zura, on the dunes. I suppose I just like the idea of her walking a path I've already wandered alone. If only for the knowledge that such journeys of solitude can impart on a soul. Initially, I had planned to arrive here last night. But we got here early enough in the day. We'll be here for two more nights. It's not just the hike to the ocean across a mile of dunes I plan on us accomplishing tomorrow, it's what we'll be doing on Tuesday. That's why I booked the yurt long ago for the Day of Eros. A good place to be alone, had I left the Emerald Realm alone. An even better place for our love to grow. Honeyman's Dunes. I rented the yurt so there would be somewhere for Zura to stay, because we can't take her on the ATVs.

We spent an extra night at Rialto, it was just too perfect there after our swift coming together and unified departure. She had found a path safe enough for Zura's bare paws to come with us and explore *Hole-in-the-Wall*. So we set out early the morning of the fourth, prepared to spend most of the day beyond the tunnel and its shallow waters, where most people don't venture to. We could have left after sunset, but we wanted to stay that extra night, for the stars. Such darkness is rare to find along the West Coast.

The fifth and sixth were spent at Kalaloch, one night in a bluff cabin, the second at the campground in my tent. I showed her the sparkling driftwood of the Winter morning, it all dazzling in her eyes in the early sunlight. Then Haystack Beach for three nights, with last night at a bed-n-breakfast in the Valley of Dark Water, and two nights camping in-between, both days and locations; somewhere near Yaquina City. Finally got into the bookstores in Haystack Beach and Yaquina City. And Sleepy Monk Cafe well exceeded her expectations, as I knew it would. We've got enough coffee beans to last us at least six months.

It's been a bit of a whirlwind so far, as I had hoped. What fun is it when everything goes to plan? I had thoughts for us to be at the northern entrance to El Sur Grande by the eighteenth, but we'll only be leaving from here on the sixteenth. On my own, with reason, I could easily cover the 650 mile, twelve-hour drive in forty-eight hours, and that's at leisure. I've seen most of what we'll be passing though, so, alone, I'd have little reason to stop. She's seen none of it. I suppose we'll end up there, at that northern entrance, in no less than two weeks.

<u>Third of March</u>

No less than two weeks... It's been sixteen days since we left Honeyman's Dunes. Boardman's Seastack Park came next, then Jed's Redwoods after crossing the border into the State of Gold. The Mountain Redwoods thereafter. One night in that previously unnamed port town. Two nights each in that Little Coastal Beach Community, the Vineyard Valleys, and the City of Fog; three times crossing its Golden Bridge they painted red for a night on a houseboat, in-between the two nights we stayed in that city. Well, it's the third now. We're in the Mountain King's Town, just north of El Sur Grande. I've never stayed here, only passed through getting coffee once.

I had thought to be in the Land of Eternal Summer three days from now, but this adventure has been too fun to rush anything. And of course, there's the stars. If there is any stretch of coast along the southern portion of this Western Frontier that holds a sky nearly as dark as that corner of the Pacific Northwest, it's here, along this preserved winding coastal route, El Sur Grande. I booked us a cabin with a check-out on the seventh; we'll spend tonight here in civilization.

One excursion worthy of mention, before the days on the Coastal Dunes, Lookout Cape and its Spit. We did exactly as I had hoped, had thought to do, when I first spotted the Three Arch Rocks three years ago. Eleven miles, out and back. Just sharing spliffs and my flask, telling of our lost years apart, playing fetch with Zura, enjoying the light of the *Golden Hours* going both ways.

There's not much to mention of everything else. As I wrote, we were basically just retracting paths I'd previously taken. All the Capes, all the Seastack beaches; most notably, Kiwanda. And the places I had yet to see, most notably, Boardman's Seastack Park and Jed's Redwoods; it would be hard to translate those experiences with my pen... Seeing a landscape for the first time as the darkness is lifted is one thing. Seeing it for the first time with love at your side is not something easily turned to words.

Tenth of March

We arrived in the Land of Eternal Summer today. She has a place for us to stay. One of her old monthly rentals, where she had previously lived. Our first stop though, the Little Beach Town near the Cliffs Where the Sun Sets that I called home for four years. The dog beach there, Zura deserved it after such a long journey. Tacos from South Beach, and ice cream waffle sandwiches from the ice cream shop next door. We're not really sure how long we'll stay in this city, but my heart is still determined to escape the White Curtain.

Sixteenth of March

I suppose I should write about the rest of our adventure south, the days after our night in the Mountain King's Town. I've just been lost, well, we've been lost, sharing our secrets of this city with each other. I'll get to all that later though. For the purpose of chronology.

It was the night of the fifth, morning of the sixth. Only a couple days after the new Moon. There was no scheduled meteor shower, but the night before, we noticed an abundance of fireballs cutting through the night sky. So the next night, the night of the fifth, morning of the sixth, we decided to enhance the random celestial event.

It wasn't the first time we had eaten mushrooms together to watch the falling stars, but we consumed little that first time for the Perseids of Year One. Also, we were not *alone together* then, and had not yet fully connected at that point. This night was different. We let ourselves be fully consumed by the dark moonless firmament of El Sur Grande.

The atmospheric streaks seemed to last so much longer, and be all the more visible, even under a sky so crowded with stars. It was like Persephone, embodied by her constellation Virgo, was painting with light, her wheat sheaf as the brush, her wings, the source of her projectiles. Sure, in an altered state of mind, we might see things that aren't actual. But these glowing lines that remained spread out above and across the horizon, after the meteor that caused them had turned to dust, they are actual. It's similar to radio waves that slowly dissipate, or the cosmic background radiation of the Big Bang.

I first noticed this heightened sense of my vision on that very stretch of coastline, some years ago. I was entranced by a waterfall. There appeared to be, what looked like, little green ghosts, or souls, floating up the cascade, just behind the first layers of falling water. My mind quickly understood what I was actually witnessing. It was just the trees reflecting off the more dense layers of water, those dancing first layers creating the visual effect. The cause, it was the heightened sense of vision, the ability to discern that faint green reflection due to my slightly altered state. That altered state, the catalyst.

We were more than slightly altered this night. Our sense of vision, simply far more attuned to seeing beyond the normal capabilities of the human eye. At times, the sky looked as if light was pouring through astral fissures, like blood surfacing from the thorn scratches collected on the hands while picking blackberries. I'll miss that greatly about the Emerald Realm. The Summers of wild-berry picking.

Light started to return, the stars disappearing. We thought to head off to sleep, but were both riding a second wave. I asked her directly, for the first time, "Have you ever actually witnessed the sunrise?" Her response, "Of course! You know sunrise is my favorite!" My reply... "Many have watched the Sun rise. My question is, have you ever actually witnessed it?"

This intrigued her enough that she decided we should stay awake a bit longer. I made us coffee while she rolled a few spliffs. We smoked one and waited. First, the re-emergence of blue from the darkness. How interesting it was, the ocean horizon, the height of the cliffs we were nestled upon, the mushrooms combining with the effects of the coffee and spliffs; we were able to see the firmament's border. The transition in the sky between dark and light. The fringe shadows of this world.

"Is that what you mean?" she asked. I didn't respond right away, far too entranced by the spectacle of seeing the *pinnacle of light* in such grand fashion. But eventually her question reached me, maybe she even repeated herself once or twice. "Sorry," I responded, "I was in a bit of a trance. No, that's not what I mean. That vision is new for me." I got up from the nest of blankets we had made for the night's viewing and walked over to Halcyon. I thumbed through an old journal, some philosophical allegory of nature I had created from an interaction I had with the *Lady of the Lake*. Something I wrote later, in Year One, when Zura and I were about to settle into the City that Imprisoned Me.

I read from it to her. "But that thought I'd been struggling to formulate... Have you ever watched the sunrise? Not just watch our star rise from the horizon, but witnessing the surrounding earth being bathed in sunlight, inch by inch, second by second? It was the view facing westward that I most vividly recall. Waiting so eagerly for the Sun's emergence. I first noticed its rays touching the southern peak that climbs above the lake. Then behind me, that westward view, the top of the tree canopy starting to glow, with each gap to the forest floor below becoming illuminated. Watching the world, slowly, yet almost all at once awaken with the first touch of light."

She seemed to already perfectly comprehend, as her eyes lit up, reflecting the fully illuminated horizon. I continued on reading, "I still stood in the shadow, of the eastern wall that had been hiding the already risen Sun for more than an hour. Then, its spires crowned that wall of granite, and drenched me in the same light as the mountain forest that towered behind me."

As I finished reading those words, the Sun finally crested those forested coastal mountains of La Sur Grande. I was reclined, facing east; sitting across from me, she gazed west, legs folded, back straight. At that moment, as I finished reading to her of witnessing the sunrise from that alpine lake where I first began to understand my love for her; at that moment, the Sun's pointed halo rose directly behind her, crowning her head in the divine light.

Twenty-Second of March

There wasn't really much of anything eventful after departing El Sur Grande. We spent a night at a vineyard in the Pass of the Oaks. We passed through the city named for the Saint of Mothers next, a night there as well. Then the next day, night, and morning in the Angelic Kingdom. Visited with friends we both have in that city. Lunch with some, Tinseltown dive bars with others, breakfast with the last, but not least. Then, off to the Land of Eternal Summer. She's already back bartending at a place she previously worked at. I start work in a few days, some restaurant, serving the pretentious yuppies their food and drinks, as I had done so long ago. Before I left my desert beach home, before the cannabis delivery service.

But we're both more than happy just being here together. A momentary stationary life is quite enjoyable after nearly a month and a half of constant travel. But I think in our hearts, we're both ready at any moment to start moving again. The desert will be warming soon, and Spring is about to show its bursts of life and color in the Valley Wonderland.

The secrets of this city, our individual places of respite from the commodified world. Mine were naturally more plentiful, being I lived here six years longer than her; also having had the use of Aether to quickly transport me across the islands of neighborhoods that comprise the Land of Eternal Summer.

But what quality her secrets have been made of! That spot in City Park, that in all my time here, I had never stumbled upon. It was a secret garden born of fairy tales. There was that hidden beach cave up in North County. And the hidden park along the southern edges of the mesas above the Missionaries' Valley.

Of course there was my secluded cave as well, just south of Jewell Cove. The far less traveled trails of Torreyana and the Cliffs Where the Sun Sets. My lonely trees and pockets of water scattered about in isolation around the Missionaries' Paths. And most importantly, all of the best surreptitious bars I still knew of, whether because of the views, the product quality, the overall atmosphere, or some combination thereof.

She had her spots of recognition as well, though more centralized than mine. Naturally, our top selections intermingled, as they had in all of our first moments together in the Emerald Realm. Great minds… Well, eclectic minds would be a more fitting description in this instance. That burger spot she took me to, best damn burger I ever had.

First of April

New Moon tonight, we're in the Valley of Death. No fooling… Not quite the Super Bloom I witnessed six years ago, still though, it's far more lively than a typical Spring in the desert. We came here two days ago; staying in a room at the Furnace Inn. It's not too hot during the day, nor too cold at night for camping. But the terrain isn't very friendly to Zura's paws in most of this park. And there's little shade for her to rest under. We took her on a great dunes exploration earlier though, so she had plenty of fun.

We've just been racing across the park in Halcyon, taking turns at the wheel; exploring every colorful mesa, every ravine, every pocket of wildflower fireworks. The remote dunes were the best experience though. Sunset came on fast, but I had planned for this; knowing how quickly the desert Sun disappears from all my previous excursions. We were near Halcyon, so I went and retrieved our pile of blankets and some firewood, as she dug two holes, one for our nest, another for the fire.

Knowing we couldn't spend too long there, with Zura alone back at the hotel, we kept it simple with wine and spliffs. That was two nights ago. Even with that dunes area being more remote, and the crescent sliver of the near new Moon being below the horizon, the sky still seems darker, and the stars brighter tonight.

She wanted to go off alone with Zura tonight, with Halcyon of course. So I just wandered a trail up to the top of the Mesas near the hotel. Same one Zura and I climbed six years ago when we spent the night at the Furnace Campground.

This is it, escape, personal freedom, with adventure and love. The greatest liberation I've ever found. As I wrote, I don't need to leave this country to escape the White Curtain. It's only that I came to the realization long ago, that I could never escape within its borders in solitude. We both love this West Coast, and its terminus metropolises, the Land of Eternal Summer to the south, and the Emerald Realm of the Pacific Northwest.

Sixteenth of May

I've made it, another lap around the Sun. It turned the Moon blood red in spectacular fashion last night. We came to the High Desert of Yuccas for the event. The Hidden Valley and its boulder piles. Zura is with a friend back in the Land of Eternal Summer, the heat already being too much for her during the desert day. I've only ever truly explored this park when I had Zura with me, so I could never explore very far, or for too long.

We've been just enjoying portioning off our preserved magic, exploring the oases, the areas of desolation, the stacks of boulders and their mazes of crevices and caves. It wasn't only for this park of Yuccas that we came this way, but to explore the vast Mountain Desert that surrounds it. All the unpaved roads, the various sand seas, with their waves of dunes, the dried craggy mountains with their vistas, and of course all the random oases we stumbled upon, some with no more than a dozen plants with small shallow puddles that would do little slake any animal's thirst.

We started the trip with a straight drive to the Casino City. Two nights there. Most of the time that we spent in the casinos was profitable for our personal entertainment, as most of the time we were just enjoying our game of people-watching. Making bets just between us two; who would walk away from a slot machine first, or a card table. She usually won, such perceptive intuition. We went to some show the second night there, just for something to do. We're both always so disappointed whenever we think some commodified entertainment will be worth our time. Still, the food and drinks we were served were worth the experience. Other than that, we mostly just drank far too much and got kicked out of fountains we decided to play in.

Then we started our journey to get here, among the Yuccas. Halcyon was packed with our camping gear, cargo racks on the roof, stocked with firewood, extra gas, and the spare tire Halcyon didn't come with. We had to make a few U-turns, but we always covered the distance we needed to, to ensure we'd get here for Selena's Witching Flower Moon. The deep blood red of a lunar eclipse.

The night before last, we spent at a hotel in the Desert Palms City. Poolside with drinks during the day, just relaxing after the two nights of debauchery under the casino lights, and the three days we spent crossing the wild desert. We're camping here again tonight, then back to the Land of Eternal Summer, back to Zura, back to our lives of rebellious acceptance behind the White Curtain. We'll completely free ourselves soon enough.

Fifth of July

We left the cloak of the White Curtain two days ago, as everyone else was readying to celebrate what they've been told is freedom. Freedom to me, it's the landscape framed by Halcyon's windows, passing us by at 110km/h; it's Zura's face as she recognizes a new place to explore. The passion, it's in the Atmosphere's eyes, a mixture of fear and excitement as she grips the steering wheel. But this is no longer revolt, it is an absolute *revolution*.

It will be a long journey, hell, it already has been. I've been enjoying it greatly though, we both have. We've only been gone a few days. The first 1,800 miles went by fast. But now, our pace has slowed, and will continue to do so. She just really loves flying on the wings of Halcyon. It's quite wonderful really, to finally be a passenger on a road trip, to be able to fully see the surrounding terrain, instead of just viewing it in my periphery.

Of all that we have planned, this stretch of nearly one thousand miles is my greatest concern for Halcyon to cross without issue. The miles are going to continue to add up, but we're prepared for mostly anything. Why take any unnecessary risks when choosing a life so full of them? Extra fuel, firewood, plenty of cargo space. Tent, sleeping bags, emergency lights, a satellite phone, and enough food and water for at least a month. This part of the journey will only take five days if everything goes as planned. Of course we have plenty of whiskey and wine, and cigarettes and spliffs. And all we'll need to make fresh coffee every morning.

We spent last night in a rest area, only for a few hours though. She curled up in the back with Zura, as I had so often done on our excursions of solitude. That's all for today I suppose. We should be at our destination by the time the stars appear, if they even do this far north. I imagine there'll still be some faint blue left in the sky by the time we arrive to meet Prince Rupert, where he's set to provide us with shelter, and then ferry us off to Hardy's Port Town with the rising Sun.

Sixth of July

We didn't stop any more than needed on the way to our northernmost destination, though I had expected at least one side excursion. So we arrived earlier than planned; there wasn't just blue in the sky, the Sun was still well above the horizon. Sunset was at 10:15, we checked into our hotel around 5. After a short nap and showering, we drove around the island, stopping briefly to familiarize ourselves with the ferry boarding area. Sushi on the water for dinner. Then we watched sunset from the beachfront park. The Sun doesn't drop from the sky this far north, not even in the Summer. Instead, it seems to slide from south to north, skimming just above the horizon, removing its blinding fiery robe as it slowly settles into the icy arctic waters.

I didn't think we'd have so much time to explore this town. Coming up this way was more about taking the ferry through the Inner Passing. A fifteen-hour journey south, passing all the little island clusters that lead down to Northland Island. We plan to wake up for sunrise, departure is at 7:30.

<u>Seventh of July</u>

Sunrise was beyond stunning, a mystical display of light ascending over the Coastal Mountain Range. A true fjord-land. What a wonder this must have been for John Muir and the other travelers of this route, before it was spoiled by commodification and environmental damage. I believe we're just passing through the McKay Reach right now. We've been on the water for five or so hours. I don't know exactly, I left my phone in Halcyon. But I figure five or so hours, the Sun being near its midday height.

The morning waters opened up almost instantly upon leaving the land behind. Clouds randomly floating, hardly infringing upon the Sun. We quickly left the expanse to the Chatham Sound's southern portion, and entered the Grenville Channel through the Arthur Passage. The passage acts as a funnel into the channel. Even on this cruise ship-sized ferry, the surroundings make one feel small. But the Grenville Channel has been the highlight thus far.

Forty-five nautical miles, sandwiched between Pitt Island and the mainland. At its widest point, it's only two-tenths of a mile. All of this making me quite excited for that day we pass through the Strait of Gibraltar, with Europe visible to the north, and Africa looking south. Surely very different landscapes though. Every mountain peak we passed, through that strait, seemed taller than the last, and more heavily forested. I'm certain the shadows changing with the rising light played some part in the illusory spectacle.

After a few hours in the narrow passage, the waters once again open up into the Wright Sound, first passing Promise Island, which obscures any possible view of the small fjord-like village of Hartley Bay. We saw a pod of orcas thrashing through the water here, toward the south, near Gil Island. The sea lions must have some good intuition, they all seemed to be harboring themselves on the shores of Gribbell Island to the north. We spotted them just as we passed McKay Reach, the northern point of Princess Royal Island.

As beautiful as this all is, we certainly would like to return one day, free to explore under our own sails; free to explore all the various shorelines of this marine wilderness. The land is about to enclose around us again. The channel named for the aforementioned island off to the west. The Princess Royal Channel. The mountains don't appear to climb as high, but still, I'll write more later. Time to live in the moment. This adventure, all of it, it is our current destination. The destination is the journey.

Eighth of July

An eighth of mushrooms. She split them evenly enough, handing me my portion, and said to me, "It's both. The journey is the destination as well." She had been looking over my shoulder as I finished writing those thoughts on the ferry early yesterday. Still, I disagree, she planned on us taking this secondary trip of the mind. That makes the *moment* the destination. Moments are concrete aspects of existence, therefore, they can be destinations.

But I digress. To the visions we had, the visions we shared. The trees, the water, the changing light, the movement of the clouds, the mountains, their peaks still crowned with snow. Sunset wasn't until almost ten, so we had mostly returned to our earthly state by the time the golden hour had arrived.

The best vision though, about two hours in. It was time to check on Zura, she volunteered. I went off to the stern's upper deck. But with what I saw almost instantly, I couldn't wait for her to return. So I entered the parking deck. The time for pet visits was predetermined by the ferry operation service, so all the other passengers were taking their dogs out as well. So many dogs, almost all barking, the echoes of their voices, it was a bit of a sensational overload. Zura was her ever-quiet, well-behaved self, but I found them easily. Zura, calmly lying on the ground, eyes closed, while the Atmosphere gazed outward, transfixed on what I was sure had to be exactly what I sought her out to show her. I said nothing, returning to the upper deck, to the view I assumed we had both found; the trail of the ship's wake.

Some moments later, I don't know how long exactly, time essentially ceases in such a state; but some moments later, I heard her voice clearly, as I had so long ago, "Oh my gosh." I turned to look behind me, she wasn't there. I peered over the railing, she hadn't moved. Zura was stretched out, belly up. But I knew, there was no way her voice had carried up to me over the noise of the engines. I looked off in the direction she was so transfixed upon. A pod of humpbacks were following us, just off to the port side stern of the ferry.

That all happened yesterday of course. Right now, we're about to set off from Port Hardy. Heading to Tofino. It's a six-hour drive. She thinks we're just staying one night, but I already called ahead to arrange an extra night.

* * * * *

She finally found me up on the upper deck of the stern, where I was still having plenty of fun with the vision I had discovered. "Did you see it?!" The excitement in her eyes was almost overwhelming. I responded as she normally does, with the Socratic method of questioning. I knew she was speaking of the whales, but I was curious if she had also seen what I saw from staring at the ship's wake. "What is it you saw?" "You didn't see the humpback pod," she shouted with exasperation. I laughed, "Only because you directed my attention to them. I was far more lost in something else."

I realized then, it was the elevated view from the upper deck that was creating my vision. "Look right there, right where the wakes calm, toward the center, where the water seems nearly motionless." Thirty seconds passed as she fixated her gaze on the spot I had pointed out. She initially started to dodge out of the way of something. I wasn't laughing at her exactly, just her reaction. But I knew two things at that moment; she had been witnessing something else when I left her undisturbed on the car deck. And also, that she saw exactly what I did from above. It was similar to that time with my friend, with the red stairs in the Emerald Realm, on my birthday of that Year Zero. The day before I met her.

The vision though, gazing off the ferry's stern from the upper deck, how similar it was. The increasing magnitude of waves, the intensity of the light filling my eyes, all so the same. Large waves are real though, Hell is not. I must confess, I too, upon my first glance at this vision, started to initially dodge out of the way of the phantom rogue wave.

The rest of the trip was immensely pleasant. We knew we'd be sweating while coming down, as mushrooms tend to cause one to do. So we returned to the car, to speed up the sweat session. A cigarette would have been great before dinner, but the food was quite welcomed anyway, as was the wine we smuggled up from Halcyon. The ferry pulled into dock around 11, just when the blue was finally fading to allow the stars to shine.

We're in Tofino now. That six-hour drive took nine. Nothing much to mention from the drive, just a lot of pulling off to the roadside for the scenery. We also explored a plane crash site for a bit, just outside of Tofino. Checked into our hotel after that. We're about to get dinner. Surfing tomorrow. She still thinks we're leaving in the morning.

Tenth of July

There wasn't much to write about yesterday. We surfed, the water was fucking cold. She asked me why I didn't rent kayaks instead, but I could see it in her eyes, as she understood why, after her first successful wave ride. We wandered around town, went on a hike, found three amazing spots for breakfast, lunch, and dinner.

The whisky has tasted particularly good everywhere so far, but something about last night. I suppose it's the calmness and steady flow of a resort town, rather than the hustle and noise of a port town that suddenly seems deserted at the end of the work-day. Of course Zura enjoyed the beach greatly, after her mostly just being our stow-away for the past several days of travel. Not that she hasn't joined us on most of our side excursions, we've just all been spending a lot of time in Halcyon. I knew those two nights in the same location would be welcomed.

Tomorrow we're set to enter back behind the White Curtain. I've never returned by sea. I guess I never have by car either... Train, plane, bus, but never by boat. And I've never crossed a border in a car until this trip. I didn't even think about it, she did. Our perishable and dried provisions, especially the dried ones, they need to be consumed or discarded. She already made some friends, here in the southernmost city of the Northland Island. We're going to a bonfire party tonight. I doubt we'll actually be leaving tomorrow; we'll see what happens. Maybe she'll just decide she wants to stay here, us living free, with the White Curtain always in view, at least on the days when the sky is clear.

Fifteenth of July

We stayed that extra night up in the Northland, as I figured we would. We're back in the Emerald Realm, with its path of shimmering golden light, guiding adventure across the waters of the Sound. The truest freedom I've known has been found by painting on canvas with only the wind.

She easily mastered the language of the wind, the charts of safe passage, possible signs of a dangerous horizon. Apparently she spent our years of separation learning to sail. We floated and flowed through numerous clusters of archipelagos. Who knew freedom could be found in *chains*. But it was only momentary freedom, as it was with the Northland. The White Curtain still drapes over us. Our freedom is across a continent and ocean.

That bonfire party though. I'm glad we had a nice hotel room for Zura to stay in, and for us to return to at sunrise, when the fires had all gone out. We pretty much slept until dinner... The dancing flames though, they were particularly vibrant and lively, thanks in most part to the dried fungi we consumed with our new friends.

As it has been, the whisky had its enriched flavor. I thought I already knew how freely she could move; an elegant graceful flow, like the Autumn leaves performing a tango in the breeze.

But on that night, it became far more wild. We, together, were a river and the sea clashing in a chaotic storm. Only the break of day was able to quell our passion.

Twenty-Second of July

One thousand miles, were it the most direct path we had taken. This was closer to 1,500. Four days spent traversing the spine of the Cascades, passing along the chain of volcanic mountains that lead down to the Northern Territory in the State of Gold, and into the Golden Range that harbors the Valley Wonderland.

The wildflower meadows have been plentiful along our entire route. But something about the blooms of the upper reaches of this valley, along the shores of the alpine lakes, they seem all the more mystical, as if the flora were fed by the ichor of the gods. We'll be camping here for a few days, then back to our lives of servitude in the Land of Eternal Summer. But she assured me, our escape is imminent. She said she's been working on our plan to break free, that by Christmas we will find our liberation.

Twenty-Third of September

Sailing today. Well, for three days. We set out this morning, she doesn't know where we are going. I only provided her with the GPS coordinates, so she can do the sailing; and so there is some surprise to this present. She's a far better captain than I am anyway. We're going to Catherine's Island, the southern end, Avalon.

I've much planned. We'll spend tonight moored on the sailboat, before even touching shore. Tomorrow night, I almost booked a hotel. Initially I thought to rent a cottage, but the hotel seemed the better option. The best option though, in a tent, under the stars, about halfway up the trail that reaches the Garden to Sky Summit. Still, I decided on a hotel for the third night, so we can go on a scuba adventure that day. Obviously just renting the equipment and taking it back to the sailboat for the day would be preferable, but neither of us are certified. Hell, neither of us have ever been scuba diving. Snorkeling sure, but we want to view deeper, for longer. And of course, I have some mushrooms for us, to enhance the dive.

I know staying in a hotel the third night will keep us longer than my original plan to be on the sailboat and leave that next morning at first light. So I reserved a fourth night for the boat. That will be down in the Eternal Bay. I had a thought to book a room at the Hotel Del as well, but I know she'd prefer her birthday night on the sailboat. And anyway, we can spend a night or two at that hotel anytime, it's just a short drive across the Eternal Bay Bridge.

Twenty-Sixth of September

The Caribbean. We've been talking madly of it. Road trip. The Western Key for the Winter, bartending. Maybe eventually get a small sailboat to live on, if her plan for our escape doesn't work as we hope.

But I'm certain things will fall into place. She's been posting our adventures, using my writings, building us a following. Apparently there are a few companies interested in sponsoring our nomadic journey through life. We'll need to build our knowledge of the sea if we are to cross the Atlantic. The Caribbean seems a far more enjoyable location to better our skills than the frigid waters of this West Ocean.

That's neither here nor now though. We're in the Eternal Bay at the moment. She's resting. We'll be sailing out before sunrise. Not just to witness sunrise, but to be within it. And to see the open night in every direction, several miles off into the vast Pacific. We thought to just leave from Avalon even later than we did this morning, and stay the night at sea, but dinner at Hotel Del was something we both wanted more. We knew it would be all the more enchanting anyway, to set sail under the brilliant moonlight, to guide us safely into open waters, to join the dark abyss reflecting the gleaming diamonds above. The Moon accompanying us far out to sea, before we pivot for our return, the rising Sun creating a path of golden light to escort us back home.

It's just a day off from the Harvest Moon. It would have been an incredible sight, to see both celestial spheres glowing above the horizon, resting in the tranquil embrace of the calm, early Autumn ocean. Tonight though, there'll be an extra gleaming jewel in the firmament.

Scene Three: Liberation

There is no ideal freedom which will suddenly be given to us one day, like a pension which one receives at the close of his life. Freedoms are to be conquered one by one, painfully, and those which we already possess are the milestones, insufficient to be sure, on the way to a concrete liberation...

-Albert Camus-

<u>Twenty-Fifth of December</u>

S he wouldn't want me living like this... Nature can be so cruel. All I can think, why couldn't I have been there? There was no way to know what would have happened that day. I wasn't there because it seemed inconsequential. A beautiful Autumn day in the Land of Eternal Summer. I was working. She wanted to go sailing; she took a friend along, and Zura. It's not like there were any storms out on the ocean, there were hardly even any clouds. I know because of the photo she sent me. Her and Zura, both smiling in the Sun, the horizon, a calm flat line in the background.

I know, I wrote it twice, that no one really dies in this story. But that's the trouble with writing a story before you know the ending. Her friend Morena told me what happened, she was lucky enough that the dinghy was detached and was floating near her. With the emergency beacon she was quickly rescued. But it wasn't quick enough for Saraia and Zura. Nothing could have been so quick, other than the rogue wave that crushed our boat. We had bought it after our sailing trip, after she claimed that earthly gem on her birthday; she named the boat Avalon, for where we stayed on Catherine's Island, and for the place that name held in her heart.

I felt it when it happened, the fear and anxiety that welled in my chest. It was just like that time around when we first met, in the Emerald Realm, when she had to jump into the Lake of Green to save her dog. I wasn't there that day either, and I was clueless to our connection then. I thought it was my own neuroticism, that she didn't respond then because she wasn't interested in me. It wasn't that though, her phone was on her when she plunged into the lake in a panic.

It's kinda funny, in the Greek tragedy sort of way... She had told me once, when she first named me the Ocean as we were gliding across *that* Lake of Green, of how she feared the deep waters of the open sea.

I didn't get a response on that Autumn day either. I told myself she was likely just out of cell service range. But still, my intuition sat heavy in my gut. I knew instantly when I received a call from her friend Morena. Still, I hoped to hear Saraia's voice, that her phone battery was just dead, or that she dropped it in the water. But it was Morena's voice. My heart sank. I dropped to the floor. Essentially catatonic. I was too numb to cry.

She came over the next day, Morena, to tell me what had happened. I was still in a daze, I didn't really hear much at that moment. I must have appeared like Meursault to her, completely apathetic to the story and her flowing tears. My heart, the archaic heart, it just didn't want to believe what my mind was relaying to it. My subconscious, it kept echoing, "it must be a joke, Saraia's just fucking with us." But there was no doubt to the truth, Morena's tears and story were as honest and actual as they come.

I didn't hear much at the moment, but I heard it all; like my unconsciousness realized both the conscious and subconscious were incapacitated, and hit record on what Morena was telling me. She began fairly calm, "It was so beautiful, next thing I knew, we were thrown from the boat." Her eyes grew watery, just slightly glistening in the fragments of light cutting through the shades I had left closed. A short stutter of sorts as she tried to compose herself. "It, it, it... the wave, fuck! It was my fault! We were just inland enough, she wanted to sail farther out. I didn't want to, so we were just on the edge of that first shelf, before the ocean gets deep. The boat, it was suspended in the air for a moment." Another long pause. "Then that wave hit us. In that moment though, before the boat was smashed, she had raced to the back of the boat, to release the small boat. I saw her, marginally struggling, but still above the water. She was frantically looking around, for the dog. Then another wave came. Much smaller, the little boat was tossed around a bit, but it didn't flip me... What's the point of a life vest?! Ray and the dog were both pulled under. I saw her come up once more. She dove back down, probably looking for the dog. A third wave came, smaller again, but still, the wave was gigantic. I didn't see either of them after that wave passed."

I cried that night though, and for, I don't know how many days after that. But that's what happened. I'm at my parent's place now, in the State of Lonely Stars. My brother came to check on me in the Land of Eternal Summer. Forever the Land of Eternal Darkness for me now. That's it, that's all I can write about for now. I thought this would finally be our first Christmas together... She wouldn't want me living like this.

<u>Fourteenth of February</u>

She's gone. She's really fucking gone! It's Eros's Day. The God of Love. I've learned, these past few months, how actual that feeling in my chest was, cause it's gone now too. I learned how the Silence never truly existed, that it was always the Voice when the Atmosphere was dispersed. I hear nothing now. I feel nothing. "I can't feel anything anymore!" That's from her favorite movie. Her favorite quote from it, "God is in the rain." It's raining today. Maybe we'll have better luck in another life...

Of course I miss my dog too, Azzura, more than I can truly express. Excluding the few brief months Saraia and I finally had together, Zura was my only constant companion for nearly a decade. But with her on the precipice of old age, I feel somewhat relieved for the both of us. That she wouldn't have to endure whatever shame it is a dog feels when they can no longer control their faculties. And that I won't have to be witness to her death.

I always thought of that with intrigue. I know it's been well documented that animals know, or rather, they can sense when they are going to die. But do they have an actual understanding of death? We humans are lucky, we can at least die without fear in our eyes, without panic in our minds; with an understanding that *our time has come*. Still, I think fear would come all the same to their minds, and a short moment of panic seems merciful compared to months or years of shame.

I left last month, from the State of Lonely Stars. I'm in that Western Key, as we had planned. I've been in contact with that man I met here three years ago, Link. I'm moving in with him next month, into his mansion. Not for long, just a place while I prepare. It's a room in the attic; it reminds me of the room I had in the Underground, in that City that Imprisoned Me. But the views are of freedom, rather than the feet of all the passersby; and the noise, oh the sweet noise. Waves, and crickets, and the wind rustling in the palms, telling me to find my sails. I've just been bartending. Obviously her plan for us to escape was drowned, along with her and Zura. He said he'd pay me to help him out around the property. To help me escape. He also has a sailboat he's going to let me use, once he feels I'm proficient enough, just to sail around this lovely turquoise sea.

Third of March

I guess I should mention the year change. Year Five now, since I met her in the Emerald Realm in May of that Year Zero. I suppose this should be a Year Zero, but I'm not sure how to move on still. After the years of separation and solitude, to finally be together, and for her to be taken away from me so soon after we finally fully connected. After we finally began to plan our future *together*; though with what we had been speaking of, we certainly wouldn't have been *alone*. Such is life, I suppose.

I met some people through Link, they'll be sailing across the Atlantic toward the end of April or just after May begins. It depends on when the caravan is leaving. A few hundred sailboats, all crossing the East Ocean in tandem. There's safety in numbers of course. So I'll be leaving then. They said they'd welcome my help, so long as I could do the work. They don't have a cabin for me though, but I told them that it was fine. I'd rather sleep under the Sun and stars.

<u>Fifth of April</u>

With helping Link, though more accurately, with Link's help, I was able to quit bartending. And he requires little from me. I'm sure it's just sympathy from a kind old man. But it's appreciated nonetheless.

I've been taking his sailboat out, days at a time. Alone. I suppose I'm somewhat tempting fate, hoping for a rogue wave of my own. But mostly, I've been living as we would have, as she would want me to live. Island to island. All deserted. The best stars I've ever seen. Other than the ones I saw in her eyes when she gazed into mine.

I'll be leaving here on the first of May. If all goes well, we'll be passing through the Gateway to the Mediterranean on my birthday. I'm sure they'll all be celebrating at that moment, the crew of the ship I'm crossing with. I already know, at that moment, I will never have felt so *alone*. That was our dream. The Strait of Gibraltar, Europe in view to the north, Africa gazing south. I always enjoyed heading south.

EPILOGUE
ContentMentality

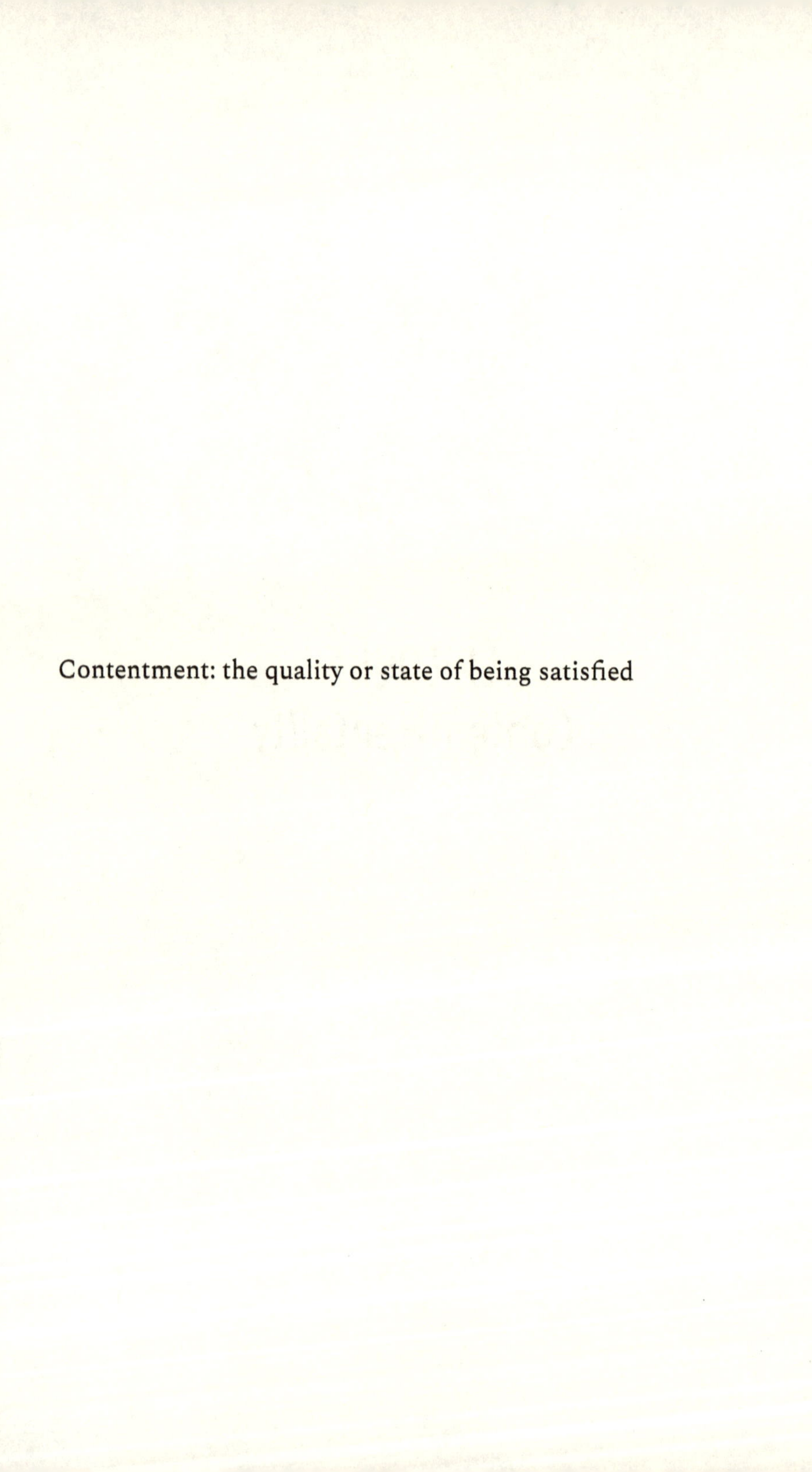

Contentment: the quality or state of being satisfied

Act VI: Year Nine

The Last Day of Winter

*In the midst of Winter, I found there was, within me,
an invincible Summer. And that makes me happy. For it
says that no matter how hard the world pushes against
me, within me, there's something stronger – something
better, pushing right back.*

-Albert Camus-

I once wrote that everything is in constant motion. That's
not true though, history is not in motion. As I also wrote,
moments are concrete aspects of existence. History is comprised
of past moments, they are stationary. The past does not move.

All of this traveling with you in my spirit, it taught me the
meaning of adventure; if your heart isn't grateful for every new
view, every new destination, you're merely seeing things, rather
than experiencing them. It taught me the truth about risk; if failure doesn't break your heart as much as achievement overjoys
it, then you don't truly love whatever it is you're taking a chance
on. And it taught me that love, a true and pure love, it can only
exist through the connection of two souls.

All those years of writing for you, to you, with you in thought;
the journals I've kept, they've formed quite a story. I made it
though. I escaped the White Curtain. Crossing the Atlantic was
fun, but I still have yet to pass through the Strait of Gibraltar.
The crew I was sailing with decided to take a detour after our
brief stop in the Azores. We went south from there, to the
Canary Islands, then back north, along the African Coast. We
docked in Casablanca after that. That's where I departed. But
that's a story for another time.

Before I had left that Western Key, I bought some cheap property in Spain. It was just a stone hut on a hill near some village time had forgotten. I figured once I traveled a bit, that it would be a great spot for a home base. After a year or so, I was broke, and it just became home. I had a garden, and a stream up behind the hut. I just bartered for anything else I needed. And luckily, the guy that sold firewood, we became very close friends. He'd feed my fires, I would feed him fish and vegetables.

Something just clicked one day, on a lazy Sunday in the Summer. My friend and I started a business. At first, I was just baking bread, but then, together, we started selling sandwiches on Sundays. And eventually we partnered with the local cafe. It was run by a woman who reminded me greatly of you, but she didn't have your adventurous spirit. My friend was quite taken with her anyway...

With the success of our business, and the improvements I made to the property the stone hut was on, I came away with a sizable profit. So I left again, as I'm prone to do, to adventure around the continent. After a month of travel I found work in Madrid, bartending and teaching English. I stayed there through the end of the Summer, through Autumn, and into the closing days of Winter. I left yet again, only two weeks ago, to buy a sailboat.

Initially, I thought to purchase one in some Mediterranean port city, but similar boats in the lowland countries of the north were available at far less of a cost. A forty-eight foot seaworthy vessel, one I can handle all alone. I found it for sale in some tiny harbor village in Kattegat Bay. Around the northern horn of Denmark first, and I unfurled to full sail, as the waters opened up into the North Sea.

I had my destination set long ago for this moment. That's where I am now. The Faroe Islands. There are many places that claim to be the mythical island of Avalon, but if I had to guess, I'd say it's here. Somewhere among this mystical archipelago covered in mist. One of the few things I took with me, that I still have with me, the last collection I had made for you. The dried flowers in the bottle.

I know you always wanted to see the Auroras, so I've come here, to bury what I have left of you under these Northern Lights. I couldn't have hoped for a better showing than the one before me tonight. The green bands of the magnetically charged atmosphere, dancing in the solar winds. A proper burial for a goddess.

I'll be docking the boat near Venice, once I make my way south and through the *Gateway of the Mediterranean*. Probably stop a few times along the coast. Gibraltar first, then a few Spanish port towns. Across the Azure Sea and around the boot tip of Italy, then up the Adriatic to Venice. I'll be there around the beginning of May, then off to the City of Lights. Paris is supposedly quite lovely in the late Spring. The sailboat I bought, I named her the *Atmosphere* of course.

You taught me that good and bad are subjective, a matter of human perception. The White Curtain, it was the consumerist shroud I was born under. Now, they are the white sails that guide me to freedom across the waters of our Earth.

I was born facing death, an obscure soul pulled into life, along with millions of others residing in or around Liberty Metro. After years of aimless wandering, I embraced my calling as the Ocean. But now, I can flow across all oceans, on the canvas wings of the Atmosphere. I go by Giovanni now, I am *The Prince of Madrid*.

The Auroras though, I wish you could have been here with me to see them. They're pure magic. They bring me hope. It's only in absolute darkness that we can see the most light.